THE
CHOICE
TO REMAIN IN HEAVEN

Cheryl Garrison Garrett

ISBN 978-1-64468-388-0 (Paperback)
ISBN 978-1-64468-389-7 (Digital)

Covenant Books, Inc.
11661 Hwy 707
Murrells Inlet, SC 29576
www.covenantbooks.com

To John, Lisa & Rose —
I love you with all
my heart!
Chris

For anyone who thinks Heaven is a figment of one's imagination.

PS 139

ACKNOWLEDGEMENTS

These are the given names of those who inspired me or encouraged me and made my first novel possible: David, Webb, Vera, Rubie, Tim, Beverly, Kelly, Tim, Kim, Kate, Sandy, John, Rowe, Lisa, Nan, Pat, Bronwyn, Danny, Andrea, Angela, Janis, Robin, Sonja, Kim, Stefan, Maggie, Gretchen, Brent, Lori, Laura, Naomi, Bob, Fred, Leo, Jim, Linda, Ann, Anne, Ron, Janie, Steve, Victor, Wesley, Karl, Ronnie, Jennifer, Magic, Ginger, Tracy, Sarah, Sara, Howell, Deb, Donna, Virginia, Renee, Debbie, Jonas, Elsa, Gene, Naoma, Clyde, and *The Covenant Books Team*.

PART ONE

Arriving

Psalm 1:1 Blessed is the man that walketh not in the counsel of the ungodly...

CHAPTER 1

First Heaven—The Waiting Room

Jared Walcott did not believe in a physical Heaven, so when he arrived there, he had no idea where he was. A vibrant light radiated behind him, and although aware of its presence, Jared was not compelled to turn toward the light.

He had the sense that he was floating and looked down, but he saw no feet, just a bench—a crudely carved wooden one that reminded him of the church pews he sat on as a boy.

With his back to the light, he hovered in place and peered into a massive chasm. It was dark gray, rock-filled with no sign of life. He knew that if he pushed forward too far, he would have a mighty long fall.

While everything in front of him was gloomy and gray, the light behind was just the opposite; and in its presence, he felt safe, strong, unrushed, and energetic. He knew who he was and sensed that he could move about, stay, or leave. A familiar scent of lemon oil rose around him and brought with it a childhood memory of times spent dusting and cleaning stair railings, chair rungs, church pews, and carved wooden claw-shaped feet of a dining room table at his grandmother's house in Gaffney.

As he thought about these chores, the dark-quiet expanse in front of him brightened. Jared watched the dull nothingness transform into a space filled with radiant, billowing, cumulus clouds that generated the sound of rushing water and presented vivid, color images of him as a child, a teenager, and a man.

He saw himself climbing Chinaberry trees, skipping stones over quiet lake water, and casting a fishing line off the back end of a paint-peeling rowboat. All the images were separate; yet he saw them simultaneously as if they were taking place at just this very moment.

Eyes pinched, he moved forward to investigate, but he stopped when he felt a tugging at his middle. He looked down and discovered that he was fastened to an elastic gold thread that knotted at his navel, passed through his center, sprang out his backside, and hooked onto the bench below him.

His restraint did not upset him because he felt that it was there for protection more than restriction and somehow he knew that he could unfasten the tether at any time. Now, it seemed natural for him to settle on the bench. Anticipation of a hard landing was exchanged for the experience of gliding onto plush cushions covered in purple, yellow, red, and blue brocade fabric. Its softness reminded him of a feather bed he had slept on as a child, and its colors were like intricate woven tapestries he had seen hanging in the Biltmore House in Asheville, North Carolina.

He sank onto the cushions, got quiet, and began to examine the expanse that stretched as far as he could see to his left and to his right. Occasionally, cumulus clouds formed over the expanse and presented an ensemble of intermittent soft "poof" sounds and flickering of lights. Colors or the image of a familiar face emerged then disappeared along with the sounds and cloud formation as if scolded and claimed by the dark. Looking into the enormous void, Jared mumbled, "I wish someone would explain what this is in front of me."

Within moments of his request, Jared sensed movement behind him.

"Who's there?" he asked, but the only response he got was a warm breeze.

Strange, he thought and he shrugged, turning his attention back toward the dark expanse before him, which now had become still. In spite of this, Jared scanned its surface for details and was drawn to its middle portion. As he did so, clouds began to take shape and started to illuminate with familiar scenes of flimsy bridges crossing the Pacolet River, brick cotton mill buildings belching black smoke, and rows of sunflowers planted along the backside of his yard. At first, an image sparkled in pale yellow, lime green, or cerulean blue, and then it flickered; just as Jared determined what the image was, it evaporated like a magic act with a loud "poof" followed by silence.

"*Humph*," he grunted prompting more movement behind him.

"Who's there?" he asked again, brusquely this time.

Turning to his right, Jared was unprepared for what he saw.

CHAPTER 2

The Guest

An object that resembled freshly dispensed shaving cream floated to the end of the bench and bobbed there as if awaiting orders. A caring energy radiated from its center.

"Greetings, Mr. Walcott," a cheerful voice rose from the white fluffy shape. Jared was impressed that the shape moved in rhythm with each syllable.

"Welcome," the voice added and bubbled for emphasis. "May I join you?"

Believing that this being might be able to explain matters, especially the unpredictable movement in the expanse in front of him, Jared shifted to make room on the bench and answered, "Sure, why not?"

A mild spurt of static was exchanged between him and the new arrival sitting next to him on the bench. Jared wondered if he had made a mistake sharing his space.

"Pretty, isn't it?" the voice said happily.

"Pretty?" Jared smirked, "You call this one-seat, cloud and wind-breaking performing arts theater pretty?"

"Oh, excuse me, I forgot. You were not prepared for the Waiting Room."

"The what?"

"The Waiting Room—the place we call First Heaven."

"First Heaven? There's more than one?"

"Yes, there are three."

"Three?" Jared repeated in disbelief. "How do you explain that?"

"*Welllllll,*" the bench guest said rising up and floating out of sight. "I will be glad to try so that you may understand."

Jared heard rustling—like papers or note cards being shuffled. He couldn't distinguish the direction of the sound, but he decided that the noise had something to do with the disappearance of his guest and his question about three Heavens. Jared groaned, certain that he was about to be given a long, boring sermon.

Without commenting about Jared's grumbling and suspicions, the bench guest reappeared and said brightly, "The Waiting Room is First Heaven, Second Heaven is where you come to understand, and Third Heaven is God's Kingdom, also known as paradise."

"Whatever the case, if I'm in Heaven, that means I'm dead."

"*Wellll*, not exactly," the bench guest said dragging out his words as if to stall for time. "You are in Heaven, but you are not dead. You died—sort of."

"Sort of? Dead, dying, dying, dead, what's the difference?"

"Dead can be final, whereas dying is a process."

"So being sort of dead means I'm not finished dying?"

"Not for now, and here you will never be dead."

"Oh great," Jared said with sarcasm. "Now I get riddles. If I died, then I'm dead."

Because of his mercy training and having studied the dossier of Jared Hamilton Wolcott Jr., the bench guest did not comment on the remark of this being whose formative years were peppered with loss.

CHAPTER 3

The Brief

Jared was born in Gaffney, South Carolina, in 1944 and his mother Julia died giving birth to him. Soon after, his father abandoned him and Jared was placed in foster care and then court ordered to live with his father's parents: Pop and Mom Wolcott in Indianapolis. Jared adored Pop but he was afraid of Mom. Pop always had time to read with Jared and play hide and seek and Pop laughed a lot. Mom was stingy, cruel, and moody and she despised Jared's best friend Percy because of his skin color. Jared's maternal grandmother Grandma Robinette wanted to adopt him, but the courts would not allow it. She was a widow who had to work full time and would not be able to stay at home with a child. Besides his best friend Percy, Pop and Grandma Robinette were the only loving islands Jared cared to visit. When he was five, he nearly died of scarlet fever and the disease caused permanent heart damage and hearing loss. When he was eight, he witnessed the accidental death of Pop, and later that day, alone in his room, a frightened Jared begged God for his daddy or to let him live in Gaffney with Grandma Robinette; but his pleading did not persuade God to do either, so Jared gave up on asking God for anything. He remained with Mom who promptly remarried a drunkard named Walter whose exchanges were single syllable grunts, brutal whippings, white supremacy tirades, vulgar imperatives, or false accusations. This early conditioning of love then loss, physical and mental abuse, and denial and rejection fostered distrust and produced a young man who could not accept God's love.

Jared might have rejected Heaven if he had not married Priscilla, his second wife or met and became good friends with C.W., a chaplain. Their combined encouragement and support helped mend Jared's old wounds, but his doubts about Heaven and lack of trust in God remained and restricted his ability to be direct. He chose sarcasm to express himself, especially when he felt something was out of his control. And because souls arrive in the Waiting Room with their personalities intact, Jared's sarcasm naturally followed him into Heaven.

CHAPTER 4

The Helpful Bench Guest

"If I'm in First Heaven, a place you call the Waiting Room, and I'm not finished dying and will never be dead, then what's happening to me?"

"I cannot tell you that," his companion said.

"Why not?" Jared asked.

Wanting to be helpful, his companion offered, "It has to do with time, choice, and the process of dying."

Jared turned to get a better look at the shaving cream fluff sharing his bench, but a gurgling noise from the chasm distracted him.

"What was that?" he asked.

"The gurgling noise?"

"Yes, that! What was it?"

"It is part of the process."

"Of dying, you mean?" Jared asked then added, "My death? Is that what's happening?"

"*Wellll*, not exactly," his helper said.

"It is more about changing time zones," he continued. "In a while, all this will make sense for you. Presently, I am limited in what I can tell you because I am not qualified to share too many more details. But I can tell you this much, so that you do not feel lost. Things are different here and many souls have no clue what to do when they arrive."

"Yeah, I know. I'm one of 'em," Jared snorted, patience thinning. His mood changed from somber back to sarcastic. "Maybe I'm dreaming," he muttered.

"You are not dreaming, I assure you."

Something about this comment triggered a sensation of familiarity for Jared. He asked, "Do I know you?"

"Not directly, but your wife helped my mother a few years back."

"My wife? My Priscilla helped your mom?"

Again, Jared thought he saw a glimmer of light in the clouds covering the dark expanse, but he shook his head in disbelief and asked, "Helped how?"

"She helped my mother deal with my suicide."

"Suicide?! You killed yourself and you get to be in Heaven? How does that work?" Jared's voice was a mixture of shock, surprise, and sarcasm, but he also wanted to know because he had a favorite teacher who had died that way.

"I was told that suicides go straight to Hell," Jared said.

"Some do go to Hell, but yes, people who died by suicide can be eligible for Heaven along with a lot of other souls you might not expect to be here. As for me, I was out of my mind. I was deeply depressed and had lost the ability of rational thought. I would never have gone through with it if my brain had been working properly."

Thinking this sounded like something out of the Joseph Heller novel, *Catch-22*, Jared asked, "Are you saying that if your brain isn't working right and you commit suicide, it doesn't count?"

"*Welllll*, not exactly. Suicide is complicated. People can take their lives because of abnormal brain chemistry or because they are selfish."

Jared thought of people in great pain, dying of cancer, and wondered how suicide could be a selfish act.

"You will come to understand that in another realm," his companion said and Jared flinched wondering how his bench guest knew what he was thinking.

"In my case, it was brain chemistry. When your brain chemistry is okay but your final act is one of willful disobedience, that is, ending your life to escape something you want to avoid, then what you are doing is selfish and wasteful. You are rejecting God. You are saying to Him that you know better than He does. In these cases, when the soul leaves the body, it will not come here."

"You mean Heaven?"

"Correct."

A rapid vibrating energy surrounded and passed through Jared. It hummed and expanded, surprising him. Before he could ask about this energy, his bench companion asked, "Did you feel that?"

"I did," Jared answered and assumed that his companion did as well. "Was it an earthquake?"

"Wellll,"

"Not exactly," Jared interrupted anticipating his companion's quirky response to questions that could not fully be explained at the time. His companion laughed and congratulated Jared on his keen observation but did not reveal to Jared that this method of stalling was out of respect for timing and choice.

Because he had another question about suicide and trusting that the bench was going to remain a safe place, Jared settled in and asked, "What about assisted suicide?"

"That is a different matter and one that will be discussed in detail later—but for now, you need only to see and understand what happened in my case."

Jared accepted the limitation and listened.

"Once I got here and understood, I felt sorrow for having offended God by ending my life."

"That must've hurt," Jared said, setting aside his sarcasm.

"More than anything you can imagine. Ironically, if I had waited a mere three hours, I would have gotten exactly the help I needed to deal with my depression. The worst part is that because of my faulty thinking, I was unable to consider the people who had to deal with the mess I left."

He didn't know how, but Jared was able to see the suicide scene. Glowing on the cloud before him were images of memories that did not belong to him. A gray-haired man was sitting on the floor of a single room sparsely furnished squalid trash-filled apartment, his legs stretched out and his arms cradling a blood-covered faceless body. Features of eyes, nose, lips, and teeth had been obliterated by a self-inflicted shotgun blast. With care, the man pulled from his back pocket a white cloth handkerchief, shook it open, and draped it over the faceless being. Caressing the docile figure to his heart, the man let out a haunting, guttural cry. A mature woman was near the man's side. She bent down, gingerly moved the firearm out of the way, and walked a short distance where she stood with her back to the scene. With arms crossed over her chest, she held herself and rocked back and forth, sobbing, moaning, and then screaming out—she cursed God.

Jared felt a chill. "Who are these people?" he asked.

"My mom and dad."

Curtailing his usual sarcasm, Jared spoke with reverence, "How terrible for them."

"Yes, it was. Mom had a nervous collapse. Unable to sleep because of grief, she became despondent. She slept in my old room, clinging to things I had worn. She yelled at God and snapped at people from her church who tried to comfort her. Dad suffered. He was also grieving, but worse than that, he felt helpless to console his wife. His prayers for her were passion-filled as he continued to call out to God, but the opposition gripped my mother's heart, showing her failures and shortcomings, making her believe that my suicide was her fault. It was your wife, Priscilla, who was able to comfort my mom with words of hope."

A feeling of sorrow rose around Jared and his companion, but it didn't last. Warmth penetrated the surroundings, and shadows of sorrow were replaced with healing, mourning light.

"Ah, relief," his companion whispered. "I do not enjoy reruns of that moment, but if seeing them can serve to help you get oriented..."

"Oriented?" Jared interrupted, resuming his sarcastic tone, "Oriented to what? This gigantic, colorless, dark-gray canyon here in front of me?"

"Ah, yes. Many new arrivals to the Waiting Room wonder about the expanse, which appears different to each being, but it is essential for decision-making and orientation."

When Jared said nothing, his bench guest continued.

"It is used for boundaries and for Rapid-Replay which is seen in Simulvision. Would you like a demonstration?"

"Jared hesitated. He had never heard of rapid replay in simulvision. He paused a long while before saying, "Sure, I guess so."

"Brilliant!" his bench guest exclaimed. "Just remember something about your life and watch the expanse."

CHAPTER 5

Joy Ride

Jared's eyes widened like a surprised three-year-old when the dull-gray space in front of him filled with hundreds of colored billowing sheets. On their surface, scenes of childhood happenings fluttered, disappeared, or came into focus. One in particular was a tender moment of discovery when Pop showed him how to use a bubble-making toy. After dipping the wand into a colorless liquid, Pop handed the watery filled ring to Jared and told him to blow gently.

Watching an iridescent bubble expand and then burst, scattering its evidence into the air, was magical. But the last part was the best, when a reminder of the bubble's existence drifted back as an invisible wet spray tickling his face.

Jared grinned, and while he savored the recollection, vivid royal blue, pumpkin orange, and bold mustard yellow colors united. They formed waves that washed over the surface of the clouds with a strong, unseen undercurrent of order. Like the steady ebb and flow of an ocean's edge, the waves cleared the image of his exchange with Pop and replaced it with another.

"What am I seeing?" Jared laughed. "Flowers? Herbs? They certainly are not weeds," he remarked as another childhood memory appeared with details of a summertime visit to Gaffney when he was six. Crawling past Grandma Robinette's flower beds, he brushed against a variety of sweet-smelling plants. His destination was a secret hiding place underneath the raised foundation of the house where he lay back on the cool red clay and let his imagination develop into scenes filled with heroes who showed up in the nick of time to rescue him from bandits. Underneath the house, pleasant fragrances wafted into his theater, overriding the musty smell of the wood subflooring above him. When it was time for supper, Grandma Robinette called him out of his hiding place to play a game with him. Together they would choose flowers and herbs for the table. With eyes squeezed shut, Jared was challenged to guess which plant his grandma clipped and waved beneath his nose. In time she taught him the names of herbs and flowers by their scent.

"I know these," Jared declared. "I can smell them: rosemary, mint, and honey suckle," he laughed and felt himself rising. He rolled, tumbled, and floated in unison with the colors and fragrances; then he enjoyed another surprise: sounds.

Initially, these were delicate tinkling noises like crystal wind chimes or a fine gold charm bracelet dangling from a young girl's wrist. But then, as if turning up a rheostat, sensations sped up. An unseen gentle but efficient force grabbed hold of Jared. With it he bounced, soared, and twirled giddy with joy.

"*Wheeeee, ooooooo, wheeeeee, heeee—heeee,*" he whistled.

His energy whirled, spiraled up, and then merged with the sounds, fragrances, and colors. United they burst into striking jewel tones that reminded Jared of a kaleidoscope, but this one was different. He was part of it, tumbling and rolling, contributing to the spectacular display.

"Where had I felt this way before?" Jared whispered to himself. "White River Amusement Park?" he asked. "No, it was another place," Jared thought as technicolor light rays shot up around him.

"I remember this," he declared. "I saw this when I was a kid, on a trip to Canada. It's the Northern Lights, the aurora borealis."

Jared's excited energy expanded then retracted slowing him down. He was almost breathless from his fun-filled ride.

"What could possibly happen next?" He asked.

As if responding to a command, the dark expanse lit up, exploding with detail. Appearing as simultaneous happenings, Jared saw things from Lake Junaluska: lush green, mature tree-filled hillsides; tall white wooden lifeguard stands; a variety of wooden, aluminum, or fiber glass fishing boats bobbing on the lake surface; and raccoons tearing into trash cans. And then he saw twin towers in Manhattan turning into dust, hot pretzel sidewalk vendors near Grand Central Station, high prancing, fast-moving trotters at the Indiana Marion County Fair, and deep aqua blue water-filled quarries in Bloomington lined with IU students waiting to make a breathtaking jump into the cold water below.

Mesmerized, Jared breathed in and out evenly. His gazed was fixed on the images. Each one captured a unique moment in time, but he could see all of them simultaneously. His companion smiled knowing that Jared was impressed with how time works in Heaven.

But Jared was not paying attention to the thoughts of his bench guest. He was still watching his life in a single snapshot of time: Pop Wolcott showing him how to properly hold a fishing rod and taking him to the banks of White River to practice setting the hook; he saw Grandma Robinette sweetly scolding him for reading *Mad Magazine* and putting a finger to his lips to hush his best friend Percy as they tromped in the Indiana woods looking for Sasquatch—the hairy man—and calling out "*E aqi*" when they got separated. He saw birthdays, holidays, and getting a pocketknife, Denver's Bronco brown and gold striped socks,.22 rifle, cross bow, putter, track shoes, compass, baseball glove, magnifying glass, Magic 8 Ball, and multicolored marbles.

There were images of him playing checkers with C.W. and him holding his first son Matthew. He saw Rita, his first wife, Matthew's mother. Images danced before him of his fraternity house at IU and hitchhiking to Georgia. He saw his Emory University diploma arriving in the mail, his first day on the job at Coca Cola in Atlanta, and visits to Old Curt's, a favorite Gaffney neighborhood gathering place for young men to tell their stories about college days or fighting in Vietnam. Multiple prints of blue jays, cardinals, wild flowers, and raccoons he had created with watercolors came into focus along with the birth of his twins Marcia and Philip. He saw them at different ages and stages of life. Then he saw her: their mother, Priscilla, his second wife—the one he affectionately called Cilly—a godly woman who tried to help him understand the difference between knowing about Christ and knowing Christ.

Thousands of images of their life together flooded the expanse, yet all were perfectly in focus. One in particular held his gaze. It was their twentieth wedding anniversary; they were slow-dancing—moving expertly to the music, crisscrossing their feet as they twirled to the throaty, soulful, lush sounds of Etta James singing "At Last."

As he held her, Jared looked into Priscilla's hazel eyes and saw love reflected back to him. She nestled her head on his shoulder and pressed into his neck. Her hair was fine and smelled of lavender. Smiling, his cheek touched hers and as it did, he reminisced about their first kiss. He could taste it.

"Is this possible?" Jared asked himself.

Then he heard her say. "My dearest one, my precious, I love you and I'll be with you again someday."

A high-pitched sound yanked the images off the cloud. Jared felt himself gaining energy and increasing in size as if he was everywhere at once, yet he was still whole and near the bench.

"What happened?" he asked, astonished. "The colors, the music, Priscilla, the memories, where did it all go? What was that high-pitched sound? How is it that I could hear my wife's voice, like she was here with me? How was it possible to see everything at once?"

Jared expected his companion to have the answers, but because it was not time for him to fully understand about transformation and arrival, his bench guest replied instead: "Like I said a moment ago, we call it Rapid-Replay in Simulvision and it, too, is part of your orientation—I will explain if you wish."

Anticipation was traded for grumbling and Jared remarked, "It seems there's a lot to explain."

"Actually, there's a lot to understand," the bench guest said, and when Jared did not comment, his companion asked politely, "May I orient you now?"

CHAPTER 6

Time Straddler

Distracted by the fascination of seeing his entire life take place simultaneously, Jared missed the offer to get oriented. He wanted to know about the technology that allowed him to see his entire life at once. "So are you going to tell me how you do that?" he asked.

"Do what?"

"Make everything appear all at the same time but separate."

"Ah, the technology. Eventually, you will understand everything. For now, I can tell you that it is a supernatural time-energy thing."

Jared accepted the brief answer because another question was crowding his thoughts. "Okay, okay, going back to the dying thing, if I'm dead, rather, dying and I'm in Heaven, how is it that I know exactly who I am? I mean, I'm still..."

"I know precisely what you mean," his companion replied. "You are still you."

"I am? How is that possible?" Jared asked.

"This is an aspect of Heaven that many people find difficult to fathom. You see, souls come to the Waiting Room with their personalities intact. Each person has a unique imprint, given to them by God through their parents. And one's soul is a culmination of all events in life on this imprint, which shapes one's personality. If you were a sarcastic or blunt or timid or reserved, cheerful, meek, or outspoken being, you remain so when you arrive in the Waiting Room. Souls also arrive with their LHT intact."

"LHT? What's that? An illness, a disease?"

"In a way, yes. It is a limitation. LHT stands for limited human thinking. We acquire this type of thinking during our Earth journey, the period of probation."

"Period of probation? For what?"

"The period of probation is more like a period of opportunity," his companion remarked and then added, "An opportunity to make a specific choice might be a better way to describe it."

"Choice? You mean to be good?"

"Not exactly," his companion said in a more serious tone. "Being good is important, but that is not the most critical decision we make. The purpose for being born is to choose God. We don't have to, and even when we do choose Him, we can still fail to trust and depend on Him. We can continue to rely on ourselves which increases limited human thinking.

"There's more to be said about L-H-T, but the short version is that here, we infuse it with spirit and transform it into L-I-G-H-T—but only if you permit it. You see, here, just as you retain your personality and all of your memories, you also retain your free will. I would not do anything intentionally to interfere with your free will. Did you notice how I wait for you to ask a question or how I get your permission before doing something?"

"Who *are* you anyway?" Jared grumbled sarcastically.

"Hallelujah! I am so glad you asked. I have been waiting to tell you that. Sonny. Sonny is my name. I am your greeter."

Jared watched the feather pillow-like object next to him change into a red-haired young man with freckles and green eyes. He wore brown corduroy pants, a blue and yellow striped rugby shirt, red sneakers, and white socks with red "IU" letters on the sides.

"This is what I looked like when I lived down there. I thought you might like talking with someone who looks less like a marshmallow and more like a person," Sonny said and Jared laughed.

"That's quite a trick," Jared remarked.

"Oh, everybody here knows how to do this," Sonny said matter-of-factly.

Thinking he would like to know more about Sonny's abilities activated clouds over the expanse; the moving screen filled with details about his bench companion. Sonny grew up in Indiana, was an accomplished horseback rider, attended Culver Academy before transferring to Thomas Carr Howe high school, fought in Vietnam, had a master's degree in math from Indiana University, and was an accomplished rugby player. He enjoyed serious lectures about education, had a winsome sense of humor, and was known for his corny jokes. He had the ability to talk with anyone: the academics over coffee at the IU Student Union Center, the dishwasher at Sully's Oaken Bucket, or the rough and tumble Mudsharks, his fellow IU rugby players.

"So what else would you like to know?" Sonny asked, surprising Jared.

"Everything, I suppose."

"Oh, this is just amazing," Sonny declared happily. "A cooperative, free willer. I love CFWs."

LHT, now CFW. How will I ever keep them straight? Jared thought to himself.

"I will help you," Sonny said.

"You heard that?" Jared asked, astonished. "I thought I said it to myself."

"You did, but remember, earlier when I told you things are different here. When souls are on the same frequency, they share thoughts."

"Frequency? We have a frequency like a radio signal?"

"Oh my, there I go again giving out too much information. I forgot to activate the guardian shield."

"What's that?" Jared interrupted.

Sonny knew that he was drifting away from his assigned task: to get Jared oriented. He prayed for wisdom and guidance to get back to his mission.

"Sometimes greeters have to protect against thought leakage," Sonny began. "We get excited about our work and think about things too advanced for a soul's level of understanding. So occasionally greeters and discussion leaders will need to hide details."

"That doesn't seem fair," Jared grumbled. "You can read my thoughts but then you get to hide yours."

"Trust me, Jared. If we choose to camouflage a detail you are not ready to handle, it is a blessing. We are not keeping secrets, just doing our job to make sure that some thoughts do not get out inappropriately. In time, all these hidden details will be revealed to you, but for now, you and I will be selectively aware of each other's thoughts, which might be funny, embarrassing, or sad. Remember how you saw my suicide but did not know how it was possible for you to see it?"

"Yes, I wondered about that," Jared said.

"It is because I thought it. I relived it, and you saw it. We shared the memory."

Amazing, Jared thought to himself.

"Yes it is," Sonny said, surprising Jared again. "You will get used to it in a while."

"There it is again, that phrase: in a while," Jared said. "This must be code for something," he decided.

Again, Sonny prayed, this time for a strong guardian shield and for better control of his blurting out disorder, which often caused him to share too much with newly arriving souls, especially the ones who are surprised when they find out Heaven exists. He was brimming with eagerness to explain to Jared that he was presently straddling Earth time and Heaven time and that his decision to remain in Heaven could still be reversed. Sonny knew that Jared had to get oriented soon, but the choice to do so was Jared's—not his.

CHAPTER 7

Individually Guided Understanding

"Okay," Jared said. "How do I get rid of limited human thinking? How does LHT get spirit-filled and turn into LIGHT?"

"Ahem," Sonny began; "This happens when something learned is replaced with understanding. For example, while on Earth, you learned things wrongly from a worldly point of view. Your thinking was self-limiting. Here it is not. Here you can think rightly and understand matters from God's point of view."

"Oh no you don't!" Jared blurted out. "I tried that once and it nearly destroyed me. I asked God to humble me so that I could be more like Him, see things His way and love everybody. What a mistake," Jared complained. "I concentrated so hard on loving everyone that I turned into a pressure cooker of nerves. I would be sweet and smiley to people, when actually I wanted to punch them in the gut or kick them in the shins."

"To begin with, Jared, you were operating on worldly soil," Sonny said, "which is filled with the weeds of might and power driven by emotion. Here, once your soil is free of those weeds, you will be driven by the spirit of love, not emotion."

"Isn't love an emotion?"

"*Ummmmm,*" Sonny hesitated then said, "Not like it is down there."

"I don't understand," Jared complained.

Sonny knew it was out of his realm to discuss love, but he felt Jared needed some clarification on the difference between emotional love and agape love. He prayed for wisdom of word choice and then said, "Emotional love is born out of a needy heart. This type of love is exhausting. Agape love is born out of a pure, giving, and unselfish heart. This type of love energizes."

"I'm still not sure I understand," Jared said wondering about the emotional ups and downs of a heart needy for God.

"You will in time, Jared. Leaders especially chosen to help you understand the difference are on their way right now. Each one is handpicked by God just for you."

"Leaders? Handpicked by God for me?"

"Amazing is it not? God is big on the details of individually guided understanding. And once you achieve understanding and love as Christ loves, you will be ready to choose how you want to spend eternity. Some choose to be artists. Some choose to be inventors, pilots, explorers, engineers, athletes, gardeners, dancers, musicians, writers, teachers, greeters, discussion leaders—"

"Hold on a minute," Jared insisted. "I was told that Heaven was a place where you lay at the feet of Jesus in lush green meadows, listen to harps, and watch angels fly around."

"I know. You did not believe in a physical Heaven or a physical body in Heaven, but in a while, you will experience both," Sonny said, thinking that he might need to consult with Einstein for proper word choice.

"On Earth, we are influenced by people who try to convince us that Heaven is a figment of our imagination. When we have faith in the existence of God but do not understand what is written in the Bible about Heaven, we can doubt. But you can see for yourself, Heaven is not an imaginary place."

Sonny's words did not completely expel Jared's doubts. Sensing this, Sonny tried another approach—one that a child might grasp.

CHAPTER 8

It's Okay

"Let me ask you a question, Jared. When you were a child, did you ever wish you could fly?"

"Oh yeah," Jared answered with enthusiasm.

"Well here, you can do that," Sonny said.

"Did you ever want to walk through walls, be invisible, be at two places at once, and see other galaxies, planets?"

"Of course."

"Well here, you can do that too."

Soothing pale colors emerged from the expanse and reached out and swirled around Jared. His energy sped up, vibrated, and hummed. "I like this," Jared laughed to himself, unaware that he was the one generating the colors and the sounds. Sonny did not remark on Jared's production of hues and humming, rather he assured his charge that there is no limit to the joy he will experience once he is perfected.

"You can choose to be solid and physical or you may choose to be pure energy," Sonny continued. "As pure energy, you will have the capacity to be everywhere at once, see everything at once, and you will have powers beyond any you knew on Earth. In Heaven, the soul creates, shares, laughs, plays, dances, and knows peace, joy, and love forever. And yes, sometimes that does include being at the feet of our Lord Jesus, listening to harps, watching angels fly, or just resting in a lush green meadow. Heaven is the ultimate, where experiences are amplified beyond any earthly measure, and you have it on good authority that this is true because here we cannot lie."

"Incredible," Jared sighed. Sonny's description of Heaven was better than anything he had learned from his grandparents, preachers, teachers, or friends. None of them talked about Heaven as a place where it was okay to laugh, dance, clap, and sing. They all made him think Heaven was a place to get punished before you could pass by St. Peter and enter the gates to God's kingdom.

Sonny was glad to be there for Jared. He knew that this soul would wobble, hum, shudder, expand, heat up, and cool down numerous times before he understood matters from God's perspective. Sonny guarded these thoughts from sharing because explaining this was not up to him. Rather, he concentrated on the Waiting Room inspiring a question from Jared.

"The Waiting Room, where I am now, are there others here?"

"Oh, yes," Sonny answered promptly.

"Why can't I see them?"

"Because of privacy issues," Sonny said.

Jared appreciated privacy and was relieved that others would not share his space during this time of discovery. He asked, "Does the Waiting Room look the same for everyone?"

"No, it appears different to each soul. Some people see themselves waiting in line, sitting on a beach, walking, running or playing in a meadow or on a pathway, climbing stairs, or as a passenger on a boat or ship. The possibilities are many. But whatever a soul perceives the Waiting Room to be, it is not a place of fear—and I sense that you have another question," Sonny offered.

"I do. I want to know how I get from where I am now to where I am able to do all those things you told me about."

"You mean being able to walk through walls, be invisible, be two places at once, see other galaxies, planets?" Sonny asked.

"Yes, those things."

Before he spoke, Sonny prayed that he not violate the principles of Heaven and God's time and that he would be wise in his choice of phrases so that Jared could be inspired to move toward orientation.

"Once you are oriented," Sonny began, "you will have the opportunity to visit several realms. Some refer to them as many rooms. Each realm is perfectly appointed by Christ and specific to a part of your worldly life that you did not understand from God's perspective. There is a complete list of the realms you will visit posted in the Doors of Wisdom. Examples of topics of discussion can include family, pride, love, lust, offense and defense, humility, charity, attitudes, church, tithing, prayer, shame, the self, and the father of lies also known as Satan, Lucifer, or Baal-Zebub. Around here, we call him the opposition. The length of your list depends on your progress while you were on Earth which is documented in the Doors of Wisdom. After orientation once you complete a realm here and you understand, you gain wisdom and refinement, which can change the order and number of realms you visit."

"Tell me more about the Doors of Wisdom," Jared said. Sonny sighed; he preferred that Jared choose orientation—but since he was the one who brought up the subject Sonny grimaced but answered promptly, "These are Heaven-tech, supernatural doors that hold details of all things imaginable. Anything ever said, done, or thought is recorded and stored beyond these doors."

Jared considered the Internet and how easily he could access answers to things he wanted to learn about. Sonny did not remark on the difference between learning and understanding at this point rather he said, "Solomon attends the Doors of Wisdom. His office is under the Vanity of Wise Living Cloud. You can visit him and the doors once you are oriented."

Still missing the fact that he had to ask to be oriented and not yet longing for wisdom because of lingering childlike curiosity, Jared asked.

"Okay, so after I go through these realms and understand things from God's point of view, what happens then?"

"You love," Sonny said, unable to stop himself.

"Love who?"

"Everyone."

"Impossible," Jared mumbled, remembering how he had tried that once before and was miserable.

CHAPTER 9

First Love

A tender authoritative nudge kept Sonny from explaining that God's love is more about giving than getting. He knew that Jared's version of love was based on emotion, which is a fragile type of love, and easily shattered when expectations of feeling wanted and worthy fail to become real. As a child, each time Jared loved, he lost, which conditioned him to believe that love began and ended rather than being eternal.

"Can you remember the first time you felt loved?" Sonny asked.

These words came like a warm breeze passing beneath Jared and into the expanse. A wispy cloud formed on its surface. Jared saw himself as a two-year-old being led by the hand into a simple but quality furnished house. He had come to live with Mom and Pop after being with foster parents while authorities searched for his dad. In this recollection, dinner was over and Pop had taken Jared into a sitting room, a place where he liked to relax after the meal. Pop was trying to make Jared feel at home and eventually the ritual of joining Pop in the sitting room became an event that accomplished Pop's goal.

As the recollection rolled onto the clouds, Jared saw himself sitting on the floor next to Pop's overstuffed chair. Beside the chair was a floor lamp with a fringed shade. Each night after leaving the dinner table, Pop rolled his ample body into this chair, turned on the light, and prepared to enjoy his evening pleasure of filling, lighting, and sucking on his favorite pipe. The tobacco he used smelled like sour cherries, but the most exciting thing was not its aroma. It was the smoke.

When Pop sucked in on his pipe, Jared could hardly wait for him to exhale. As he did, the smoke drawn by the heat of the light bulb swirled predictably upward into the lampshade. It soared, pivoted, and fluttered above the top of the shade in such a way that it made Jared, who was almost three at the time, giggle. Pop in response laughed too. Because of the close proximity of the chair, Pop's jolly laughter shook the lamp, causing the fringe on the bottom of the shade to jump like a line of tap dancers.

This delighted Jared. Pop delighted Jared. Together they dug in the garden, buried seeds, turned on the spigot, and watered the soil. Discovering the first evidence of success—fragile green furry leaves poking up from the dirt generated a duet of whistling, jumping about, and pointing at each new sprig of life.

Besides gardening, teaching Jared how to make barnyard animal sounds promised long episodes of odd "*aaahh-hh-heeee-haaaww*" braying donkey sounds or chicken cluck-cluck and rooster morning crowing. These noises were always punctuated with side-aching laughter. Pop also taught Jared how to throw a ball, bait a hook, and land and clean a fish. He took him to Globetrotters basketball games and ice-hockey games and to play miniature golf—where Jared got a hole in one.

At the age of eight, Jared was standing on the side of the road, a short distance from where Pop was changing a blown tire. Before Jared could process the unfamiliar sounds of impact and the peculiar scene of Pop's body gliding without resistance into the air, Pop was no longer alive. He had been struck and killed by an automobile steered with hands of a frantic anonymous person who sped away. Jared had never seen a person killed before, let alone someone he knew and loved.

The split second that claimed Pop's life and the image of his quiet body splayed out on the road replayed in Jared's young mind, especially at nighttime, often exchanging precious hours of sleep for pools of tears that soaked his pillow.

CHAPTER 10

Holes

"After Pop was gone," Jared said, "I decided that I would lie, cheat, and steal as much as I wanted and get saved in the last split second. Like jumping up before a plunging elevator hits the bottom, I could just go on sinning and—snap! I could confess my sins and join Jesus in paradise just like that criminal on the cross did. It worked for him. Certainly, it would work for me. But after all, I was only eight or nine at the time."

"God knows this," Sonny said, his words soft and gentle. "Children do not think like adults, but this I assure you, God never stopped loving you. In fact, He was only one breath away from you at all times. All you had to do was call His name. He would be there and never leave you."

"Never?" Jared asked, sarcasm filling his voice.

"Think about it. He created you. Why would He abandon you?"

"Well, my dad created me and abandoned me. Why wouldn't God?"

"Our heavenly Father is nothing like our earthly father," Sonny said.

"I always thought that my dad abandoned me because he didn't love me. And he didn't love me because I was worthless. I grew up thinking that God agreed with my dad," Jared said.

Sonny sighed but did not speak.

"I spent most of my teen years trying to prove myself to someone," Jared said, "an unknown father and an unseen God. When neither one showed up to help me, I decided that I was on my own. Remembering how cocky and quick-tempered I became makes me wonder how I could possibly make it here."

Sonny remained quiet. He knew about Jared's rebellious teenage and young adult years and his attempts to prove himself worthy. But for now, he wanted to comfort Jared.

"It is because of your heart," Sonny said. "God knows what drives you. He knows your pain, suffering, wants, and needs. And when you misbehave, God understands. He sees into your heart, your core—the true you. Because of this, He has faith in you and His faith, unlike ours, does not come in degrees. He knows that in time you will feel His Love and overcome any notion of unworthiness."

Sonny paused then added, "Only one thing will cause Him to turn away."

"What's that?" Jared asked.

"Rejecting Him, that is the only sin that is not forgiven, and it destines a soul for Hell. When you accept God's gift of salvation—"

Before Sonny could finish his sentence Jared's center heated up.

"I remember something important," Jared declared and his energy field increased in size.

"I was on a train to South Carolina to visit Grandma Robinette. A crippled old man in an army uniform took the seat next to me. His uniform smelled musty and he grunted when he sat down. At first I was annoyed and wanted him to go away. I had been crying and angry with God for taking Pop who hugged me and replacing him with a drunkard who beat me."

Sonny listened; he knew the story and the outcome.

"This old guy talked with me most of the trip. He told me about forgiveness and God's mercy. He said that God's grace was not a trophy given because we are worthy but a gift offered because of His love and that God so loved us that He sent His only son not to condemn us but to save us. The choice is ours: we believe this or we do not."

Jared's recollection of the train ride generated flickering light in the dark expanse. Simulvision clouds materialized and displayed the poignant details of that moment in Jared's life; a tingling sensation swept through the center of his energy.

"What was that?" Jared asked.

"A hole got repaired," Sonny told him.

"A hole? I have holes?"

"Yes. All souls do."

"What?" Jared sputtered. "How does a soul get holes in it?"

"Holes are caused by sin," Sonny said.

Jared interrupted. "I thought once a sin was confessed, it was forgiven and forgotten."

"With God, yes, but with sin, there is residual—deep scars," Sonny clarified. "To us it looks like a hole and only understanding can mend it."

"How so?" Jared asked.

"When we sin and confess that sin, we are forgiven, but we still are left with the consequences. This is when our faith in God is put to the test. After a person accepts responsibility for the consequences of a sin and strives to not repeat that sin, the father of lies gears up with every bit of ammunition he can muster to assure that we fail. A sly trick this wicked one uses is to convince a person that his sin is not forgiven. And because the pain, shame, or consequences of that sin remain, it is easy for a person to accept the false notion that God could not possibly forgive them. Satan's goal is to make a person believe that because of sin, God's love is taken away."

Jared knew this trick; it had worked on him—he remembered how afraid he was of being abandoned and how his drunken father replacement made him feel ashamed by calling him a loser, bastard kid, and stupid and telling him that he ran like a girl.

"Fear, intimidation, humiliation, and feeling unworthy are powerful and wicked drivers," Sonny said startling Jared. "Not yet accustomed to sharing thoughts?" Sonny chuckled.

"No, it's a strange feeling, but I'll get used to it, I guess."

"You will—in a while," Sonny said. Jared smiled at the choice of words. He was enjoying his time with Sonny and didn't want it to end.

CHAPTER 11

Evil? Really?

"**W**icked drivers lead to shame and shame makes us vulnerable to rejecting God," Sonny said in a subdued voice. "A vulnerable person drifts away from God and onto Satan's prey-ground. On this soil, disciples of the father of lies thrive, and evil is poised to strike anyone who stumbles in."

Sonny's words caused Jared to wobble like a two-year-old learning how to walk and he nearly fell off the bench. His movement generated rings of instability. In support of Jared's moment of imbalance, Sonny moved closer. He knew what he had to say would be upsetting, so he braced Jared for what he was about to hear.

"In evil's territory," Sonny began, "Satan coos, strokes, cradles, or rocks a person onto islands of self-pity, bitterness, depression, shame, and doubt. Satan can even glow if he must. All he needs is a tiny speck of shame, fear, or doubt to get a person to look his way. As soon as he hears words of defeat, 'What's the use? Why pray? God's not listening, anyway,' Satan slithers in, latches on, and drags God's beloved into places where they can be pummeled, beaten, kicked, raped, stricken with disease, and experience financial ruin or intense heartache and loss, and when they are attacked, if they blame God rather than lean on God, Satan is delighted because this soul is primed to change sides."

Jared shuddered as he recalled a time when he mocked God and claimed to be an atheist. He gazed into the expanse and watched the memory. He had been taken to Community Hospital in Indianapolis to recover from a brutal beating by thugs who felt entitled to his night's poker game winnings. With a broken jaw, four cracked ribs, a fractured collarbone, and a lacerated spleen, Jared was fortunate to be alive, but he didn't see it that way. He laughed when C.W. a chaplain at the hospital asked if he could pray for him. Jared spat in C.W.'s face and bellowed "I don't believe in God." Now Jared was ashamed of what he said to C.W. about God being a cruel tyrant who takes a mother from her child or a loving grandfather from his grandson and puts in their place a drunkard who whips, beats, and belittles. Jared watched the scene of himself crying like a tiny child when C. W. encircled his shoulders, held him close and with tenderness told him, "I don't believe in that God either." "Evil is real, isn't it?" Jared said. "Indeed," Sonny answered.

CHAPTER 12

Losers' Hall of Fame

Sonny ignored another nudge from authority reminding him that he was about to drift out of his realm. "In the Losers' Hall of Fame," he began, "we feature a long list of men and women who were spectacular at messing up but in time got turned around. Take Manasseh, for example," Sonny said.

"Manasseh? Who's that?" Jared asked.

"That is right. You did not read the Old Testament much."

"It scared me."

"The opposition at work," Sonny sighed.

"How so?"

"Why else would you be afraid to read the Word of God?"

Startled by a zinging sound that zipped past Jared's ear, he looked up. A dragonfly pulling a sheer banner floated across the dark expanse. Words on the banner lit up the Waiting Room: The Bible! More than six billion in print! 350 different languages! Get yours today! Discover the Divine text and God's love and mercy today!

Jared watched the banner float past; he didn't expect to see such a sight in Heaven, but it did remind him of the early years with Grandma Robinette and how she loved the Scripture and encouraged him to know his Bible.

"My grandma told me once that when we pray, that's us talking to God, but when we read the Bible, that's God talking to us," Jared said still watching the banner float off into the expanse.

"I like what your grandma told you," Sonny said. "My brother, Tim, leads a discussion about the Bible. You are welcome to visit his realm. His audiovisual aids are indescribable. You just have to see them to believe them. He covers the 'if word,' 'missing parts,' how a preposition can change the meaning of scripture, and Third Timothy."

"Third Timothy? Is this one of the lost books of the Bible?"

"Not really. Tim calls this the repository of things mistakenly attributed to the Bible. He reminds us that we ought to study numerous translations and transliterations and meditate on each one. And he stresses how vital it is for us to ask the Holy Spirit for wisdom and perspective as we study God's Word because many human beings get feisty and argue over scripture that they think is contradictory."

"Well, there are some things that don't make sense," Jared said remembering how defensive he became when he and C.W. talked about Cain leaving home to get a wife.

"I know," Sonny said. "We have seen some monumental word hurling between people who use scripture to shore up their point of view, to scare or judge someone. It pains us to see the Bible used this way."

"You mean by Christians?"

"By anyone who is using God's Word in a hateful, scare-tactic, demeaning, or demoralizing way. Although words may appear contradictory, the message never changes: God is faithful, loving, and merciful."

Jared thought about a conversation he had with C.W. when he argued that the Bible was just a bunch of books written by ordinary men. C.W. never raised his voice, remained calm, and then asked Jared: "What if God intended mysteries and contradictions to remain in the Bible just to see how we would handle these differences as brothers and sisters in Christ? Would we hammer one another with opinion? Or would we be encouraged to delve deeper into God's word?"

"Love one another as God loved us," Jared whispered.

Sonny knew that he had a mission and needed to get his charge focused; doing so was the mark of a good leader—something Sonny was striving for.

"Tim's discussion sessions about the Bible are deep, thoughtful, and assure increased wisdom," Sonny said. "I encourage you to call on him for further understanding and you might be interested to know that I will be joining him too once I get you oriented."

Again, completely missing the part about getting oriented, Jared asked, "So you are still learning?"

"No. On Earth we learn things. Here we understand things. Learning does not always lead to wisdom."

Jared hummed wondering why Sonny felt he lacked wisdom. He was about to find out.

PART TWO

Discovering

Psalm 1:2 "...but his delight is in the law of the Lord"

CHAPTER 13

Blurting Out Disorder

"I am easily distracted and say things without thinking," Sonny said. "I get overly stimulated with all the beauty and potential of Heaven. When a soul asks for clarification of some issue, I have a tendency to try to help them understand things that are outside my realm. Sometimes I blurt out things ahead of schedule and generate lively discussion, far above my level of wisdom."

"I know the feeling," Jared offered in support. "I used to blurt things out without thinking."

"Yes, the mouth can get us into a lot of trouble," Sonny agreed. "I almost never see that blurting-out thing coming. Anyway, Tim will give you greater details about Manasseh. For now, I can tell you Manasseh was a terrible person. If you read about him, you might put him in the same category as Adolf Hitler—who is here by the way," Sonny blurted out unintentionally.

"Whaaaat? Whaaaaat?" Jared howled lifting off the bench. "Hitler is in Heaven? I *cannot* believe it. I won't believe it. How can that be?"

Jared's energy was so charged with astonishment that he bounced off the back of the bench, nearly snapping his tether and propelling himself over the cliff and into the dark expanse.

"Oh brother, I did it again," Sonny sighed and then attempted to calm Jared who was not at a level of wisdom to understand how Hitler could be in Heaven.

"I am really pushing my boundaries," Sonny said, "but since I am the one responsible for premature information sharing, it is my duty to get your frequency reset—perhaps I can do this by revealing one tiny bit."

Jared still bloated with bewilderment did not want to doubt God, but he also could not imagine such an evil person being permitted into Heaven. Of anyone, Jared believed that Hitler was the most cruel and hateful person to ever live.

Sonny took a deep breath and said, "When Hitler was given the Final Offer, he accepted."

"Final offer? You've got to be kidding. Bottom line, are you telling me that Adolf Hitler did all the horrible things and then God invited him into Heaven?"

"Bottom line, yes," Sonny said meekly. "But if you will give me a chance to explain, you might understand."

"Final offer, final offer," Jared grumbled. "Sounds like a real estate term."

Sonny brightened. "It is in fact a real estate term, but here the definition of real estate is different. Here it is about a place we inherit by God's grace in exchange for our debts."

Sensing Jared was not yet satisfied, Sonny added, "With the Final Offer, a soul is given one last chance to call on the name of the Lord for mercy. A soul can remain loyal to the self, take the defensive, and hang on to all debts claiming these were not his fault—that they were created by someone else or a soul can do the opposite. He can claim ownership of these debts, his sins, and hand them over to Christ. He inherits accordingly hell or paradise."

"Are you talking about the paradise Christ offered the criminal on the cross?" Jared asked.

"I am," Sonny said beginning to feel he had returned to his level of wisdom.

"And you are telling me that Hitler inherited just like that guy, just like the Reverend Ken Hutcherson, the Reverend Billy Graham, Maya Angelou, Pastor Samuel Rodriguez, Dr. Charles Stanley, the Reverend Dr. Martin Luther King?"

Jared would have continued with a long string of names of people he felt were entitled to inherit God's kingdom, but he was too jangled about Hitler to name anyone else. It wasn't making sense to him. He decided to give Sonny a chance to explain things but he was feeling like God had made a mistake.

"God is incapable of that," Sonny whispered.

Jared jumped, startled by Sonny's shared thought.

Tempted to talk faster, Sonny knew that if he could only get the words out, Jared would be okay with Hitler being in Heaven. He resisted rushing the discussion and said, "God never gives up on us—even until our last breath."

CHAPTER 14

All Sinners Welcome

"Hitler in Heaven, this just doesn't sound right," Jared snorted.

"Do you think the sins of Hitler are worse than yours?" Sonny asked.

"Absolutely!" Jared bellowed.

Sonny remained quiet allowing Jared to consider his response.

My sins? Jared thought. *They certainly weren't on the scale of what Hitler did. Or were they?* "Sin is sin regardless of degree," he remembered telling his son Philip. Now he was emotionally charged, unable to accept his own words. He realized he was trying to change his son's behavior with advice that he did not apply to himself.

Jared did not want to displease God. Obviously if Hitler was here, God allowed it and he felt the need to understand why. Straining for recollections he remembered having a discussion with Priscilla about Hitler. He had asked her, "How could anyone possibly love Hitler?" She answered, "If he were your son."

Her comment made him think about his two sons: Matthew, the one he abandoned, and Philip, the one who abandoned him. If he could be with either of them now, he would be glad to ask for their mercy, their forgiveness. Recalling these memories caused a swell of regret to rise. Jared changed his tone and humbly asked, "Why does God continue to love us when we are so terrible? Why does He keep trying?"

"You will understand in a while," Sonny said.

"I want to understand now!" Jared insisted.

"I cannot tell you now," Sonny said realizing the consequences of taking on extra duty outside his area of expertise. "My job is to get you oriented."

Jared again missed the point about getting oriented. He was unsettled, trying to grasp the idea of Hitler in Heaven. Regardless of how much energy he put into understanding, he continued to wobble, shiver, and shake—he felt pinched by an idea that was too extreme for him to embrace.

"I promise, you will come to understand," Sonny said.

"I know, I know...in a while," Jared added with sarcasm.

"Would it be all right to change the subject?" Sonny asked, hoping that Jared would agree. As encouragement, Sonny thought about fishing on Lake Junaluska, North Carolina, which redirected Jared's thoughts. Humility oozed in, calming Jared to think about his later years with Priscilla and how he wanted to be a better man. He recalled how easy it was for him to backslide and find his temper or offend someone with his political leanings or his opinion about the church.

"What if a person who's trying to live a life of obedience messes up and sins?" Jared asked Sonny.

"When a man accepts Christ, he has God's supernatural power to stop sinning," Sonny replied.

"But this does not mean that he will never sin again. It is inevitable that he will. Even when a person is surrendered to Christ, he will sin daily because his thinking can be faulty or he is unable to resist a temptation and spends too much time in the dark. There, for certain, he will stumble.

"When we walk in the light, we can see better what is on our path," Sonny told Jared who was weighing the meaning of the words fall and stumble. He liked the word stumble better; it carried hope.

"Yes, it does," Sonny said, having shared Jared's thought. "You trip up, but you can get back up, ask for forgiveness, and try all over again. That is a promise of the relationship with God. He will forgive you—if you ask."

"Well, what if a man knows this and just keeps on sinning?"

CHAPTER 15

Willful Disobedience and Heart-Set

"God knows the heart," Sonny said. "He knows when an action is a performance, a test, or a sincere confession. Being Heaven-bound is all about a person's heart-set."

"Did you mean to say mindset?" Jared asked.

"Heart-set is the correct term. The mind can play tricks on you. The heart cannot."

Jared wanted more information about the heart; he knew if he got still, Sonny would deliver.

"When a soul is departing from the body," Sonny began, "the heart is in control and has the capacity to hear the voice of Christ. If it does, this soul will know which direction to go as the body releases it. Others will not."

Jared couldn't resist, "It is beyond me that Hitler would ever have accepted Christ. I just cannot picture him capable of doing that."

Sonny had hoped Jared was past the issue of Hitler, but since he obviously was not, he knew he had to resume attempts to help Jared understand. He said, "I know, it is baffling. Sometimes we are so certain about who we will see in Heaven and who is bound for Hell."

Jared sighed. As he pictured Hitler, all he could see was a hideous, hateful murderer.

"Right now, you are remembering Hitler as a cruel person who organized and allowed unthinkable atrocities," Sonny said. "He was all of those things, but you do not yet understand the ways of God. You will. I assure you. You will eventually know that each arriving soul is unique and once oriented will have specific experiences needed to see things from God's point of view."

Preoccupied with the thought of Hitler and his cruelty Jared said, "I hope his experiences were rotten." Immediately he had an unpleasant twinge and his unmerciful thought was replaced with one of conflict causing his energy to become unstable and give off a discordant buzzing sound.

With compassion, Sonny spoke, "In the Realm of Empathy, Hitler's faulty thinking was corrected."

"Realm of empathy, what's that?" Jared interrupted.

"I'll get to that..."

"I know. In a while," Jared scoffed.

Sonny prayed for wisdom. He had requested this extra duty so that he could be more refined. Now he was wondering if he could deliver what Jared needed to move him toward orientation before it was too late.

"In the Realm of Empathy, Hitler was given the opportunity to understand mercy and the meaning of Christ's commandment to love others as He loves us." In a subdued and measured tone, Sonny continued, "Hitler experienced the terror, panic, agony, despair, depression, hunger, thirst, neglect, abuse, pain, injustice, loneliness, hopelessness, and cruelty he caused each and every person in his life, as well as what he did to his loyal dog, Blondie."

Jared interrupted Sonny. He was thinking that Hitler bombarded by all of these horrible experiences surely felt fear. "I thought you said that in Heaven there is no fear."

"Ah, good point," Sonny said. "I did tell you that and it is true. Here oriented souls can experience these moments empathically, but fear is not present because the Holy Spirit hovers over them as an assurance of hope. The fear that is absent in Heaven is the fear of being abandoned. But what Hitler caused others to feel, he experienced. Sonny paused, then asked. Can you imagine knowing the terrifying emotion that you caused another to have and all the while you are aware that in spite of your atrocious behavior, the presence of the Holy Spirit is with you, loving you, protecting you, helping you to understand things from God's merciful perspective?"

Jared's energy twitched and puckered. He knew he lacked the wisdom to fully grasp this reality; he decided to keep quiet and listen to what Sonny had to say.

"Hitler met each soul whose free will he took," Sonny continued. "One by one, these souls helped him understand the potential that he destroyed and the beauty that potential would have brought to others."

"I know you said the Holy Spirit hovered over him, but was he on his own?" Jared asked. "I mean, was there a person-like soul in there with him? Was he by himself?" Jared was surprised by his moment of caring and asking such a question. Still he wondered.

"No, he was not alone," Sonny said. "Henry Gerecke, Dietrich Bonhoeffer, Dr. King, and a young Jewish boy were with him."

A warm sensation washed over Jared and he was struck by the exquisite irony. *Good and faithful servants*, he thought. Could he be that faithful, that unselfish to look after and care for such a heinous enemy?

Jared's thought shifted when he heard Sonny say, "In the Realm of Empathy, God provides the soul an opportunity to feel the same mercy that was given by them to another on Earth."

"This sounds more like judgment to me," Jared remarked.

"Judgment is a one-on-one with your Creator. Empathy is a one-on-one with other souls."

"Oh, I see the difference," Jared said.

"'Glad you do. Glad I could help," Sonny said.

"I know that I will face judgment, but will I go through the realm of empathy?" Jared asked.

"Absolutely!" Sonny blurted out unintentionally.

CHAPTER 16

Sympathy, Empathy, Judgment, and God's Wrath

Realizing that he had once again provided detail prematurely and delayed orientation, Sonny prayed. Graciously he was given the insight to handle topics of discussion that he never before had managed. He was inspired to be serious with the next few topics and to concentrate on getting Jared to orientation.

Sonny began, "What sympathy, empathy, and judgment have in common is the opportunity to understand matters from another perspective."

"So judgment is me seeing how God sees me?" Jared asked.

"Almost," Sonny said. "Judgment is shared with Christ alone—only Christ can judge us, because only He knows our truth, our heart."

Jared's frequency revved up, "You mean, when I go through judgment, no one else will hear about my atrocious behavior?"

"No, in judgment, they cannot."

"All my life," Jared said. "I pictured judgment day taking place in some massive auditorium, the audience filled with all of mankind, me standing center-stage, bright lights glaring, and a monstrous sound system broadcasting the sordid details of my miserable failures."

"No, it does not happen like that—whatever the sin, it was against Him only and as such, judgment will be up close and personal with Christ alone."

Sonny's comment startled Jared. He realized this encounter could hurt more than any embarrassing moment in front of other sinners. His energy changed from excited to somber as he thought about the many times he chose to be disobedient and what those moments would feel like in the presence of God.

No excuses, he thought. *I made the choices. I could have given all my hurts, worries, and anger to God. How different would my moment of judgment be if I had done that all along?* Jared asked himself.

"Everyone asks that," Sonny said, again surprising Jared not yet accustomed to thought-sharing.

"Everyone?" Jared asked.

"If they choose to come here, they do," Sonny said.

Heaven was becoming a place Jared wished he would have taken more time to prepare for. He once had asked Priscilla about Heaven and she told him a story that sounded like science fiction. She said that she had visited Heaven after giving birth to their twins, Marcia and Philip. At the time, her story seemed like a dream but it did make him wonder.

"Many people wonder about Heaven," Sonny offered. "But that is all they need, a tiny spark of wonder. The Bible provides splendid detail about God's kingdom, but sometimes people misinterpret passages and get scared that God is after them to hurt them—this especially happens with young children or those who fixate on passages about fear and God's wrath."

Jared remembered Grandma Robinette reading passages out of Jeremiah that frightened him. He said, "Reading the Old Testament was not something I did much, but Priscilla loved it. When I asked her about the revengeful, cruel God of wrath, she told me that God was incapable of cruelty. His wrath was delivered to those who demanded it over repentance. They had used their free will to test God's warning about the dangers of holding onto sin. She told me that she believed with rare exception some of these defiant beings died, got a glimpse of Hell, and came back to be a better man—willing and wanting to please God."

As the memory of this conversation dissolved, something occurred to Jared and he asked, "You say that my judgment is with Christ alone. But what about the angels and others that are witnesses on judgment day?"

Sonny knew that answering this question was going to take him out of his realm. Trying to explain things to a soul still connected to limited human thinking is as difficult as trying to describe a dream to someone. Not until one is oriented to Heaven and understands omnipresence and omniscience can he comprehend how judgment day is a corporate experience yet with Christ alone. Sonny loved his job and didn't want to violate heavenly principles; so again he prayed and was able to camouflage his immature thoughts by concentrating on one of the "strange battles" of the Civil War.

He asked God for wisdom in what to say next about angels on judgment day.

"That is a good question, Jared," Sonny said. "I know it is a struggle, but in a while, everything will make sense."

"Humph," Jared grunted. "There it is again. In a while, in a while—everything in a while."

Sonny did not comment. He had a job to do and realized that he and Jared could talk for a long time and delay the inevitable. Since he had introduced the terms sympathy, empathy, and judgment, he needed to finish up with descriptions of these words. So he concentrated on the word "empathy" until Jared asked about it.

"So, tell me more about empathy," Jared said.

"Of course," Sonny said, glad that he had curtailed his drifting.

"Empathy is feeling what another feels," Sonny said.

"So, it's like I'm in their skin?"

"Yes, and in the Realm of Understanding Empathy, there are two chambers. One is called echo. The other is called Reflection. The Echo Chamber is where your words are echoed back to you.

Anything you said in anger to anyone such as your parents, brothers or sisters, grandparents, children, friends, your boss, or God is shouted back at you. It is a sobering moment to hear your own voice yell, "I hate you!" or "Go to Hell!"

"The Reflection Chamber is..." Sonny stopped himself and said, "Forgive me."

"Forgive you?" Jared asked, puzzled. "Hasn't that been done?"

"To the point," Sonny explained, "forgiveness here is about respect for others. Another discussion leader is in charge of describing the Reflection Chamber. And another one covers Heaven etiquette."

"There are rules of etiquette in Heaven?"

"Certainly, but these rules are more like manners for those going through the various realms," Sonny clarified.

"Martha leads discussion on Heaven etiquette. She also covers time management. Her personal story is a classic. It is a good example of things we can miss when driven by 'shoulds and musts,' Sonny said. "She knew the Master when He was down there," he added.

"Is she the one who complained about being overwhelmed with fixing dinner and cleaning the house for company while her sister Mary was rubbing oil on the feet of Jesus?"

"Correct," Sonny said, pleased that Jared remembered scripture. "Martha helps you understand the limitations of 'shoulds and musts,' noble acts, rigidity, being strong-willed, driven by a need to be needed or loved, and the value of time. She wraps up discussion with Heaven etiquette. I love her. You will too. In fact, you will love everyone here. It comes naturally," Sonny could not resist adding.

"There seems to be a lot to understand," Jared said. "But the more I hear, the more I want to hear," he added sincerely.

Sincerity, that is nice. Sonny said without speaking.

"I heard that. I did. I heard you say 'sincerity, that is nice,'" Jared declared, amplifying the vibration of his energy and expansion of his colors.

"That is how it works here," Sonny said. "You and I are on the same frequency, so we see and hear things about one another. Heaven etiquette is essential once you master sharing thoughts."

Realizing that they were at risk for drifting and knowing that there was a lot to cover, Sonny asked if he could review the differences of judgment, empathy, and sympathy and move toward orientation.

"I don't remember anything about sympathy," Jared said. "I understand that judgment is one-on-one with Jesus, that empathy is one-one-one with another soul, and God's wrath is about disappointment, but I'm not sure what sympathy is. Isn't it feeling pity for someone?" Jared asked.

"Correct. Sympathy is just that," Sonny said. "But if a person is not careful, he can get snagged by feeling pity for someone and be conned."

"Conned? How in the world could having pity for someone set you up to be conned?" Jared asked.

Sonny knew that it was Martha's responsibility to cover con jobs, self-pity, and discernment in another realm. He needed to get Jared back on course to orientation.

"Me and my blurting out disorder," Sonny laughed. "Martha covers con artists. You will be with her soon. Until then, I hope you'll have patience with me."

"Why wouldn't I?" Jared asked. "You've been patient with me and did your best to answer my questions—in fact one comes to mind right now."

"What would that be?" Sonny asked.

"It's about holes. If holes are healed when we ask for forgiveness, then why do I still have them?" Jared asked.

"Good question," Sonny said. "Holes are not healed when we ask for forgiveness or even when we understand. They are repaired, fixed, or mended, all of which leave scars. The healing of scars requires a massive amount of the purest type of love— His type."

"You mean God?"

"Yes, God the Father, the Son, and the Holy Spirit type of love. When we stumble, and sin, we ask for forgiveness," Sonny said. "God gives us that, but the consequences of the sin remain. These are scars which can turn us into bitter people wallowing in self-pity or they can cause us to be people grateful for wisdom. In either case, God will make beauty out of our messes."

Sonny's words reminded Jared of something he did to a man who had parked in his driveway. Greatly offended because the man did this without asking his permission, Jared called a towing service and had the man's car towed away.

"I'm ashamed of that now," Jared said and felt a tingle. *Did a hole get repaired?* He wondered.

"Affirmative," Sonny said causing Jared to smile.

Sharing thoughts with Sonny was becoming easier. He liked his greeter and was grateful that Sonny was chosen for the job—but Sonny knew that he had not yet done his job. Jared was still stuck on the bench because his greeter had taken on extra duty and talked too much.

CHAPTER 17

Messes Become Beautiful

For a moment, Jared felt the urge to rise up off the bench but resisted it and waited for Sonny to speak. Asking permission from authority to cover this one last lesson, beauty out of messes, Sonny promised to stay focused. He made his request on a frequency that Jared could not hear and felt confident that he could inspire Jared to move from the bench to orientation.

"Your story is a great example of how God does just that," Sonny said. "He makes beauty out of our messes."

Jared listened; he liked hearing stories about himself. Or so he thought.

"At first, your action triggered pride. The driveway was your territory. How dare this person park there without permission?"

The bench was getting uncomfortable; Jared was not sure he wanted Sonny to finish the story. But Sonny pressed on.

"The opposition was delighted with your conclusion and sent you two neighbors to congratulate you on your fine work. The neighbors, one of them a disciple of the opposition, told you how appropriate it was to call the tow truck on this guy. You and the two neighbors got a good laugh knowing that it was Friday and that the owner would not be able to get his car until Monday. You felt triumphant."

"I did," Jared said, now wondering how he could have ever felt good about making some other person suffer.

Pleased with Jared's show of compassion, Sonny shared, "God never revealed to you just what happened to that man, but you will get to learn about it in the Realm of Empathy."

"Oh no, not that," Jared cried out.

"You can calm down," Sonny offered. "Since later in life you became remorseful about what you did and asked God to forgive you, the pain of that man's experience will not be so bad for you. After all, he did break the rules. He should not have parked on your private property, especially since you had such large and prominent signs warning against trespassing."

The use of the word trespass generated a ripple of familiarity in Jared. He repeated the words he learned as a child: "Forgive me my trespasses as I forgive those who trespass against me."

"Now I get to understand how that feels. I'm going to feel what he felt, right?"

"That is empathy," Sonny replied, "feeling someone else's pain. It's different from sympathy, which is when you feel sorry for someone, or take pity on someone. Being sympathetic can drive us to fix things that God intended to use to refine the individual. Being empathic does a better job of helping us understand and offer comfort rather than a solution. In this case, it will not be so bad. You'll see. Actually, you will enjoy the man's story. It has a surprise ending."

"Oh tell me, please. I need to know what happened to that guy," Jared begged.

Sonny laughed and then said, "Okay, since you need to know."

Jared's energy bubbled with anticipation. He liked tidy endings but he was especially eager to know about this one, because he had carried a lot of guilt over what he had done.

"Since the man did not have his car, he and his family were not able to go to their regular church, a mega-church where they were not growing in their relationship with God. Instead, they walked to a little church in their neighborhood—and that's all I'm going to say on the subject," Sonny said showing restraint.

I always wanted to find that man, reimburse his towing charges, and ask him to forgive me. I was young, stupid, calloused, and smug. I'm glad to know that in spite of the mess I created, it was turned into beauty for this man."

"God will not waste any part of you Jared. Sonny said. "He will use your failures, pride, greed, or even your anger if necessary.

"He knew the journey you would make before you are born," Sonny said. "He knew that you would find Him, ignore Him, doubt Him, challenge His love, and wrestle with Him. He also knew that one day you would desire to connect with Him. Remember the moment you did that? When you and God connected?" Sonny asked.

"I do. It was incredible," Jared whispered. "Like I was on the highest peak of the most magnificent mountain—the air crisp, cool, refreshing—nothing was going to go wrong, but this feeling didn't last. In fact, soon after, life became miserable."

"I understand," Sonny said.

CHAPTER 18

MT Experiences

"The mountain-top experience can generate giddiness and feelings of self-importance, which produces boasting that yields anxiety and worry driven by 'shoulds and musts.' But this encounter can also generate joy, sobriety, and refinement which grows our understanding of God's ways. Wisdom and peace are the fruits, Jared. In this state, we are calm, meek, and able to give a testimony that is not arrogant, threatening, or judgmental but one that creates a yearning for the listener to know Christ in a personal way. We do not long for the mountain top experience, rather we appreciate the benefit of having had one."

Jared noticed the change in Sonny; he liked it. Sonny seemed more mature and Jared wanted to be in tune with him.

"You will know the answer to this," Jared said. "When I was younger, I learned that with every euphoric moment, sadness and depression followed."

"That makes sense, Jared. When we brag about a supernatural encounter with Christ, it is draining. But when we 'just be' the proof that we are changed by the experience, it is exhilarating. Do you remember when Jesus healed a leper, a blind man, and a deaf man? He told one to go back to his town and tell what had to happened, but the others he told to be quiet. He knew that one man would act out of joy and gratitude, where the others would act out of happiness and greed for another MT experience."

"Grandma Robinette told me that 'happiness depends on happenings' but joy is permanent because it comes from a right relationship with Christ."

"That's right, Jared. How we come down from the mountain, happy or joy-filled, will dictate how we view life. Will we expect God to make our lives free of pain and suffering? Or will we know that God's promise is to be with us constantly whether we are on the mountain top where the opposition is uncomfortable and rarely goes or in the valley where the opposition has unlimited resources and roams unchecked?"

Sonny's words made Jared feel like a tight-rope walker losing balance, "I've been in that valley," Jared said. "It was awful."

As the memory rose on the cloud, the two shared it silently. At a political rally, Jared met a man who convinced him that with his connections the two could make a lot of money if they went into business together.

"Stupidly, I did," Jared said out loud. "Taking money out of our savings to start the company. This nearly destroyed my life with Priscilla. Around him, my old ugly habits came back. I started using foul language, lying, looking at other women, and enjoying X-rated movies and TV shows. I ignored my children who were babies at the time. I drank too much and stepped up my smoking habit from two packs a day to three. Priscilla and C.W. saw what was taking place in me. I was like an addict being fed 'power'—my drug of choice. But they stood by me, patiently guiding me back to safe ground in spite of the access I gave to this con artist. When the truth of this man's plan became clear, I wept with sorrow and embarrassment and now shudder at the thought of how close I had come to destroying our lives."

"Near misses always make us shudder," Sonny said.

"Yes, I know. I was fortunate to have a loving wife and C.W., a good friend who was an expert in relationships. He asked me to do something that I'll never forget."

"What was that, Jared?"

"To name the three things I cherish most. I told him my wife, my children, my work, and he told me to give these to God."

"And you did this?" Sonny asked.

"Yes, I did."

"What and how did you feel then?"

"Relief, free. Like the burdens of duty on my shoulders were lifted off. I saw Priscilla, my children, and my work not as my responsibility but as blessings being cared for by a power more capable than me."

"And what happened after that?" Sonny asked.

"The con-artist business partner disappeared along with all the money in the bank account—the reality of the near miss hit me hard. I had made the choice to become partners with this man—even when Priscilla warned me that she did not trust him. I cried in Priscilla's arms and asked for her forgiveness for being so proud and feeling superior—feeling like I knew better than anyone, including her."

"And what did she do?" Sonny asked.

"She told me that the cost of refinement can be painful, but together, we would work through the loss and be restored, if we did this with gratitude and not for the sake of amassing a lot of money. Her kindness deepened my love for her. She could have railed on me, blamed me, threatened me but she didn't."

"This was a spiritual flash point," Sonny declared.

"I don't understand that term," Jared said.

"You will. It is key to who you are. But I do not have the authority to cover the meaning of this term. Another leader is in charge of discussing it, but I can tell you this much, it is a point in time that redirects a life. After orientation, you will understand."

"Orientation—what is the purpose of orientation and your job as a greeter?" Jared asked realizing that he had not been curious about Sonny's job.

Gratitude for the opportunity to move his assigned charge closer to orientation surged through Sonny. He bubbled with gladness and said, "While on Earth, you doubted that Heaven was an actual place. Therefore, you did not know how to get oriented when you arrived. You needed someone to help you. This is where an intercessor steps in and provides assistance. In your case, the intercessor prayed that you be turned to the light. Immediately, I was sent by our heavenly Father to greet you. Part of my job is to stay with you as long as you remain in the Waiting Room and until you choose to be oriented—that is, turned to the light and on your way to understanding. This is my job, my sole purpose—pun intended." Sonny smiled, but Jared did not see it. He had a question.

"So if someone prayed for me to go to the light, why am I still looking at this dark, quiet expanse?"

"Simple," Sonny replied, "the prayer went to God, not to you. Remember, you were not convinced that there was such a place as Heaven. How could you possibly know anything about it if you had doubts about its existence? You are here because you accepted God's gift. If you believed in a physical Heaven, you would have skipped over the dark, quiet expanse and immediately be oriented. In cases of doubt, like yours, there are delays. Someone on Earth has to pray for you to turn to the light. God answers that prayer and sends a greeter—a companion—like me. I can wait as long as it takes, but you are the one who makes the choice."

"Really? Then what am I waiting for? Orient me. Now," Jared cried out.

"Oh, thank you. I will," Sonny said relieved and grateful that Jared finally asked.

The best part of his job was about to take place. Sonny was going to witness an orientation—each one a miraculous display of peace, love, joy, humility, glory, power, and awe.

CHAPTER 19

Orientation

To turn Jared, Sonny needed to merge their energies—a delicate move considering the billions of colors involved in the merger. Exhibiting a skill reserved for Heaven, and to allow Jared to get accustomed to the tingling sensation, Sonny offered his energy which lifted Jared up from the bench. New colors formed a mosaic of mutually contributed hues.

Jared felt enriched, exhilarated. Because he trusted him, being one with Sonny and giving him control over his energy was effortless. He sensed himself revolving, turning away from the dark, quiet expanse. As he was turned, he got a glimpse of something majestic, magnificent—splendid—a golden-white light, pure, rare, and irresistible. As he completed the turn, the light spread out before him—it was immense—it expanded in endless billows of bright shining energy, wrapping completely around him; it moved in a way that could not be described because words were insufficient to express the splendor he was witnessing.

Jared felt no fear. He felt connected: calm, drawn to, and wanting to permanently join with this radiance. He inhaled deep and slow and as he exhaled, he released Sonny, who, once separated from Jared, watched with love as crystal tears of joy poured from him into Jared's colors. Like a ribbon fluttering to the ground, Jared crumpled onto his knees. Solemn with awe, he wept. His sobs were deep and heart-felt. His hands slid out in front of him and turned upward, reaching out. He could not speak; he could barely breathe. The light was electrifying, strikingly beautiful yet peaceful and loving—Jared had never before felt this type of love. It was pulling him—forceful as an ocean's undertow.

"Ah," Sonny whispered. "You are now filled with The Longing. It is different from the emotional mountain-top experience on Earth, isn't it?"

"Yes," Jared breathed—the word barely audible.

"You are witnessing the power and splendor of your Creator."

"My Creator? Is this what God looks like?" Jared gasped.

"No, it's what He feels like. You are not looking at His face. You are seeing only the peripheral band of His splendor because you are not prepared to be face-to-face with Him. The Longing will remain with you as a reminder of the joy you will have for eternity. It will serve as your motivation, your driver, to move you through the realms where you will eventually understand all," Sonny said.

Jared reached out trying to touch the light. He wanted to follow this remarkable, indescribable, peaceful, loving energy but something held him back. He turned to Sonny and cried out, "This Light consumes me but I am not afraid. I want to join it. Why can't I? It won't go away, will it?"

"This light will not leave you," Sonny said. "It is permanent and it will not fade. It will only increase as you are refined and come to understand."

"Thank God," Jared whispered.

Sonny was delighted. He loved orientation.

CHAPTER 20

FAQs

"The light, where did it go? How far away is it? Where is Heaven anyway? What will we look like in Heaven? What color will we be? I want to know. I want to understand," Jared cried out to Sonny who knew he was at risk for drifting outside his realm of responsibility if he tried to answer all of Jared's questions.

So he prayed for wisdom in what to say to Jared.

"First, Heaven is up."

"You mean like the opposite of down?"

"No, up as in vibration."

"We vibrate?"

"Yes, and we all have a frequency."

"Why?"

"We need it to experience this dimension."

"What dimension?"

"A state of being where earthly solid matter..." Sonny stopped. He knew that this discussion was not meant for him to lead.

"When Dr. Einstein discusses vibrations, mass, density, frequencies, and energy, he will explain all of this to you."

"Einstein? You mean Albert Einstein the 'E-equals-m-c-squared' guy?"

"Yes, one in the same," Sonny replied.

"But he's an atheist isn't he?" Jared asked, unsure how an atheist could be in Heaven.

Sonny postponed the answer to Jared's question. "Einstein will tell you all about that when you meet him, but you have a few other realms to visit before his. To address one of your other questions of what color we will be, I can tell you that everyone will be white."

"White!" Jared gasped.

"I said, white, not Caucasian. That's because all colors moving at high speed become one and appear white."

"Uh, okay. I seem to remember that from fifth-grade science class," Jared told Sonny.

"One more question," Jared said. "I know that you told me I could not see others here in the Waiting Room because of frequencies, but are there many others here?"

"Sure, there are, but their frequencies are not compatible with yours."

"Are you telling me that I will be limited in who I can see in Heaven?"

"Eventually you will be with all who are here. But you must progress at God's speed and understand from His point of view before you are prepared for such an encounter."

"God's speed?"

"Yes, where you neither linger nor rush. Meanwhile, Dr. Einstein will address your questions about sound, energy, matter, dimension, darkness, and light."

Sonny added, "One of his discussions that I find quite pleasant is the example he gives of light and darkness. I don't think he will mind if tell you this much. He says darkness obscures light much like a heavy cloud layer obscures the sun's light. The sun is ever present, but you just aren't able to see it. It works the same way with our light. Darkness can obscure it but never destroy it. And you have the power to make darkness disappear."

"I do? How?"

"Remember the moment when you could see images in the dark, quiet expanse?"

"Yes."

"As you began to recall things from here, your power to do so was generated by light, not fear—even unpleasant experiences could be seen in the light," Sonny explained.

"Then why did the light go away?"

"You lost confidence and limited human thinking obscured your field of vision."

Jared sighed; he was disappointed.

"Don't feel too bad, Jared. Peter, one of Christ's disciples, nearly drowned when he lost confidence taking his eyes off Christ. It's easy to do. And before you reach the gates, you still have the potential to get temporarily distracted—would you like me to demonstrate?" Sonny asked.

"Sure, I guess so."

"Okay look down."

Jared obeyed but gasped, "There's no floor. The bench is just floating. God help us!"

"Good reflexes Jared. And you are correct, the bench is floating and there is no floor."

"And this is because I lack confidence?"

"Yes. You lack confidence about where you are. But in a while, your confidence will be a matter of certainty once you realize."

"Realize what exactly?"

"How much God is looking forward to seeing you face-to-face."

Jared did not speak; he was reliving his moment of orientation.

"Come on," Sonny offered cheerfully. "Let's pick up a copy of your itinerary."

"I have one of those?"

"Certainly. Every soul gets one."

Unsure of what to expect, but trusting that Sonny knew what he was doing, Jared asked where they were headed.

"Right here," Sonny said. "Take a look at this," he told Jared as a list appeared before them. It floated overhead and the words looked like they were written in water. At first Jared was unable to read the items on the list, because the words wiggled too much. Sonny nudged the liquid letters bringing them into focus long enough for Jared to read the ones that were not written in Greek. Discussion leaders were listed first: Sonny, Ronnie, Martha, Deborah, Einstein, Chris and Channon, golf pro, mystery guest, and restoration crew. Realms were listed next: here, there, everywhere, and plenary session. As Jared read them, the words flipped and rolled like the arrival/departure board at an airport.

"This itinerary is impossible. It keeps changing," Jared grumbled.

"It will do that for a while, but soon your journey will become clear. Meanwhile, all the discussion leaders will see to it that you get to the appropriate room," Sonny said.

"For what?" Jared asked.

"Refinement and understanding."

Jared waited for more details, so Sonny clarified. "In each room, you will have the opportunity to ask an expert about an issue you struggled with as a human being. Some leaders are knowledgeable in multiple areas and may repeat things you have already talked about, but these repetitions increase your level of knowledge and refinement, which will take place before you meet your Creator. So if you'll follow me, I'll get you on course," Sonny said with love, having fulfilled his heavenly duty to this soul.

CHAPTER 21

Broken

Sonny moved away from the bench, taking Jared along with him. They paused outside the entrance of a cave. Jared enjoyed exploring caves as a boy and now was excited to find out if the ones in Heaven were similar to ones on Earth. Sonny ushered him inside and told Jared that his realm discussion leader would be along in a little while. Jared thanked Sonny for his work as a greeter and for getting him turned around. A warm breeze brushed past his energy and Sonny was gone.

For a moment, Jared missed his bench guest, but an ambient light made stalagmites and stalactites visible and captured his attention.

"These are exactly like the ones in Kentucky," Jared laughed—and one wall brightened with an image of him, Pop, and Percy struggling through the narrow troughs of Fat Man's Misery, a featured room in Mammoth Cave, National Park, in Kentucky.

Pop's ample size created a side-splitting round of laughter when he got stuck in one of the turns.

"I'll pull," yelled Percy as he climbed in front of Pop. "You push."

Together they grunted, pushed, pulled, laughed, and shouted trying to pry Pop loose. Eventually their cackling was heard by a park attendant who had to bring in an extraction team to pull Pop from the rock formation that would not let him go.

"I gotta lose some weight," Pop told the park ranger.

"Pop," Jared whispered, "I sure do miss you."

A snorting and sputtering sound outside the cave caused the image on the wall to fade. An energy entered the cavern, but Jared was still watching the wall wanting to restore and prolong the childhood memory of a time of innocence and joy. He remembered Sonny telling him that a realm discussion leader would be arriving soon, but he did not turn away from the cave wall to see who had joined him.

"It all seems so simple," Jared whispered to the being who now stood behind him.

"I'm here, because I accepted a gift."

"That is a fact," the being said. "God makes it simple, but that doesn't mean it's easy."

Jared understood. He had been "saved" several times, but the one time when he was fourteen, he believed, would be permanent. And with that thought, a burst of light ignited the simulvision clouds, which surprised Jared when they formed inside the cave. As large cumulus clouds brightened and filled with images, Jared watched the events of his brokenness, confession, and surrender to Christ.

He and Walter his step-grandfather, who he called the Drunk, had gotten into a physical battle over a .22 rifle Jared received on his fourteenth birthday—the gift had come from a stranger, but it was the one thing Jared had hoped and wished for; and when it arrived, he would not put it down—which made Walter angry. "Put that damned thing away," Walter shouted at him. "Or I'll take it away."

Their argument over the rifle became so fierce that it escalated into face-punching fight, a careless toss of a burning cigarette, and an explosion setting the backyard garden shed on fire. As a remedy to the war between her demanding husband and her unruly grandson, Mom took the rifle away from Jared and made arrangements to put him on a train to Gaffney to spend the summer with his Grandma Robinette.

Cavern clouds filled with more detail: Jared saw himself riding on the train from Indianapolis to Spartanburg with a stopover in Cincinnati. Here he would need to change trains, which made him anxious because he feared he would get on the wrong one. He liked the high ceilings and oily smell of the railway station and especially liked the Ohio travelers aid representative who helped him make the proper connection for South Carolina. At fourteen, Jared felt grown up but secretly was grateful for someone who was familiar with schedules and track locations. The aide had ushered Jared to an empty seat next to the window where he could watch railway employees and travelers with different intentions scamper and race in opposite directions. The activity outside his window did not diminish his built-up thoughts of hatred for Walter. His nostrils flared and his breath fogged his window as his anger smoldered about to erupt.

A bent-over elderly man wearing a musty smelling army uniform plopped down onto the seat next to Jared. He was carrying a satchel which he placed on the floor and then opened it. A waft of sour cherry tobacco fragrance rose from inside and reminded Jared of Pop. The man smiled but did not say a word; rather, he pulled from his satchel a Bible, spread it open across his knees, and began to read, silently tracing the words with one bony finger as he read.

Jared glanced at the frail old man, and then turning away, he smirked, and under his breath, he called the man a fool. Where was God when Pop was killed? Where was God when the Drunk was beating him? Where was God when his father abandoned him? What kind of God takes a mother from her newborn baby? God was a real disappointment, he decided, and the man next to him was wasting his time trying to find God in the pages of this book called the Bible.

The cave clouds continued to feature Jared's recollection. The being, which was the realm discussion leader, remained quiet so that Jared could have an uninterrupted memory of this journey on the train. It was important for Jared to see his rage-filled tears, his struggle to withhold them, how the old man reached out to comfort him, and how he spoke of a love that could not be taken away. Jared watched the image of himself on the cave clouds and saw how he responded. He saw himself accept Christ—but grimaced at the images of his return trip to his life in Indianapolis, when he drifted back into a life of sinful rebellion.

Feeling shame for ever offending God with his flagrant disregard of the grace offered to him, Jared confessed to the unseen being standing behind him.

"I remember having for a while a great sense of freedom, but it didn't last long. Once I returned to Indianapolis and to the flood of criticism from Mom and Walter, I felt imprisoned and looked for ways to be free again. In the next years, I ran with high school dropouts who liked to drink, smoke pot, gamble, and lie about being in love so that they could take advantage of some poor girl wanting to be married. I was no exception. I pressed Rita, a local teenage girl, to have sex. We were only sixteen. She got pregnant and neither of us wanted to raise a child. A Greek woman who lived in downtown Indianapolis gave Rita some pennyroyal tea to drink—the woman told Rita to drink several cups a day, but she couldn't do it. The tea made her sick and she ended up at the hospital where a nurse changed Rita's mind about having the baby when she let Rita listen through a stethoscope to the heartbeat of the child she was carrying. It was then that Rita declared that she was keeping the baby, and she insisted that we be married. I felt obligated, so we married, but I didn't love her. I don't think I knew at that time how to love. In fact, during most of the pregnancy, I was ashamed of how scraggly Rita looked and often I yelled at her making her cry."

"Making matters worse, we had to live with Mom and Walter. Cramped and under their constant prying eyes, our arguments were daily and my real self showed up. I used God's name in vain, did not go to church, did not read my Bible. And when our child, Matthew, was a year old, I tried to escape by enlisting in the army, but I didn't pass the physical because of a heart defect from scarlet fever when I was a child."

"Angry, I returned to my street buddies and rarely came home at night. Fed up dealing with Walter and my selfishness, Rita took Matthew to Louisville to live with her mother. After a while, she asked for a divorce because she had met a nice man, an auto mechanic who loved her, loved Matthew, and wanted to marry Rita and raise Matthew as his own. At first, this was convenient. I liked the feeling of financial relief and personal freedom to be with my buddies and have fun drinking, telling filthy jokes, while we gambled and smoked pot. Often I was a big winner and left the table with ten times the money I could have made in a weekly paycheck honest job. After a brutal beating, when all my winnings were stolen from me, and I was left for dead in an alley, I changed—but not for the good. I wanted possession of the things taken from me, even though I had neglected them. I felt entitled—and this ramped up my attitude of defiance, blaming others for my loss: my ex-wife for robbing me of being a family man and God for robbing me of a father and a mother. I whined and complained about how unfair life was and wallowed in self-pity and then took that wicked attitude with me to Bloomington and university life where my path of self-destruction was in full force: destroying the reputation of young women and drinking myself into a stupor."

"With a track record like that, how do I deserve to be here?" Jared asked, his voice, now louder, echoed off the cave walls surprising him like an unexpected slap in the face.

"None of us deserves to be here," the realm discussion leader replied suppressing the loud echo. "It's a common misconception that our 'goodness' gets us into Heaven. It does not. We confess our sins, submit our hearts to God, and do our best to honor Him each day.

"What we do not prepare for are the clever tricks of the opposition that cause us to drift into his control zone. He has one purpose only: to win us back. He succeeds if we reject God."

Jared wanted to make a case for good behavior, "Still, it doesn't seem fair..."

"Forget that thought," the discussion leader said crisply. "Although you are here, you have a great deal of work to do before you can enter God's kingdom."

"So is this limbo?" Jared asked.

"No. Limbo is a place believed to be for souls that are barred from Heaven because they were not baptized."

"Isn't baptism essential?"

"It depends on your understanding of baptism. God's gift is not dependent on specific words, special clothes, oaths, or rituals. The baptism Christ is seeking is of the heart, which only He can see. You can't fake it. If He sees a contrite heart, you're His. You're in. It's that simple.

"At the time of your surrender, in the company of that elderly man, your heart was contrite, Jared. You were broken for Christ, and He knew it. But He also knew that you would live a shallow, squalid, selfish, sinful life for a long while."

"And this didn't matter to Him?" Jared asked.

"It mattered greatly, but it did not change His love for you. The opposition crawled in shortly after you surrendered your heart to God. You were distracted by pressures and temptations laid on your path by the father of lies."

"But I didn't stop believing in God's existence," Jared offered in defense.

CHAPTER 22

Oh Hell

"That's true, but believing in God's existence and having a relationship with Him are quite different," the discussion leader said.

"But I must have had potential, or I wouldn't be here, right?" Jared asked.

"Everyone has the same potential in God's eyes, but not everyone gets the same opportunities. In your case, seeds of knowledge planted in you by Pop and your grandmother Robinette when you were a child gave you an unshakable foundation on which to build your relationship with Christ. At first it was difficult for you to accept the fact that He died for your sins and rose from the dead. You doubted this. And the opposition took advantage of your lack of faith. It was easy for the evil influences around you to make you feel ashamed and unworthy of God's love."

A queasy feeling came over Jared as he thought about the power of evil on Earth, because he knew that once he accepted God's gift, it was up to him to protect and cherish it. He remembered something Sonny had told him about rejecting God and being ushered to hell. As a boy, someone told him that hell did not exist.

Jared shuddered and asked, "Where is hell anyway?"

"It is a place where a soul has the longing and understands that it cannot be satisfied, ever," the discussion leader replied.

Before Jared could ask for more detail, the leader asked Jared a question. "Have you ever made a decision that you regret so deeply that it haunts you for years? One that you would give anything to go back correct?"

"Sure, I have. It was torture knowing that I could not rewind time and make a different choice," Jared said, thinking about his sons.

"In a small way, that is what souls destined for hell will experience. You see, every soul is given the Final Offer to accept Christ. Once a soul rejects this offer, they have two more experiences before heading to Hell. For the lover of the self immediately after choosing their heart's desire, this soul witnesses God's wrath. It terrifies them. Next, they witness Christ's passion, when He says, 'Depart from me.' This is when they realize the horrible consequences of their choice."

"At that moment, millions of angels gather to usher the lover of self to Hell, and as they are led away, they have the 'knowing' of who God is and that they are dead to Him. As they grasp what they have done, they are plunged into a lake of fire. They emerge with their throats parched and their hearts aching for this thirst to be quenched—but it will not be. Across the chasm, what you call the dark expanse, they see Heaven and souls enjoying memories, understanding, experiencing refinement, and readiness for God's kingdom. For the hell-bound, the longing intensifies and a persistent fire burns inside of them as they begin their endless journey in torture."

"A dark silence envelopes them," the leader continued. "They see nothing but pitch blackness in front and behind them. They kneel in fear as invisible walls press toward them until the sides are so close that they cannot turn left or right. They cannot turn around. They cannot get up from their knees. They can only crawl in place. And they do so with the knowledge that they are eternally alone. Their cries for help go unheard except to ceaselessly echo back to their own ears, further adding to their torture. They understand that they will never see or hear another soul, ever. They have only the Longing burning in their dark hearts and endless tears of regret."

Jared's energy sputtered, "So hell is an actual place."

"Absolutely, just as Heaven is an actual place."

"And there's no hope for these souls who go to hell?" Jared asked, surprised by his feeling of sorrow for these hell-bound beings.

"None," the leader replied. "They were given the same opportunity as anyone, regardless of their sin state, to choose God. Remember the man on the cross next to our Lord and Savior Jesus?"

"Yes, I do," Jared replied, his tone changing. "When I was younger, I was annoyed that getting into Heaven was so effortless for him. He lived an entire life of sin and then 'snap' he gets to come to paradise."

"As a matter of fact," the leader replied, "everyone gets the same chance."

CHAPTER 23

Atheists, Agnostics, and Believers

"Everyone gets to come to Heaven? Jared bellowed in disbelief. Even atheists?"

"Anyone, if they so choose," the leader replied.

Jared was confused. He thought only believers in Christ as their Savior were permitted into Heaven. It bothered him that an atheist, agnostic, Mormon, Muslim, Catholic, or Hindu might be close by.

"Everyone has a body, soul, mind, and spirit-room which is the heart," the leader began. "Everyone bleeds red blood and breathes in and out the same way."

"What does this have to do with getting into Heaven?" Jared asked, annoyed.

"We are all created to be the same."

"That's not true," Jared snapped thinking of deformed, mentally ill, or foreign-looking people.

"Have you ever heard what people call the 'death rattle?'" the leader asked.

Jared had heard it. It is a long, eerie-sounding final breath expelled as a person dies.

"God breathes life into each creation and then steps back to allow free will. When an Earth life ceases to be, God is present as that breath departs. While it does, Christ receives the innocent and to all others He extends the Final Offer..."

"Wait a minute," Jared interrupted, "if the final offer is for everyone, why don't I remember it?"

"You will in a while," the leader told Jared and then continued before Jared could get confused about timing. "When the Final Offer is acknowledged, the soul makes its choice: its declaration to be harmonious with Heaven or Hell."

"But if a person cannot speak, how can they declare anything?" Jared asked.

"It is not a declaration of the voice that comes from the mouth, but the voice that comes from the heart. It is when the heart acknowledges paternity. If a heart is blackened with self-love, greed, hatred, revenge, whore-mongering, murder, idolatry, or love for the father of lies, the voice of the opposition will prevail over the voice of Christ. The lover of self will become a fool yearning for what the opposition has to offer which appears to the dark soul as the bright lights of Babylon.

"Christ knows who has faith in Him. He also knows his lost sheep, the ones who have become misinformed, misguided, misdirected, misunderstood, or doubted."

"Like agnostics and atheists?"

"Yes, they too are given the Final Offer. You would be astonished at the number of people who seek proof that God exists, but in their heart they wonder, which is all God needs, a tiny spark of wonder. The Final Offer is their moment when wonder is replaced with knowing."

"So agnostics and atheists are in Heaven?"

"No, only former agnostics and former atheists."

"So, this means that otherwise they go to Hell?"

"Precisely, along with many souls who professed to be Christians."

Jared's energy sputtered. He felt lopsided from the idea that an agnostic or atheist even a former one can be in Heaven but not some Christians; that good is good, but not good enough that the most despicable person can make it to Heaven and that our hearts, not our brains, are the decision-makers. He had also known some very nice atheists and wished he had tried harder to help them know God. He could have ignited a tiny spark of wonder, is this what Christ meant when He told us to make disciples?

Jared heard the realm leader take a deep breath, let it out, and draw it back in again before saying, "Some people require a lifetime before a spark of wonder is ignited in their heart. This ignition is not dependent upon labels, religions, or fancy words, but it is dependent upon infection."

"Infection?" Jared repeated. "Infection makes you sick."

"There is a powerful infection that makes you well because it cleanses the heart. A doubter, disbeliever, or ignorant person catches this infection from a believer, not from what they say but how they are. God's love permeates a believer's physical, emotional, and spiritual being, allowing Christ to work through them, not by them. Their modesty, humility, self-control, and patience are sometimes the only thing that will ignite a tiny spark of wonder in a stubborn heart."

"Like an agnostic or atheist?" Jared asked.

"Ummmmm, yes. The tiny spark of wonder is possible for the hearts of declared proof-seekers, nonbelievers, and the Godless good. A great number from these groups choose to come here."

"Really?"

"Indeed. These individuals possess the raw material for knowing God, not as a person that instills fear and humiliation but as a force that is in all creation. Although emphatic in their declaration that God does not exist, they lived a life that declared the opposite. They exhibited a love of justice, showed mercy, and were not haughty when explaining their nonbelief. Agnostics and atheists are usually highly intelligent, and igniting a tiny spark of wonder in them must come from a trusted source, not from an emotional display of evangelic imperatives. In almost every case, these individuals eventually find themselves among believers in Christ and want to be like them. Ironically, an atheist who has a change of heart and accepts Christ for who He is will become a person of great influence. CS

Lewis is one example. Einstein is another. The list of conversions is growing because the need for people of good infection is great."

"C.W. told me that a tiny spark of wonder can become a flame that fuels a love story."

"Your friend is correct," the leader said. "And when a person feels the warmth of this flame, they want it to remain. Acceptance of responsibility for wrongdoings and handing over their sword of disbelief becomes natural for this changed heart. At the split-second moment a person asks His forgiveness and surrenders his heart to Christ, the heart is given a love implant that is impossible to purge—diminish, perhaps—but not destroy. As lovers, we may fail Him, but He will not fail us. If our surrender is sincere and God knows when it is, we have only to do this once in a lifetime and the heart will know His voice. Disease, mental illness, sin residual, life achievements, or failures will not override the heart's ability to return to the love it once knew."

This sounded familiar to Jared. He was remembering something Pop and his Grandma Robinette told him about love. They said that once we surrender our hearts to God, we are knitted together in love. The old man in an army uniform on the train told him the same thing. Jared thanked God for Pop, his grandma Robinette, and for the old man, but he felt something tugging at him that he needed to better understand.

CHAPTER 24

Surrender, Faith, and Trust,
Best Bank in Town

Jared's energy stream accelerated, causing instability and producing a concern that reflected onto the cave walls. He saw it in upper case neon colored letters: TRUST.

"I think your interest is better addressed by someone at the bank," the leader said.

"There are banks in Heaven?" Jared asked, wondering if these banks had vaults and if so, was the Book of Life kept in one of them.

"Certainly, we have banks up here. I'll show you," the leader said and encouraged Jared to come out of the cave for a while.

Stalagmites and stalactites retracted and were replaced with bursts of jewel-tone light rays indicating the way out. Jared liked the cave, but knew that he needed to leave. He followed the light rays toward the mouth of the cave. As he approached the opening, his frequency increased when the light rays merged and took hold of his energy. Bound by the light, he sped past massive granite walls that flickered as he raced by. His pathway was obscured by blankets of light mist but as he rounded a bend, these barriers to clarity rolled away like a midday fog giving way to sunlight. Looming before him was a billboard-sized sign. Its phosphorescent letters pulsated: Surrender, Faith, and

Trust—Best Bank in Town. Directly below was a byline: "with convenient branches located everywhere."

Jared's fascination with the glowing words was interrupted by a chirping feminine voice.

"Greetings, Jared, my name is Martha."

Her voice bounced onto his energy causing a static electrical sensation similar to his first encounter with Sonny. He wondered if he would be able to trust Martha like he did his quirky Waiting Room greeter.

"I understand that you have a question about God's love," she stated matter-of-factly.

Before Jared could respond, Martha's colors changed from Monet-style pastels to vivid Van Gogh swirls that spiraled out beyond his line of vision. The display was spectacular, convincing him that Martha was powerful and that she had something significant to share with him.

Martha smiled, neutralizing the disruptive static between them. As she breezed past Jared, her energy caught hold of his and swept him across a valley, down a long tree lined road to a castle. He held on as they passed through two elegantly carved wooden doors which led into a massive room dripping with brocade tapestries that reminded him more of the Biltmore House in Asheville than any bank he'd seen. Martha did not hesitate. She got right to the point.

"Of all the discussion topics I lead, God's love is my favorite," she declared.

Curious, Jared asked about the other topics. Martha promptly gave him a list, "Shoulds and musts, heaven etiquette, time and waste management, church, wants, needs, worry, anxiety, rigidity, self-pity, and getting the hell out."

Martha said the word hell as if it were a stain, Jared noticed.

"Well, it can be, you know," she said, having shared Jared's thought, but this time he wasn't startled by the exchange. It felt natural for Martha to know what he was thinking.

"'Should-action' makes us competitive and feel defeated or it can cause us to become offensive and argumentative. All result in poor time management," Martha said. "'What ifs' cause us to worry which leads to waste because we are focused on something that has not yet happened. Musts make us miserable and 'if onlys' make us feel guilty about what cannot be undone, you know, like a spaghetti sauce stain on your favorite white shirt that you can't get rid of. During inspirational nourishment time, I encourage sufferers of 'shoulds,' 'musts,' 'what ifs,' and 'if onlys' to consider alternate word and phrase choice, such as could, might, and 'how would God like it to be?'"

Martha's comments ignited a "what if" memory for Jared. He and his wife were on their way to Lake Junaluska, North Carolina. At a rest area on I-26, before completely out of his car, Jared was startled by a well-dressed, thirtyish-looking man racing toward him, shouting and frantically waving.

The rest stop was a place notorious for the presence of panhandlers, even well-dressed ones. So Jared tried to step around the man, who was pleading for money. He was desperate, he declared, keeping pace with Jared who was working his way up the walk toward the restrooms. The appeal continued. The man claimed that he had to be on the road within the hour to get his five-year-old son to Asheville where the child's mother was waiting with the pediatric surgeon to perform a procedure Jared had never heard of. Only twenty dollars was needed for gas. Jared grimaced and walked faster, but the man kept pace and continued talking attempting to make his story compelling enough for Jared to break down and give him money.

Ignoring the man's persistent urgings, Jared started to run, creating distance between him and the frantic acting father. Before reaching the doors of the restroom, guilt welled up almost choking Jared.

He stopped the memory abruptly and blurted out to Martha, "I should have given him the money!"

Martha sighed, "If you had, you would have been duped by the father of lies. This man was a con artist. He played on your sympathy. He counted on you to feel guilty," Martha explained, elevating Jared's irritation rather than calming it.

"How can you know if a person is telling the truth or conning you? How do you know the difference?" Jared complained.

"Sometimes you can't," Martha said.

"Then why did you let me know that this man was a con artist?" Jared demanded. "I wouldn't give money to a con artist, but I would surely give money to a helpless person down on his luck," he declared.

"Emotions will get you misdirected every time. Emotions shut down your discernment radar," Martha warned.

"Okay, okay," Jared huffed missing the mention of "discernment radar." "Now I'm confused. First you tell me that I avoided being conned, and then you tell me that my emotions were misdirected. Which is it? Did I mess it up or get it right?"

Martha knew that Jared was conflicted about how to please God and she decided to try a new approach. "What made you walk away?"

CHAPTER 25

Thorn in the Side

Jared hesitated before saying that he didn't know. A vivid array of memories about church registered on the curved, pastel blue-colored ceiling of the bank. As a young boy, Jared attended church with Pop in Indianapolis and later with his grandma Robinette in Gaffney. He liked Sunday school in both churches but was afraid of the Baptist preacher in South Carolina who made him feel like he was destined for hell no matter what he did. As a teenager, he thought church would be a place of enrichment and strengthen his feelings of freedom, but church did just the opposite. It made him feel claustrophobic. Still for a while he attended because secretly he thought that by doing so he might win God's love.

When assassinations and the Vietnam War began, claiming lives of beloved leaders and boys he knew, he decided that church was a bad joke. For years, he did not consider going to church until he married Priscilla. His attitude about church, however, remained critical, and whenever Priscilla asked him to take her to church, he made excuses not to go. He was not about to get sucked back into a place that made him feel inferior and unworthy.

His friend C.W. gave him a Bible that included explanations of the scripture. This increased Jared's interest especially in reading the New Testament, but the more he read the Bible, the more he used it to make excuses to avoid church. He told

Priscilla that he did not need to attend church and that he was satisfied to share scripture with her at home and recited, "Wherever two or three are gathered in my name, there, I am in the midst of them."

The recollection of Jared reasoning with Priscilla about church continued to flash on the ceiling of the bank. Jared heard himself telling his wife, "Churches are run by men and nearly always become more like a club than a place to assemble for worship. As leaders of churches gain power through control, they become heady with self-importance. They create a hierarchy beginning with 'mandatory minimums' for what the officers of the club can expect from a 'giving unit.'"

Jared's disdain for church intensified when he barked at Priscilla that "a church becomes a place for members to crow before a congregation about acts of selflessness and sacrifice."

Hearing his words echo off the vast ceiling, Jared realized that his argument was laced with disgust more than reason. Martha understood; this was a common thorn in the side of many souls who thought of church as a place to make them happy. She knew that Jared wanted to avoid conflict and that he was moving away from the issue of giving the man at the rest stop the twenty-dollar bill. She provided a gentle stream of energy that nudged Jared back on topic.

"I didn't want to be a rooster," Jared blurted out. "If I gave the man the twenty, I was afraid that might happen, and if I was a member of some church, I would be tempted to do that."

"Really?" she asked. "Since you weren't a member of any church, and not at risk for crowing before a congregation, what made you feel guilty about not giving him the money?"

Jared was not prepared for this question, but he realized he was about to experience an important revelation about trying to do things to please God: damned if you do and damned if you don't because the one you are attempting to please is yourself.

Before shame could seep into Jared's energy, Martha made an offer. "May I show you a little known thought maneuver?"

"Of course, I'd like that."

"Although not often used by human beings," Martha began, "they have the power to go back and reshape a memory so that it aligns with love, not fear, guilt, or shame. Let's take a look at how this memory could have been."

CHAPTER 26

Do-Over

J ared's energy stepped up, vibrating with anticipation of a better outcome. He had heard C.W. talk about replacing toxic memories with fresh, vibrant ones. Was this what Martha was about to show him? Images flickered on the ceiling of the bank. He watched himself get out of the car and the frantic father rush toward him. Instead of ignoring the man, Jared smiled at him and asked in a firm voice, "Do you know Him?"

The man halted abruptly, his face involuntarily altered by astonishment. "Know who?" he asked.

"Our Lord," Jared answered. "May I show you?" he asked the man.

Curious, the con artist said. "Sure."

Jared pulled out his phone and linked up to the Internet to a video of Dr. S.M. Lockridge's sermon. "That's my King."

Together, Jared and the con artist watched the video, their heads nearly touching, bowed over the small screen. As Dr. Lockridge delivered his final few lines, Jared looked up at the stranger's face and said, "You and I are brothers, God's beloved children. He loves us so much that He came down here to this sin-drenched place, suffered rejection, betrayal, and physical pain. He died for our sins showing us how much He loves us. We are given one lifetime to show Him how much we love Him too."

The con artist blinked. In all the requests for assistance, he had never been given anything comparable. The man changed his request from a twenty-dollar bill to a prayer for him. Jared offered a high-five hand slap and said, "It's a done deal, brother!" Both walked away smiling.

Martha knew that Jared would have preferred this outcome. She comforted him by saying, "You were not prepared, that's all. When distracted by emotions, we react in haste which stifles our discernment radar."

"Discernment radar," Jared repeated, now realizing that he had missed asking about it when Martha mentioned it earlier. "I remember discussing discernment of evil. Is this the same thing?"

"Yes, it is the ability to know the difference between something godly and ungodly. In this case, it is to know the difference between a want and a need," Martha said. "And being prepared to meet that need."

"I wasn't prepared, was I?" Jared said.

"It's all right, your wife was right behind you and she showed the con artist the video with her phone. She also gave him a handful of King's Witness® Bracelets and a furry little toy bear for his son."

Jared blinked, "She never told me, why is that?"

"She didn't do it for you. Some people can hardly wait to promote their 'noble act.' You call these people 'roosters.'"

"Right," Jared declared and with a strong critical voice offered his definition. "Roosters hurry about, looking for the chance to do good and then strut in front of an audience so that they can crow about it. After the applause, roosters go looking for another poor soul in 'need.'"

"I understand," Martha said. "When a person crows, they get immediate gratification. The reward comes from man and is short-lived. But if one is quiet about a job well done, their reward is in Heaven and it is eternal. Individuals who are mature in their relationship with God know that they do not have to search for work. They hear God's whispers and are ready for the daily task that He chooses for them," Martha added.

"Like Priscilla did," Jared whispered, humility now replacing judgment.

"She wasn't always like that, Jared," Martha said. "She had her crowing moments too and struggled with trying to be still and listen. Most people think that to hear God's voice, they must concentrate and deliberately shut everything out. That is excellent beginner practice, but in time, with discipline, a person can be quiet and hear God's voice in the middle of chaos."

"I would guess such a person is rare," Jared remarked.

CHAPTER 27

Be Still and Know

"**I**ndeed, they are. Being quiet and able to listen," Martha continued, "prepares a person for any emergency work placed on their path. This person will not likely react with emotion when someone approaches them. They will pray for wisdom and address the opportunity to disciple to another with kindness, and they will not speak of it. They know that in their quiet, they have pleased God. When stuck in the excitement of sharing a noble act with others, a person feels offended when tomorrow doesn't produce more of the same. In an effort to recreate the event, they get noisier and chattier as they search for an opportunity to repeat the performance, rather than wait for God's assignment, which often is menial and missed because of their noise. From self-indulgence comes self-pity. And self-pity gives way to exhaustion and feeling defeated: damned if you do, damned if you don't."

Martha's sobering words struck Jared in the heart; he felt drained but mustered the strength to ask if she would help him understand how to avoid such traps.

"Sure," she said brightly. "Skill building is key to being prepared—and begins when we first open our eyes. We thank God for the day. We study scripture and we pray for protection and wisdom. Fully equipped with God's armor, we set out to do the work of this day, none other."

"What about making plans, setting goals, and schedules?" Jared asked.

"Nothing wrong with that," Martha said. "What I'm talking about is being so disciplined that whatever appears on your path, scheduled or not, your response requires no thought. You act instinctively like our Lord would if He were facing the situation."

Martha knew that Jared was feeling guilt over his encounter with the con artist; she increased her volume to say, "Guilt is a reverse process power tool. It is used by con artists to assure a sob story has a happy ending—for the opposition, that is. When someone steps onto our path assaulting us for a snap decision, causing us to feel ashamed or guilty, this is the father of lies squeezing us. If we are in touch with God, we can resist feelings of guilt. His love will fill us with wisdom for the words needed to address the moment. He will provide us with the appropriate form of charity."

Jared pondered Martha's word choice: "appropriate form of charity." "Isn't charity always appropriate?" he asked.

"Indeed, but some people think charity is about giving money when in fact it is about giving God's type of love. His type of love is to want the best for someone, even people we don't like, including the 'roosters.'"

Feeling the sting of the last remark, Jared didn't say anything. He knew she was right.

"Sometimes being charitable means being silent, doing nothing, in spite of how painful it may feel seeing someone do without," Martha added. "Feelings are not what God cares about. He wants us to love Him not as employees working to please, but as His children, sons and daughters, pleased to be working. The love He has for us is fixed, permanent," Martha concluded.

"You mean unconditional?" Jared asked.

"Unconditional sounds docile, submissive, passive—God's love is greater than that," Martha declared. "His love is relentless, high-voltage, authentic, unimpeachable, active, jealous, and pursuing. It is deep, wide, intimate, kind, patient, tolerant, and surpassing all limits, boundaries, and knowledge. His love is not given in degrees and is so unrestrained, so radical that He set aside His supernatural powers to endure a wretched, horrific, excruciatingly painful, heart-breaking bloody death on the cross to wipe your slate clean in the eyes of your Creator. He gave you a do-over and then waited patiently for you to accept this gift and to use it."

Jared felt a pang of remorse for his reckless years in Bloomington and his flagrant disregard for God's love.

Martha moved close to Jared and touched his energy; with tenderness she said, "He wants alone time with you, Jared, and then for you to invite Him into everyday moments, decisions, and relationships. He wants us to laugh, sing, and dance with Him."

"How do we do that?" he whispered.

"Trust," Martha whispered back to him.

CHAPTER 28

Trust

"Trust in God is the single most difficult but rewarding act of man," Martha told Jared.

"When we trust, we give thanks to God regardless of the circumstances or the outcomes. Sometimes things don't make sense. Sometimes people of strength and character appear to be beaten by the enemy, but they still trust God. They do not lose their faith in spite of well-meaning friends who tell them to pray more. Prayer can be fear-based, where trust is faith-based," Martha said. "When our prayer is fear-based, Lucifer knows it—especially if we are praying out loud. Lucifer will show up and pour himself into a soul, filling it up with doubt, hoping for the fatal disclaimer: to reject God. When you surrender everything you treasure, including yourself, and attempt to know how to love as God does, Lucifer's army is activated. Surrendered to God, you become an enemy and prime target of the opposition who cares nothing for the ungodly. These souls are already in Lucifer's camp. He and his disciples want you and they will pull out every weapon to achieve infidelity."

"Infidelity?" Jared repeated.

"Yes, infidelity, which is the loss of faith. The father of lies and his disciples whittle away faith by twisting God's truth, convincing you that God only loves you for your good deeds," Martha continued. "This evil one will masquerade as a messenger from God—sweet talking you into his lair where he will shout a list of 'shoulds and musts' and convince you that it is God who is making these demands."

"Well, how do you know if it's Satan or God talking to you?" Jared asked.

"Simple. God never shouts, humiliates, or belittles. He doesn't sweet talk either. He speaks in a still, small voice. He whispers—like a gentle breeze and with few words—sometimes only a 'yes,' 'no,' 'stay,' or 'go.' If our relationship with Him is not refreshed and reinforced daily, God's voice gets softer and Lucifer's gets louder so that isolation, worry, fear, and distraction will dominate. When no longer paying attention to our surroundings, we are vulnerable to the maneuvers of the opposition to make us feel abandoned and question God's love. Lucifer persuades weakened souls to see every trial as a reminder of failure and decay."

"Like Sonny's mother," Jared remarked.

"Exactly," Martha said. "Christ tells us to love one another as He loves us—that means also to love who we are, God's creation, and to not become haughty or feel superior when we are in the presence of someone who does not understand this love."

Jared thought about step-grandfather Walter and how difficult he could be: grunting orders for more coffee while sitting in the comfort of Jared's recliner and making a spectacle of Jared in public by wailing out to strangers that he was being abused.

"Generally, we tend to gravitate toward the easy-to-love people," Martha said. "They offer no resistance and require little work. On the other hand, the difficult ones, the ones that need love the most, are often cast out of a family or a church with the faulty-thinking that by doing so, the family or church body will be preserved."

"And isn't it?" Jared asked thinking about how easy life would have been if he and Priscilla had left Walter in the Hope and Happiness Rehab center rather than bringing him home to live with them. "Crotchety old goat," Jared whispered and then felt a twinge.

"Sorry," he said and then shifted his thoughts to trouble-makers in church.

"Shouldn't the bad ones, the rule breakers, be expelled? Cut off? Excommunicated?"

"If you think like a man, yes. But if you think like Christ and how He loves us and how He wants us to love others, no."

CHAPTER 29

Practice Loving, Listening, and Knowing

"Loving Christ's way takes practice," Martha said. "We cannot practice from our living room, alone in a recliner chair, binge-watching television."

"Ouch," Jared said realizing that she had just described one of his favorite pastimes and how annoyed he got when Walter took over the recliner and interrupted Jared's TV-watching routine. Martha heard Jared's thought but ignored it.

"We have to get onto the practice field to do our work," she said, "out into our community, which includes the church. Here we are guaranteed to have our feelings hurt, our emotions stoked, our desires shattered, and our hearts broken."

"Good grief," Jared puffed. "No wonder I didn't like going to church. I got enough practice with that at home," he declared thinking about how easily Walter could pick, poke, and push to him to find his temper, causing him to blow up at Priscilla.

"Our Lord's honor is at stake in how we treat one another," Martha said. "And besides home, the church is a good practice ground. We can choose to practice with the Methodists, Baptists, Catholics, Episcopalians, Presbyterians, Jews, Mormons, Seventh-Day Adventists, Church of God, Home-based, or any other denomination established by man. As such, we choose to become members of a team so that we can practice as a team.

Some teams get better at the goal: to love one another. A winning team exhibits Christ's love. In doing so, these team members are not fearful of sitting next to a sinner. In practice sessions and end-of-day evaluations, they will ask, 'Is my relationship with Christ so weak that I see this person's sin as greater than my own?'"

"But the Bible says to not even eat with such a man," Jared offered, feeling defensive.

"Yes, it does say that. What do you think this passage of scripture means?"

Jared didn't consider himself knowledgeable enough to interpret God's Word, and he was trying to keep negative thoughts about Walter out of the discussion. He knew Martha wanted to help him understand things from God's point of view. He strained and squeezed, tightening his energy to move thoughts of Walter out of the way and to allow a proper answer to emerge.

"Well, when I think about how Christ sat down with sinners, I am confused by the passages in Corinthians, Thessalonians, and Titus. It sounds to me like we ought to shun a person who is disobedient, but aren't these the very people we are supposed to help save?" Jared asked.

"It's not up to us to save anyone," Martha said.

Oh, that's right. Christ already did that, Jared thought to himself.

"Not everyone will accept God's gift, but everyone can," Martha told him. "The Good News is not always shared in words," she continued. "Sometimes it's reflected in our behavior. In these circumstances, our love for Christ dominates and is displayed in our ability to show compassion especially when someone sins. When our heart is right with Christ and our practice of asking for wisdom and protection becomes as natural as breathing, we will have no fear of whomever we sit next to in church. This is God's house, a place of forgiveness, love, and mercy."

A quivering ripple revved up and vibrated erratically in Jared's center. "God, please help me understand this," he prayed and Martha smiled. She knew that Jared's prayer was to understand the passage in the Bible and not the odd vibration in his energy.

"Could it mean that we turn them down when they invite us to join them at 'their table of sin' but not shun them in church or anywhere for that matter?"

"That's good, Jared," Martha said. "We are to shun the places of immorality. We are to decline to participate in the sin of willful disobedience with this person, ignoring the impure behavior, exhibiting love and the sincere desire to see this individual have a change of heart. All the while, we maintain our prayer for this person with the same fervor we would want someone to pray for us."

"I still don't fully understand about excommunication," Jared said. "Pop used to say, 'One bad apple can spoil the whole bunch.' He told me that the church elders were to cast them out."

"Think about it, Jared, who did Christ cast out?"

"Demons, evil spirits," Jared said with confidence.

"That's right. He did not cast out people, but the evil influences that had a grip on their hearts causing them to live a squalid life of sin. And because God can use every outcome to refine a soul, a walk with Satan may be the very journey a person needs to circumcise the heart and know God's love. These are souls in great need of our prayer and kind support. We do not have to go out looking for them. They are all around us."

"So by joining this individual in his sin, we become vulnerable to sin ourselves," Jared remarked.

"That's right, Jared. If a man is in a rage, be quiet and show him self-control. If a man is committing adultery, be quiet and show him how much you cherish your wife. If a man is using God's name in vain, be quiet and show him how you express yourself without defaming God. If a man is telling vulgar jokes and bragging about how sloppy drunk he got at a local bar the night before, be quiet and do not reward him with insincere laughter."

"Be still and know that I am God," Jared whispered.

CHAPTER 30

Our Best Game

"God is sovereign, Jared," Martha said. "We trust that He knows the heart of this person and that it is not up to us to fix them but to exhibit the type of loving, respectful behavior that honors God. We do this with persistent, sincere prayer and we can do so singularly or in a group. Often it is in a church where we can find others willing to do the hard work of steady prayer."

"Finding the right church is not easy," Jared said as he remembered something Priscilla told him about churches she had been to where she didn't feel welcome. "Hospitality," she said, "is about sharing and making a person feel at ease in an unfamiliar place. You make them want to come back not run away," she had told him.

"Each church has a personality, just like people do," Martha continued. "A church that fosters love will exhibit patience and kindness. Its members are not envious, boastful, prideful, rude, self-seeking, or easily angered. The people of such a church keep no record of wrongs. They do not rejoice in evil but only in truth. In America, you are free to choose which church you want to attend. A church can be for some a small group that meets regularly in someone's home or a massive one with thousands of people. You make the church. The church does not make you. It is not a place of rules but a place to practice love for Him and for one another," Martha said.

"When we listen to Lucifer," she continued, "and take the easy way out, sit at home, become lazy, spiteful, fill up on self-pity, feel offended, seek revenge, and become willfully disobedient or bitter, this destructive behavior lessens our ability to love. If we make too many choices from this loveless base, in time, the consequences bury us. We forfeit our best game."

"Best game?" Jared repeated.

"Yes, our best game takes practice, and to practice, we need to be around others. Church is a place where we can be around others who are also struggling for their best game. Here we practice as a team the three-strike rule."

"You mean like three strikes you're out?" Jared asked.

"Not out of the church but out of touch with love. 'Three strikes' is about how we speak to one another. When we have something to say, we ask: are the words true, necessary, and kind?"

Jared was reminded of Sonny's blurting out disorder. He realized that his strong criticism of the church had more to do with his own issues of trust. As Martha's words penetrated Jared's energy, his critical feelings about church were replaced with sorrow for thinking that church was a place to gloat, boast, and publicly punish sinners. This realization caused him to remember something his friend C.W. read to him from a book. It was about prophets, wisdom, and God's love. When asked, "What ought to be the punishment of a sinner?" Wisdom replied, "Misfortune!" Prophecy replied, "Death!" Christ replied, "Let him repent, and he will be atoned for."

Martha liked that book too. Feeling that Jared understood the requirements of this realm, she suggested that he return to the cave and to her friend, the previous realm leader to continue their earlier discussion. With that thought, Martha vanished along with all her dazzling, energetic colors.

The bank vanished with her.

And Jared was back inside the cave. But this time he was closer to the opening. He was trying to remember Psalm 1 when he heard a familiar voice say, "Welcome back."

This time Jared thought he heard the sound of spurs and a horse whinny, accompanied by the aroma of a hay barn. "My imagination," he decided.

CHAPTER 31

Ready

"How'd you like Martha?" The realm leader asked.

"She was terrific. I hope I get to see her again."

"You will, in a while," the leader said.

That's nice, Jared thought to himself.

"Nice indeed," the leader replied and Jared smiled; since his discussion with Martha, he no longer felt jumpy or startled by the thought-sharing feature. He liked it.

"Would you prefer to stay in the cave or go outside?" the leader asked.

"I'm okay where I am," Jared remarked as he inched toward the opening. *This being is different from Martha or Sonny,* he thought; Sonny was like a buddy and Martha like an older sister, but this realm leader had the energy of a commander. As waves of confidence rose in Jared, he felt at ease asking questions without being embarrassed. He was grateful because two were bubbling up.

"Jesus says that no one comes to the Father except through Him. He is our Savior. So what about non-Christians: Jews, Muslims, Buddhists, Hindus, Baha'i, Confusions, and Sikhs?"

"There are no religions in Heaven," the leader said crisply. "You either have a heart for God or a heart for evil. It's that simple—Christ meets every single soul during their last breath regardless of the religion they chose while on Earth. He knows His sheep and the ones who will recognize His voice. For doubters, He asks the same question he asked Paul, when Paul was on the road to Damascus. 'Why are you persecuting me?' Depending on the soul's response, Christ says, 'Depart, I never knew you' or 'Rise, follow me.'"

Jared was glad about the answer. He had some Jewish friends who loved God but argued that Jesus was not the Messiah. Rather, they believed that He was a teacher, a prophet, a rabbi—a mere man. Jared was relieved to know that they would get the same chance that Paul did.

"You had another question, I believe."

"Sonny told me that the Waiting Room was the first of three Heavens. Why three?"

"It's about choice, understanding, and letting go. First Heaven is the place where souls come after declaration and to await orientation. Memory does not work the same way here, so the Final Offer details are not recalled in the Waiting Room. A soul must be endued with power before those details are remembered. That's important and you will understand why in a while."

In a while, Jared thought. "Everyone here uses that," he mumbled, but his need to understand the three Heavens was more pressing than knowing the meaning of a phrase.

"And Second Heaven?" he asked.

"Following orientation," the leader began, "the soul transitions to Second Heaven, which is where refinement occurs. It is a battleground where the soul examines temptations not resisted and the consequences of sin. Realms of understanding, empathy, assimilation, the river of perfection, judgment, and glorification occur in Second Heaven."

"What's plenary session?" Jared asked recalling seeing this on the itinerary Sonny showed him.

"Everyone gathered together," the leader replied.

"And Third Heaven?"

"God's kingdom, also called paradise. It is where you will be once you are refined through understanding, let go, assimilated, and perfected for the glorious reunion. It is where you remain until the New Earth. This is God's other Waiting Room."

"There are two?"

"Yes, one for arrival, one for departure."

"Departure?" Jared said, concerned that he might be dismissed from Heaven.

"That won't happen," the leader said with authority. This time Jared was relieved that his thoughts could be overheard.

"God's Departure Waiting Room is the place where souls go in preparation for Christ's return."

"You mean we get to be with Him when He does that?"

The realm leader took a deep breath. He didn't want to diminish Jared's enthusiasm, but he needed to explain being chosen as one of God's Ready Soldiers.

"Souls coming here during this time are fortunate. When the Word of God returns, He will choose souls and angels to be at His side, but He will choose soldiers most ready to be on the front lines with Him."

"How is a ready soldier chosen?" Jared asked.

"From the Book of Life, according to their works as one of His disciples, which is how he or she lived during the time of probation on Earth."

Jared was silent. He now understood what it meant when Christ said, "You did not choose me, but I chose you."

"We don't get in based on our works but we serve according to them," the leader said.

Jared was grateful to be in Heaven and knew that he would experience freedom, love, and joy, but to be at Christ's side in battle, nothing could be more desirable.

"God isn't choosing favorites," the leader said. "He is choosing the most prepared. These souls understand sacrifice and surrender. They practiced under the most difficult circumstances: a fallen world. If they could hold fast to the truth down there, they are eligible as ready soldiers up here. They are also patient, willing to wait for God's command and provision of duty."

"What about souls like me? Do we get to serve?" Jared asked.

"Absolutely. God doesn't waste a single soul. Everyone here will have a position. It will be compatible with their level of understanding and ability."

"You mean to carry out God's commands?"

"In part, yes. Those who surrendered all earthly possessions including their lives for the love of Christ will be next to Him during His return. But other souls are needed to tend the gardens of Heaven, to lead songs with the children, to guide new arrivals, and to inspire souls still on Earth. All of us are useful, highly valued, and loved equally. None of us will feel resentment or unworthy as a result of the work we are chosen to do."

Jared felt a strong twinge. He grimaced. Now he understood the period of probation, our time on Earth. Did we spend our time acquiring stuff? Or did we spend our time in service? *This is how love grows,* he realized. *It multiplies through acts of service.*

"And it is through service that we are counted Ready Soldier eligible," the realm leader added.

God's mathematics are exquisite, Jared told himself, using a word that he never used before.

"We agree," the leader said.

Jared smiled and thought, *Most definitely, I will make a visit to the Doors of Wisdom.* Then he wondered: if I choose to stay here, will I get to inspire others?

"Once you have completed all the realms and are perfected, you will discover how heavenly inspiration works."

Jared did not ask for an explanation; he trusted that he would understand in a while. He laughed out loud realizing that he was beginning to use the language of Heaven: "Understand in a while," he repeated to himself.

The realm leader laughed with him. He was glad for Jared's level of refinement but now it was time to return to discussion about the three heavens. A cloud lit up with the words first, second, and third. It was just the right amount of inspiration to return Jared to topic.

"Second Heaven, is that where I am now?" Jared asked.

"Yes, and the reason you have a sword at your side."

Jared looked down. To his amazement, he saw an elegant sword. It was held in place by the golden thread that earlier tethered him to the bench. Light danced off its blade and its handle was filled with gemstones: sapphire, amethyst, ruby, emerald, and others Jared had never seen. Why hadn't he noticed the sword before? He wondered.

"You needed practice using it," the leader said. "Here, we practice first with words. We'll have a discussion until trust is sufficient to handle a sword properly. Once that is achieved, a soul goes into battle against misconceptions, hang-ups, misunderstandings, and offenses. As these are conquered, the sword is refined into pure gold. Where the purpose of the First Heaven is orientation, Second Heaven is understanding and refinement."

"And the Third Heaven?"

"Reward."

Jared felt the longing return and he wanted more than ever to experience the light of Christ again. His desire caused him to hum at a higher frequency, prompting another question. "Sonny told me that we cannot see others in the Waiting Room and that our encounters with leaders or others are limited. Will I ever be able to choose who I can see or talk with?"

"Eventually, you will be able to see everyone who is in Heaven," the leader said, clarifying the issue for Jared. Or so he thought.

"Which wife will I be with?" Jared asked.

"Both of them," the leader answered promptly. "But you will not interact with them as husband and wife. You will connect with them on a different level—a higher frequency. You may even choose to share a mission."

"You mean like the missionaries from church?"

CHAPTER 32

Missions

"Earthly missions can be flawed and interfere with God's time," the leader said. "These acts are counterfeit and result in self-serving pride."

"Are you saying that missionary work is unnecessary?" Jared asked.

"Hey Jared! I was just passing by the cave and overheard your question. Do you mind if I join the conversation?" Jared recognized the voice of Martha and felt good that she decided to drop in.

"Not at all," the leader said. "We're always glad to have your input Martha." "Missionary work done properly is essential," Martha began. "But some missionaries ignore the mission which is to 'Go to all nations making disciples teaching them to observe all that Christ commanded: to love one another.' Some missionaries go and are tempted by emotional pity, 'shoulds and musts,' or the 'fix-it' urge. They can get confused about the difference between a want and a need. With best intentions, they can interfere with God's plan by correcting something according to their standards, not His. Missionaries are to reflect the image of Christ in a culture and meet needs, not wants, and be joyful for this duty regardless of where it is: in a foreign country or in their own backyard."

"Priscilla and I were annoyed with churches whose leaders made elaborate trips to exotic places while ignoring people who lived within a mile of the church," Jared said.

"That's a common irritation," the leader replied. "Even well-intentioned people can miss the purpose of duty. They can go overboard and do too much. An authentic disciple provides what a soul needs: the gospel. What happens next is up to that individual."

"Like becoming a disciple too?" Jared asked.

"A disciple, a humble servant, yes. A pushy zealot, no," Martha commented, excused herself, and breezed out of the cave so that the realm leader could resume discussion.

"Some people become obsessed with a plan to 'glorify God.' They want a monument to the world exemplifying how they served God," the leader said. "Our brother John tells us that some loved the praise of men more than the praise of God."

Jared recalled his earlier conversation with Martha about trying to do things to please God, when in fact we are pleasing ourselves—choosing how we want to exhibit God's love rather than allowing God's love to be exhibited through us. *Attraction rather than promotion*, he thought.

"The opposition is delighted with exhibitionists," the leader said. "These individuals are zealots for theater and no longer a reflection of Christ. Yet, they might not be aware of this loss of similarity. Their obsession can be so great that they will dig into scripture looking for words to support their dissimulation."

"I don't know that word, dissimulation," Jared said.

"It is the opposite of becoming similar. It is becoming unlike, which is to care for the self first, above all else. True missionaries are givers of Christ's love, who are patient, kind, truthful, and merciful as they minister to the sick, the hungry, the thirsty, and the lowest of low. They are not givers of the self who boast and brag about their efforts to make life more comfortable."

Jared thought of the times he criticized missionaries. He thought they were "roosters" always crowing about their accomplishments and begging for money so that they could do more of the same. He argued with Priscilla that he could do just as much good on the golf course as he could in some far-off country. The leader did not interrupt. He knew that Jared was about to discover something important.

Had I done that? Jared asked himself. *Had I used my time on the golf course in service to God?* He recalled a time when he stomped, cussed, and threw his nine iron into the lake because he missed a chip shot that cost him the tournament. His boss, a nonbeliever who was competing against Jared, was astonished at this loss of control. Then there was the time when his son Philip who was three years old had begged to go with him to the golf course: "I wanna ride with you, Daddy." Jared didn't want to be bothered with an unpredictable toddler. As he became more proficient at the game, weekend golf outings surpassed family outings. He thought, *How unlike Christ was I during those times? I had not used my time on the golf course to serve God at all. I had served myself, ignoring the needs of my son, my most precious charge.*

These realizations were painful for Jared, and it made him think about Sonny's mention of the echo chamber.

"What do you remember Sonny telling you about this chamber?" the leader asked knowing that besides his own voice, Jared would also experience the voice of his son.

"The Echo Chamber is part of the Realm of Empathy where we feel what we made another feel because of our words. We get to hear what our words felt like from their point of view," Jared said.

"Good description, Jared," the leader remarked. "But I sense you have a question."

"Does a soul recognize his own voice as the person saying these words?"

"Indeed, he does," the leader replied.

"But are there times when the soul hears the voice of someone else?"

"Yes, but these are special cases," the leader said. "Each echo carries the imprint, the unique frequency of a soul. There's no mistake whose voice gave birth to these words. The intensity of the echo depends on how often and for what intent they used such language. Words of hatred older children say to their parents when they don't get their way are good examples."

Jared remembered hateful words with Walter. But at the time, he felt justified. He hummed at a lower frequency wondering if Walter had made it to Heaven and if he did, would he share the Echo Chamber with him? He also wondered if "kind words" were echoed back.

The realm leader did not provide Jared with that information, because it would be a distraction. He knew what was in store for this soul and that it was not his responsibility to tell Jared about these upcoming encounters. However, he could provide more information so that Jared would be better prepared for the experience.

"When souls who had 'loose and flagrant tongue issues' arrive here," the leader said, "and they make it to the Realm of Empathy, the Echo Chamber experience can be a remarkable exchange of frequency. Reverberating sounds tumbling continuously onto your energy will humble a soul, especially since the time-date stamp accompanies each word."

Jared got still, waiting for an explanation of the term.

"At the end of each word phrase," the leader explained, "another voice, the recipient of the words, calls back the time and date the words were used to hurt them."

Jared thought of outbursts, when he yelled at people in his life. He also thought about his use of irreverent babble and foul language when he was a teenager and especially during his college days at the fraternity house. He hoped that the volume on these echoes would not be too loud. During their time together, Sonny told him that the Realm of Empathy had two chambers, Echo and Reflection, but that some other realm leader was more qualified to explain them—this leader seemed to have the authority and Jared asked about a Reflection Chamber, wondering if it was a huge mirror.

"A lot of souls think that," the leader said. "The experience of reflection is with all the animal creatures who served you on Earth."

"So animals have souls?"

"No, they have 'reflections' of the people they served," the leader clarified. "If you cared for and were kind and loving toward an animal, the encounter is nice. If you were cruel or neglectful of an animal, that's what they reflect back to you. It can hurt a lot to see yourself in the eyes of these helpless creatures."

Jared relaxed; he could not think of a single animal he had mistreated, but he did remember forgetting to water Mom's African violets which shriveled and died while she was visiting a friend in Michigan. "How 'bout plants?" Jared asked. "Do we meet up with them?"

"Now, that's a superb question Jared," the leader said. "It is a rare soul who asks about plants. Although they are not part of the animal kingdom, they are living things that serve mankind by producing..."

"Oxygen!" Jared interrupted. His increased vibration activated the simulvision cloud on the side wall of the cave. He watched a memory of a heated argument with a golfing buddy, who nearly came to blows with nine irons over the topic of global warming. His buddy said that carbon dioxide was killing the earth. Jared yelled back, "It's carbon *mono*xide that kills. Carbon *dio*xide is what plants need to make oxygen."

"You were passionate about global warming and other political issues," the realm leader said. "I confess to enjoying matters along those same lines myself."

"You liked politics?" Jared asked.

"Indeed. You and I will have to share opinions in a little while. Presently, I would greatly appreciate wrapping up this discussion. I have a group meeting in another realm. But don't let me rush you."

"That's okay. You've been patient and kind. Go ahead and wrap up," Jared said.

"Because the Echo and Reflection Chambers experience can be quite painful," the leader said, "Christ provides you with comforters."

"The Holy Spirit?" Jared asked.

"The Holy Spirit is your constant comforter, but others are people who were loved on Earth and who preceded us in coming here. Examples are grandmothers who raised us, fathers who died in war or of health issues, mothers who died in childbirth or when we were young, or children who died before their parents."

Jared thought of all of the people who had died, and the one he most ached to see was his mother.

CHAPTER 33

A Shout-Out

"Sonny told me that for doubters, like me, someone had to pray for me to turn to the light so that I could get oriented. What if no one had prayed for me? Would I have spent eternity on the bench in the Waiting Room?"

"Eventually, by one method or another, all souls who arrive here and choose to stay get oriented," the leader said knowing that Jared was not ready to understand that in Heaven, there is no such thing as "eventually," because time in Heaven is all in the now.

"Intercessory prayer," the leader said, "is one way to encourage a doubter to choose orientation. A Spiritual Flash Point is another."

"Flashpoint," Jared repeated. "Sonny used that term earlier. He said that it is a point in time that redirects our lives, but I thought it was a chemistry term, isn't it?"

"It can be," the leader said. "In politics it is a moment that has a strong possibility of developing into a war. For a human being, a Spiritual Flash Point is a moment that has a strong possibility of developing into love."

"Love for God?" Jared asked.

"Yes, because when we love Him, we can love ourselves and others. That's our earthly responsibility—our commission. And prayer is one of the tools we are given to accomplish this. Intercessory prayer can ignite a flash point that heals a broken heart, restores shattered hope, and is powerful enough to turn a soul to the light—to get oriented in God's time zone."

In response, Jared bobbed toward a pale-colored stalagmite, indicating that he needed more direction. The leader offered, "We are grateful for those who continue to pray for people who are no longer on Earth."

"Isn't that praying for the dead?" Jared asked, his stability returning.

"The dead are in Hell. For those who know Christ as their Savior, there is no such thing as dead. We die but we are not dead. We do not cease to be. We are changed."

These words triggered a memory of a sermon Jared heard when he was a boy. Grandma Robinette had taken him to a Wednesday night revival prayer meeting at her church in Gaffney. He was bored and began daydreaming when the pastor startled him by saying, "Repent, you sinner, before you fall asleep and Satan snatches your soul!" This sermon gave Jared the creeps which added to his misery of being afraid to go to sleep at night. He had seen a movie called *Invasion of the Body Snatchers* and decided the technique used in the movie was the one Satan planned to use on him once he let go and went to sleep. As he got older, he knew that the snatching of souls was nonsense, at least by this Hollywood method.

He recalled his grandma talking about how people sleep, waiting for Christ to call them from the grave. Since he was in the presence of an expert on issues of Heaven, he asked, "What about all those people who are asleep? Are they safe and waiting to be ushered to the Waiting Room?"

"Your question is more appropriate for Einstein's realm, but I don't think he'll mind if I cover this one point. It is among the FAQs."

"Frequently asked questions," Jared declared.

"Correct. The sleep thing confuses a lot of people. Souls do not remain in a state of sleep awaiting Heaven. Consider this, when you were down there and you went to bed to sleep, can you ever remember the exact moment that you fell asleep?"

"Now that you mention it, no," Jared said.

"But when you woke up you knew that you had slept, right?"

"Yeah, come to think of it, I did," Jared declared recalling how relieved he had been that a body snatcher event had not taken place for him during the night. "So what you're telling me is that when someone dies, they move immediately from their body to be in Heaven?"

"If their heart's desire is Christ, then yes, they 'go to sleep' there and wake up here, in the presence of the Lord," the leader said.

"But I'm not yet present with the Lord, am I?"

"Oh, but you are. He's right here in the cave with you."

"What?" Jared cried out. His energy expanded and vibrated with an unexpected intense pleasant tingling sensation.

"Oh, my Lord!" he shouted and was amazed by the experience of being so large that his shout-out rattled the cave walls and activated the Simulvision cloud. Bursting onto the surface of the cloud was a recollection of Miss Ellie, a colored lady who attended the Baptist church he visited when spending summers in Gaffney. Predictably, Grandma Robinette selected a seat behind Miss Ellie. Eleven-year old Jared could not resist snickering when she thrust her white gloved hands upward—a signal that she was about to deliver her passion-filled, "Oh, my Lord!" shout-out.

After crying out, she would totter and fall back onto the pew with such surrender that the massive bench rocked up from the floor, convincing Jared that it would tip over and pin him in place with Miss Ellie piled on top of him. He was always startled by her outcries even though she gave advance warning.

The prelude to her shout-out was a bobbing head, arms up, body rocking back and forth, building momentum that dislodged her lace-covered wide-brimmed Sunday hat, making it flip off her head and spin onto the floor or into the lap of someone sitting nearby. Retrieving Miss Ellie's hat was a routine scowling faced mandate from Grandma. As a young boy, he made fun of Miss Ellie's outbursts. And as an adult, it disturbed him to hear explicit outcries. He thought such displays were showing off. He never dreamt that he would utter these very words with the same passion-filled exhibition. Now, he understood precisely what Miss Ellie felt when she rocked that pew off its feet and sent her Sunday hat flying. "Was this empathy?" Jared asked himself as the tingling in his center quieted. Without asking, he knew that a hole got repaired. With a deep sigh of relief, he thought about intercessory prayer.

"You said that to get oriented, someone had to pray for me. Who was it, may I ask?"

CHAPTER 34

Getting Turned

"Certainly," the leader replied. "The person who prayed for you to turn to the light was your wife, Priscilla. Would you like to activate that moment?"

"Sure," Jared said and filled with anticipation as he recalled the extraordinary demonstration of a do-over with Martha.

"Watch," the leader said directing Jared to the clouds that brightened rocky features of the cave. Images formed and Jared felt connected to them as if they were events occurring at the moment. His beloved wife was at the bedside of a man in a hospital room. Jared floated above her and realized that the body she was attending was his.

It was odd knowing that he was in Heaven with some discussion leader but also hovering above a body that was obviously in a hospital room on Earth. Jared shivered. The leader moved closer, offering warmth and comfort as Jared continued to look on his own body with wonder. He saw his chest rise and fall, but this movement did not look natural. It was too precise. Jared understood why he shivered because the body in the bed was lying on top of an ice-filled mattress.

Tubes and wires streamed from his nose, chest, forehead, arms, hands, and ankles. He saw Priscilla sitting in a chair next to his bed, leaning over him. She was holding his right hand, caressing it, rubbing it. On the other side of the bed, he saw a young man he did not recognize. The man's head was bowed and he was holding Jared's other hand, tenderly stroking limp fingers as if he hoped they would offer some sign of life.

Activity defined areas of the hospital room. People ebbed and flowed from the 8 × 10 cubicle. Expertly they attended to the wires trailing from his body and the machines that spewed details about impulses transmitted in secret by silent limbs. Some visitors to his bedside were familiar to Jared. Others were not, but all appeared to care about him. A doctor entered the room and spoke with Priscilla. He told her that he was a neurologist and explained the readings on the machines.

Once the doctor left, Priscilla sat down in the chair next to the tube-laced body of her husband Jared Hamilton Walcott. She leaned over, put her lips to her beloved's ear, and kissed it as she whispered, "Jared, my precious, stay as long as you want, but I need to unplug the respirator so you can decide. The nurse will get the doctor who can turn off this machine and remove the tube. My dearest one, my precious, I love you and I'll be with you again someday."

The realm leader remained close to Jared, knowing that the next few moments were going to be profound. Jared watched as the unknown young man and his beloved walked into the hall to get the nurse. A loud buzzing and shrill tone vibrated on the cloud. He knew exactly what had happened. This was the moment he chose to depart from his earthly, wretched body. He remembered his final breath, which seemed to last much longer than he imagined it would. He remembered the Final Offer, the moment of declaration. He saw the angels guide him to the Waiting Room and realized that for a while he had been lingering between the two dimensions there and here, something the soul is able to do for a period of time.

He understood the elastic-band sensation he felt when he arrived in the Waiting Room. "No one can snatch you out of His hands," he heard his beloved Priscilla say. Then he heard her crying out to God that he be turned to the light—and now he understood Sonny's arrival.

Jared's energy changed from erratic pulses to a steady hum as he integrated with this moment and gave thanks to God for giving him his beloved Priscilla to nurture him and help him understand God's love. His altered energy generated a unique fragrance and harmonious tones. He realized that his heavenly identity was forming. He felt different. He was lighter, larger, and more sensitive to things around him. Colors were rich, fragrances were inviting, sounds were harmonious, and conversation was shared by means of thought.

"You can still go back," he heard the leader say, and Jared knew that he could return to the body he saw lying in the hospital bed.

He didn't want to.

"With God, it is always about choice," the leader told him. "He never makes the decision for you. He allows you free will even through your last breath."

CHAPTER 35

Celebrity Praise and Worship

"If only I had a way to tell others about Heaven," Jared said.

The realm leader knew that because of Jared's choice of heavenly mission, he would help generations for eternity—but he guarded his thoughts because he wasn't authorized to show Jared this outcome, yet—Jared was still in transition and although unlikely, he could choose to go back. Telling him anything more about his life in Heaven might influence his choice.

"The peace that I feel is indescribable," Jared said and remembered scripture, "Peace that passeth all understanding."

"It's true. This peace can only be understood by someone who experiences it," the leader replied.

A memory of Priscilla rose and surrounded Jared. She told him that she died after the birth of their twins and that she went to Heaven. When he argued that the trip was just a hallucination, she was adamant that it was not. She told him that the visit was as real because the peace she felt while on that visit could not be possible on Earth. She knew without a doubt that Heaven existed and that her return to him had purpose: to help him discard faulty or fearful word meaning and replace them with faith and confidence that one day he would experience this peace as well.

The realm leader listened to Jared remember the conversation with his wife and his good friend C.W.

"Words are powerful," Priscilla said.

"With them, we can generate healthy or toxic thoughts," C.W. added. "And words though well intended do not always line up with the message. Take for example the word fear," C.W. continued. "As a child, you did not understand the word 'fear' when referring to God."

Priscilla added, "When Grandma Robinette read the Bible to you, she did not explain that the word fear meant 'awe.'"

"You were a child, and so you thought like a child," C.W. said. "Your only reference point was childlike, where fear meant to be terrified."

Before speaking, the leader waited until Jared completed reliving the memory and then said, "The opposition loves these moments. Gripped by fear and worry, it is easier for him to convince you that you have no power over such thoughts. In an anxious state of mind, you are vulnerable to rejecting God."

"Can a person say that they reject God and then change and ask for forgiveness?" Jared asked.

"Yes, because God knows when a person is rejecting Him or just rebelling against Him."

Jared had another thought about God, sin, and repentance, "I have a question."

"Yes?" the realm leader replied.

"If God hates sin so much, and He is all powerful, why does He allow sin to continue?"

The realm leader's tone changed, and again Jared thought he heard the giddy sound of a horse whinny and the clink of cowboy's spurs. He also could smell hay and freshly mowed grass. Before he could ask about this, the leader spoke.

"Not to make a federal case of it, but if God denied us the freedom to sin, people would undoubtedly complain that there just might be another way besides God's way for salvation."

"Your words," Jared began slowly. "Your voice—they seem familiar, and I believe that we never did get properly introduced."

"That's true," the leader chuckled.

"Down there, they called me Ronald Reagan. Up here, I'm called Ronnie."

"The President Reagan?!" Jared squealed like a child.

Ronnie laughed out loud, "Indeed, I am."

"Oh! My! Word!" Jared exclaimed.

"I get that a lot," Ronnie said and sensing that Jared was wondering why he was privileged to be in the company of such a celebrity, Reagan interceded. "Here, I am no more special than you are. In God's kingdom, we're all celebrities. You will come to understand this in a little while."

Jared had difficulty accepting the fact that he was as much a celebrity as Reagan. His energy hummed attempting to make the adjustment. But Jared was not quite ready to accept his own celebrity status. Instead he focused on trying to grasp the fact that he was in the same time and space as the President Reagan, the fortieth president of the United States.

He could not resist reciting a few lines that President Reagan was famous for.

"General Secretary Gorbachev, if you seek peace, if you seek prosperity for the Soviet Union and Eastern Europe, if you seek liberalization, come here to this gate! Mr. Gorbachev, open this gate! Mr. Gorbachev, tear down this wall!"

Reagan laughed. "Remember, here I'm Ronnie. All the 'hoop-la' of celebrity down there holds no value up here. A few of my friends call me Reagan—but whatever name you like best is okay with me."

"Besides leading discussion in this realm, what's your mission?" Jared asked, curious if Reagan was serious about wanting to "goof off and eat candy." Reagan smiled and was glad to have created a humorous memory for Jared.

"I am working with a freshman senator from South Carolina, to inspire the words for a bill he and a congressman will sponsor."

"To do what?" Jared asked.

"To establish the truth about the separation of church and state. I just sent Him a text message yesterday."

"A text message, from here?"

"It's not the kind of text message you used to get on your phone. It is inspiration from the Bible—the original text messaging. Besides meditating on several verses of scripture, the young senator is reviewing words I used in a speech on this topic."

Ronnie repeated the key portion of the speech for Jared, although Jared knew it by heart. "The first amendment was not written to protect people and their laws from religious values. It was written to protect those values from government tyranny."

Jared felt great and Ronnie knew it and asked which realm he might like to visit next. Jared told Ronnie that he wanted to better understand God's laws. Ronnie offered that he was going past the law library and would be glad to show him the way.

CHAPTER 36

Acts of Treason and Violation of Copyright

Ronnie directed Jared into the law library. He wanted to personally introduce him to Judge Deborah, the realm discussion leader. As they entered the room, Jared was surprised by the endless rows of leather-bound books.

Leaning in Jared's direction, Ronnie whispered, "Man's interpretation of God's law. Amazing isn't it? God put His laws on two simple tablets and then the lawyers got ahold of it." Sensing Jared was about to share a lawyer joke he motioned for him to remain quiet.

Judge Deborah was standing with her back to Jared and Reagan. She was facing a dark-skinned, trim and fit handsome young man who was sitting on the edge of a three-legged stool playing an unusual string instrument.

"That's a kinnor," Ronnie whispered.

"Looks like a miniature harp," Jared said; but whatever it was called, he liked the sounds it made. Delicate, soothing notes rose from strings, inviting him to sway. Judge Deborah sang in a passion-filled voice, "So may all your enemies perish, Oh Lord. But may they who love you be like the sun when it rises in its strength."

Reagan again whispered in Jared's direction, "This is from a song she wrote. That fella on the stool is King David. Really good, aren't they?" Jared bobbed in agreement. He had heard of King David, but he had no idea who Judge Deborah was. Sharing his thoughts, Reagan whispered, "She was the fourth and only female judge of Israel."

Jared did not remark that he thought women should not be in positions of political power. God obviously didn't agree. David rose and smiled at Jared, but he left without saying anything.

"Greetings, Jared. It is nice to see you, and you too, Ronnie," Deborah said.

Shortly after the greeting, President Reagan evaporated. So did David. Jared wondered where they went.

"They've gone back to work," Judge Deborah said out loud, reminding Jared that his thoughts were in the public domain.

"Ronnie has his governance group to inspire. David is leading some composers and songwriters working on the lyrics for an upcoming *He is Risen* praise and worship event."

"Are these songwriters here or there?" Jared asked.

"There," Deborah said. "Creative souls here enjoy inspiring creative beings on Earth."

"Isn't that interfering with a person's free will?"

"Not at all. The godly artist wants to hear from an expert. They ask for help through prayer and they are given their answer in the form of inspiration, which might occur during a dream, or witnessing a godly man or woman suffer in pain or watching a sleeping puppy, kitten, child, or a brilliant sunrise or sunset. When a prayer is lifted up by someone on Earth and answered with waves of inspiration from Heaven, it brings us joy, especially when the artist gives the glory of their accomplishment to God.

"As for David," she continued. "He also leads the realm of understanding making of a joyful noise. Presently, he is being assisted by Rich Mullins, Carl Perkins, Mary Wells, and Elias Bates. You used to call him Bo Diddley," Deborah said surprising Jared who wondered how these four were assisting King David.

Sharing Jared's thought, Deborah explained, "Rich, Carl, Mary, and Bo are helping David with musicians misled by the opposition into producing music poisonous to the mind and the heart."

How can music be poisonous?" Jared asked.

"By what it generates."

"Huh?"

Deborah knew that Jared had been down both paths. He had been ensnared and inspired by music.

"When the consequences of music are inspirational," Deborah began, "the listener feels God's presence and desires to minister and witness to others with love. When the consequences are insnarational, the individual feels alone and becomes obsessed with finding his missing piece. He has an overwhelming desire for the 'primitive pelvic thrust' dance."

Jared felt warm. Was he blushing? He remembered listening to music that made him feel raunchy. In an effort to quell memories of those moments from bubbling up and being shared, Jared quickly redirected his thoughts and asked, "'Insnarational,' that's not a word I know."

Deborah knew about Jared's college days when he had been seduced by this lusty force of lyrics and rhythm and had gone on the hunt for a woman to conquer. She camouflaged her knowledge of his pursuits by thinking of a Civil War battle scene, unknown to Jared. It wasn't time for him to address his improper behavior with women.

Her cover-up made Jared hum. He was beginning to appreciate the thought-leakage provision after repeated odd episodes of Civil War scenes or political debates randomly showed up on the Simulvision clouds. He knew at some point in time he would find out what Deborah was protecting him from seeing.

"'Insnare,' also spelled 'ensnare,'" Deborah said, "means to lure a person into a dangerous trap. For us, it means to jeopardize a person's relationship with Christ."

Her words hit a chord. Jared enjoyed music. It was a constant in his life. When he was a teenager, he listened to "rock and roll" on a transistor radio until Walter the Drunk snatched it out of his hands. As a college student, a time when he wanted nothing to do with God, his choice of music exemplified the word "insnare." Jimmi Hendrix, Marvin Gaye, and the sultry sounds of Nina Simone pulsated in the hallways of his fraternity house.

Later music was something he and Priscilla enjoyed. Slow-dancing with her to Tina Turner's "You're Simply the Best" caused a warming sensation. Before this memory could complete itself, Jared jammed thought-sharing between him and Deborah with a humorous Julia Childs cooking scene. He wanted to keep that moment with Priscilla private. Deborah smiled at Jared's choice of thought-camouflage. In spite of his reckless college years with immoral behavior and frequent sexual conquests, once married to Priscilla, he knew the difference between having sex and making love.

Changing the subject, Jared said, "I noticed that this realm is called Acts of Treason and Violation of Copyright, I can understand the acts of treason part, because disregarding the laws of God is being treacherous, betraying, or breaking an alliance with Him resulting in death."

"So what do you not understand?" Deborah asked.

"What copyright is being violated?"

"The use of God's name," she said.

"How's that violating a copyright?" Jared asked. "That's a publisher's term isn't it?"

"Yes, it is. On behalf of God, the Senator being inspired by Ronnie wants to provide a way to bring attention to the widespread disgraceful and cavalier references to our Heavenly Father. The bill being crafted will keep movie makers from using God's name in vain."

"Wouldn't that be unconstitutional, a violation of the first amendment?"

CHAPTER 37

The Cost of Vanity

"**N**ot the way the bill is structured," Deborah said. "The wording will not restrict the moviemakers from using God's name in vain, rather this bill imposes a vanity tax on those who choose to. Since most in the movie industry are concerned with profits more than content, we know that the senator's strategy works well."

"If the law is just now being written, how do you know it will work?" Jared asked.

"We can view outcomes. Would you like to see?"

"Sure!" Jared said. He was giddy with the idea that he could see things in the future. Deborah didn't tell him that seeing the future was a God's time experience and that this would become natural for him in a while.

"Watch the clouds," she told him and he looked up.

The library dimmed and its ceiling filled with plump, radiant cumulus clouds. Jared saw the words "Advance-View Generator" roll onto the bright surface and "The Holy Spirit" listed as Executive Producer of outcomes. After a brief stream of credits, activity on the cloud surface blossomed: images rose, dangled for a moment and drifted into place. The scenes reminded Jared of C-Span, a channel he used to watch when he wanted to know the goings-on of Congress.

"The woman you see standing next to the senator is a member of the House," Deborah told Jared. He was struck by the humility of the two legislators when in unison they knelt to pray. For much of his adult life, Jared thought politicians were corrupt, but he became less skeptical when Priscilla told him that prayer was ever present on the Hill. She explained that both the House and the Senate had chaplains and since 1955 there was a dedicated prayer room where any member of Congress was invited to visit. Priscilla trusted that these chaplains would be vigilant and inspiring in their opening daily prayers; she was particularly impressed by Chaplain Barry Black who asked God to forgive the Senate their pride and blunders.

Actions and events on the clouds were happening at once but it was not chaotic. People moved in slow, deliberate fashion, walking about with purpose: handing papers to one another, shaking hands, hugging, and smiling. Jared felt inspiration flowing from Ronnie to the senator and the congresswoman who were kneeling in prayer and who punctuated their request for wisdom with, "In Your holy name, we ask, amen." Jared expected them to get up off their knees, but they did not. Their heads remained bowed and he realized that they were not finished. They were listening. In a surreal exchange, Jared heard Reagan's words: "The vanity tax resolution could be constructed using the Office of Patents, Trademarks, and Copyright regulations. Since God's mark is on everything, the better use of the term is copyright and the source is the Word: 'In the beginning was the Word and the Word was with God, and the Word was God.'"

After receiving inspiration, both members of the congress stood up, smiled, exchanged a "high five" hand slap, grabbed a pencil and yellow legal tablet, slid into barrel back chairs, scooted up to a table, and started writing the bill in long hand.

"Whereas God owns the original use of His name, and whereas its first use was in print 3,500 years ago in a publication deemed authentic and in use at the time and so named the Ten Commandments, whereas these tablets inscribed with God's name were witnessed by Moses and his brother Aaron, etc...."

Deborah interrupted, "It goes on from there with more legal language, but the best part is toward the end."

Together Jared and Deborah looked back at the clouds. He saw the legislators discussing the importance of stating that a producer of any visual product including but not limited to digital, analog, holographic, robotic, artificial, and virtual productions, in existence now or anytime in the future, who chooses to use God's name, especially when it is followed by an order for God to damn someone or something, in a singular, collective, or multiple use, the owner of the film will owe a vanity tax of 28% of the gross receipts.

Jared laughed out loud. "That's some outcome," he said to Deborah who was laughing too. "There's always hope, when people work from the heart," she remarked. "Ronnie is also assisting this group with other bills: the Single Purpose bill, the Redactment Amendment to Copyrights, and the Repayment of Tax Dollars and Undue Influence bills to name a few. George, Abe, Bookie, Annie, Howie, and Fred are on that inspiration team."

"Ronnie and Abe, I know. George, I'm guessing is George Washington, but Howie, Bookie, Fred, and Annie, I'm not sure."

"Howie, you know as President Eisenhower. Others you would recognize as Booker T. Washington, Frederick Douglass, and Marguerite Annie Johnson who later changed her name to Maya Angelou."

"Oh, yes, I do remember them now," Jared whispered. The idea that good work continues from Heaven made him feel lighter.

Deborah interjected, "Not only does it continue but it expands."

CHAPTER 38

Who Gets the Credit?

Deborah directed Jared to the conclusion section of the production and together they watched a scrolling list of outcomes: the true free market restored; physicians unbound by government regulations and allowed to practice the art of medicine; malpractice lawsuits less than 1% and unemployment, poverty, and claims for disability less than 1%; school dropout rate less than 1%; marriage up by 1,000%; fathers remaining in the home up 1000%; abortions—spontaneous only; church attendance up 1000%; the national debt paid off; military pay quadrupled; and all of the US government agencies restored to their original missions without budget cuts or loss of staff.

"*Ooooooh—wheweeee!*" Jared whistled, surprising himself. Whistling was something that he loved doing as a child but got punished for when Walter grabbed him by the neck and quoted scripture: "A whistler and a crowing hen are abominations in the sight of God."

"That's in Third Timothy," Deborah said.

"What is?"

"The admonition about whistling. It's not in the Bible. Here you can whistle all you want. In fact, we delight in that use of breath."

Everything Here is encouraging and uplifting, Jared thought. He cherished the understanding he was gaining and noticed that he had become less sarcastic, more articulate, and trusting of thought-sharing and he was having fun gaining knowledge.

The scrolling conclusion on the Advance-View Generator ended and the outcomes faded into the clouds. Jared thought about the use of God's name in vain and asked, "So all those great outcomes will be the result of this vanity tax?"

"Our Creator is the ultimate in reconstruction and redistribution of wealth," Deborah said. "But there will be some challenging times during the transition. Christians still consider using 'Oh my God' or 'OMG' as perfectly acceptable expressions."

"But aren't these expressions just meant for fun or to be funny?" Jared asked.

"That is the problem. Most do not realize that each time we use God's name, we are calling Him to participate in what we are doing. If we are having fun, ignorant of what we are saying, praising Him or asking Him to damn something, He comes to us regardless. During judgment, God allows us to see these times so that we can assess for ourselves how judiciously and appropriately we called upon Him. Unless, of course, we figure that out and repent of breaking this commandment. Once you repent of a sin, God forgets it."

"But you still have the scars from holes of sin, right?" Jared asked.

"That is true," Deborah said. "Thankfully, due to awareness this vanity tax generates and the revenue derived, many of today's and tomorrow's children will come to understand the meaning of reverence and respect."

"When I was a kid," Jared said, "Grandma Robinette scolded me for saying 'gall-durn.' I didn't understand it—the words seemed harmless. And as I got older, I began to replace these phrases with stronger versions of profanity. By the time I got into college, asking God to damn something was as common as saying 'hello.' And then later, the misuse of God's name in thrilling action movies didn't faze me. Priscilla helped me to hear better, and after she did that, it felt like a punch to the gut to hear someone call God to damn someone or something. But the stories, the action, the filming, the acting were so good—it was not easy to resist watching these movies."

Jared thought about the first forty years of his life and how he watched hundreds of movies but could not hear God's name abused. Later, when he and Priscilla watched those same movies, he was astonished that a PG-rated movie used no popular profane words but included at least one command of God to damn something.

He sighed, "Desensitize, a strategy used in war and in the world. It didn't occur to me at the time that desensitizing someone is also a good path to indifference. From here, it's clear to see the ways and means of the father of lies."

Deborah was pleased with Jared's refinement. She knew that if he kept up this pace, his advancement through the realms would be swift. She gave thanks for this assignment and nudged Jared back to discussion about law.

CHAPTER 39

RALF at Work

"I f the violation of copyright is against God, who collects and distributes the money? The government?" Jared asked.

"Certainly not," Deborah said. "The money belongs to God. It is distributed among organizations, agencies, and institutions that glorify His name. However, the government is an indirect recipient of this money through fair taxation."

"Without a manager of funds, how does the money get distributed?" Jared asked remembering how corrupt people became when they were in control of vast amounts of cash.

Deborah responded with a sweet laugh. "Oh, there is a manager of funds, alright. It's all handled electronically by artificial intelligence generated by some sophisticated cyber-technology algorithms inspired by a group of scientists here. All those data collected by spying on citizens becomes a 'furtive life form.' Although not human, this life form is prone to altruism, or love of mankind. It becomes a radically altruistic life force, RALF for short."

Jared howled with laughter, "No kidding?"

"No kidding," Deborah said, laughing along with Jared.

"The distribution of funds will not involve grants, appropriations, or earmarks," Deborah said regaining her composure. "This is all accomplished anonymously by RALF which knows who to reward. Organizations, agencies, or businesses receive without notification, a large periodic deposit into their bank account, and so long as they do not get lazy and expect this money, and so long as they put in an honest day's work, rest, and are charitable with a portion of these funds, they remain eligible to receive, and the deposits continue. It is inspiring to see obedience rewarded. Like children, they all figure it out. If they are sincere, love justice and show mercy, and are moral, ethical, lawful, charitable, humble, and loving to one another, the deposits are made and increased depending upon the degree of joyful heart charity they exhibit."

Jared sighed with relief knowing that America wouldn't be destroyed. Still he was curious about cyber-technology and wondered who the scientists were that inspired the design of such a system. He especially wanted to know if there was some way to turn it off. Before completing the thought, Deborah spoke up, "Bert, Max, Marie, Leo, Eli, and Vince were responsible for the inspiration—you know them as Einstein, Max Plank, Marie Van Brittan Brown, Galileo, Elijah McCoy, and Leonardo Da Vinci."

"They meet regularly," Deborah added. "If you are interested, you can join their Inspirational Technology (IT) discussion group once you are perfected. Their field trips are exhilarating, fast-paced, and multidirectional—pure fun."

Jared tried to grasp the idea of being in discussion with such a distinguished group. He took a deep breath and told Judge Deborah, "There seems to be no limit to what a soul can do in Heaven."

"Except sin," she reminded him, and sensing that Jared had no more questions, Judge Deborah continued the discussion about God's laws. "God gave his people the law to keep them safe from sin."

"I never thought of God's commandments as a way to keep me safe. Whenever a religious authority told me to 'obey,' it made me feel like I was losing my freedom. But with God, it's just the opposite: I gain freedom."

"Nicely said," Judge Deborah offered.

"I memorized the Ten Commandments as a young boy," Jared said. "But I didn't understand them then," he added.

"That is not uncommon. God's laws are simple: Love Him and love others. But people often try to complicate or distort the meaning of His commandments. For a child, an adult's perspective of God's laws is impossible to understand, although many adults expect this of their children."

"I know, that's what happened to me," Jared said.

Deborah offered a treat. She filled the clouds with outcomes of RALF. Jared laughed as he watched images of photographs, cell phones, and computers rise on the cloud. It reminded him of a favorite conversation with Grandma Robinette about idols and machines.

"I remember something she told me about this. It didn't make sense when I was eight. She told me that machines would be our downfall."

"Your grandma knew her Bible. In Jeremiah, we are warned about idols: 'Do not provoke me to anger with what your hands have made.'"

"When I was a child, I used to think she was talking about modern appliances and air travel. But anything created to please the self would apply—if the love of it comes before the love of God."

"Good point," Deborah remarked.

"Priscilla and I worried about future generations growing weaker because of their love of contraptions and electronic gadgets," Jared said.

"Would you like a glimpse of possible outcomes?" Deborah asked.

"Sure," Jared replied, remembering the fun of activating the Advance-View Generator.

CHAPTER 40

Zip, Zoom, Bang!

Rows of library books served as the surface for low-hanging clouds to gather and display images. Judge Deborah narrated as scenes came into focus.

"Man's ability to bring machines into existence will diminish procreation—fewer and fewer babies will be born. Adoration for these man-made programmable alternatives to unpredictable spouses and friends replaces human love. A generation of souls becomes lost because of infatuation with the faux-sentient soulless beings. They lose sight of the fact that God's creation regardless of how sinful, tattered, and challenging has a soul which can communicate with the Holy Spirit. Manmade imitations of God's creation do not have this capacity. But because these artificial life inventions are programmed to anticipate wants, promote material gain, and provide instant gratification complete with door-to-door drone delivery service, every kid wants one."

Jared was stunned. He wasn't expecting to see a bad outcome.

"A few people continue to take a chance on messy but real relationships," Deborah said, easing his tension. "And they decide to limit their use of the Internet, gadgets, and social media. Unchaperoned children, however, are mesmerized by these high-tech machines and become obsessed and distracted by the toy's magical capabilities. Children do not think of the consequences and are incapable of understanding how an obsession limits their ability to form relationships. Caught up in text messages, 'selfies,' postings, and tags, children and many adults foster loneliness rather than love," Deborah said.

"They become like robots doing the 'thumb dance'—alone with their faces turned down focused on the magic box that gives them immediate pleasure but robs them of opportunities to look into the eyes of a potential new friend. The artificial sounds of the magic boxes eventually overwrite the child's God-given frequency. These sophisticated programs can alter the appearance of someone with filters or can change the image of a sweet child turning them into a talking rabbit, fox, cat, or dog."

Jared felt unstable and nauseated; what Judge Deborah described did not sound good at all.

"Unable to express their unique melody," she continued, "they are kept from uniting with their intended mate. The opposition is ecstatic over what seems a triumph for his side. People who knew how to prepare for these times try to warn others, but much like the pleadings of Prophet Jeremiah, words fall on ears that do not hear. The obsession continues to destroy relationships, cause heartache, and foster loneliness."

Her words were shocking. Jared thought Deborah was going to show him a good outcome, like she did before with the politicians. This one was not what he expected, but then he considered the cries of the few who were prepared and he sighed. He hoped that their warnings would matter.

Judge Deborah who was listening to Jared's hopeful thoughts comforted him with the rest of the story. She knew that he was concerned about the younger generation and their love for technical toys. She surprised him and reactivated the Advance-View Generator.

Pictures of a massive electromagnetic pulse attack over America that shut down all of the devices appeared on the screen. Jared's mouth opened in astonishment.

"For over a year, people were without their phones, computers, cars, electricity, and access to the Internet," Deborah said.

Jared saw how dumbfounded people were at first. Some did not survive. Those who did were prepared; they helped their neighbors and the children discover how ingenuity replaces preassembled play things.

"You can see that these children begin to take care of themselves. They plant gardens, play games, build things, and talk and laugh with one another and as they grow up, they meet, marry, have children, and come to know their Creator. Their ability to love is restored."

"Thank God," Jared whispered.

"Indeed," Deborah replied. "Ready to practice law?" She asked.

PART THREE

Trying

Psalm 1: 3 "...and he shall be like a tree planted by the rivers of water..."

CHAPTER 41

Commandments 1, 2, 3, 4, and 5

"In commandment 1, I believe that God tells us that He is the only true God. And that the second commandment tells us to not forget the first and replace Him with substitutes incapable of doing what He can do. Number 3 commands us to not do evil in his name.

"And commandment 4?" Deborah asked.

"To keep the Sabbath holy" Jared began. "We do not work for profit. This is a day of rest; a day free of slavery." And if we do not rest our mind and body, neither can rejuvenate and in time we break down beyond repair.

Deborah did not remark, but she was pleased with Jared's progress toward understanding. "And 5?" Deborah asked.

"Honoring my parents was especially tough, and I still have issues with that. It's difficult to honor someone who abandons, rejects, ignores, and screams at you or beats you without good reason."

Deborah knew that Jared was still struggling with family issues, but she also knew that if he chooses to remain in Heaven he would get them resolved before he reached God's Kingdom. She commended him for his progress toward understanding these first five commandments and said, "When you are face-to-face with God, you will have perfect clarity."

Jared thought about the next five commandments, the ones that Grandma Robinette referred to as his compass for behavior when in a position of authority over others.

CHAPTER 42

The Book of Life

J ared remembered the first time he heard the 10 commandments. He was 7 years old and sitting with Pop. "Exodus 20, Jared," Pop said. "It's in the Old Testament. Here let me show you in this Bible I got for you." Jared remembered how carefully Pop opened the front of the Bible and showed him his name. "See Jared Hamilton Wolcott; that's who you are and as you grow up, you should try never to steal or to lie." Remembering Pop's words made him think about his Grandma Robinette who also taught him the importance of telling the truth. She told him "bearing false witness" was not just limited to giving false testimony in court, where you swear an oath on the Bible. She said this commandment includes any lie, big, small, and seemingly harmless ones, even gossip. She told him that the truth requires less effort than lying because unlike truth, a lie is built on fantasy and fantasies are more difficult to remember because a fantasy is unreal. It never happened, so it cannot be recorded in your book of life.

Deborah almost shared with Jared a few times when God approved of a lie, but she knew that in a while he would discover this in the Doors of Wisdom.

"The Book of Life. Do you believe such a 'book' is kept here?" Deborah asked.

"As a child, I thought my book of life was like a bank account, filled with deposits of my evil doings and that God's copy of my monthly statement showed accounts overdrawn rather than interest earned."

Deborah smiled, "And now?"

"Everything is here in the Doors of Wisdom, I would imagine." Jared said.

CHAPTER 43

Who Invited Jezebel?

"You seem uneasy, Jared," Judge Deborah remarked.

Her loving presence gave him courage, and without hesitation, he began sharing the details about an experience he had with a young woman who worked with him on an anti-bullying program at a high-risk neighborhood elementary school. He was married to Priscilla at the time. One evening after learning bullying incidents had dropped by 60% as a result of their program, without thinking, they hugged one another. Her embrace lingered, but then she stepped back, lowered her head, and looked down at the floor.

"I thought she was embarrassed," Jared said. "But she wasn't. She raised her eyes and began praising me for my leadership skills, patience, and perseverance in spite of a persnickety, controlling principal. Her generous flow of compliments made me feel important, powerful, virile, and good about my abilities as a man. "In the years before I knew what it meant to cherish someone, I would have delighted in a meaningless romp with this woman.

"You were in the presence of a woman filled with the Jezebel spirit," Judge Deborah said.

"That's what C.W. told me. Jared replied. He explained that these women are angry with authority because when they were children, they were hurt by someone they should have been able to trust: a relative, neighbor, family friend, teacher, preacher, or a parent. He told me that inappropriate physical contact, verbal abuse, or undue punishment destroys trust and twists the meaning of love for these women."

"What C.W. told you is correct," Deborah replied. "Unnatural relationships during the formative years, especially unloving experiences with loss, rejection, or fear of abandonment, can cause a person to create toxic thoughts about themselves and others. They become vulnerable to the Jezebel spirit, and once her presence dominates, a person feels that survival is dependent upon the ability to manipulate and control through deception. Ironically, it is the unworthy self that they want to hide from the world. They do not trust that they are loved. And they themselves have difficulty loving."

"The Jezebel spirit will seek and destroy churches, businesses, and marital relationships. These women are Hellbound, shackled by such a powerful evil force that breaking free requires intense prayer, exposure to righteous relationships, and intervention by a skilled professional."

Deborah was about to add that men overtaken by the Jezebel spirit can also wreck the lives of vulnerable women. She decided to leave the issue for Jared to discover later.

"Everyone is going to be tempted," Jared said. "Jesus teaches us to resist temptation, not run from it. Resist it."

Deborah interjected, "Yes, Christ tells us to resist the devil and he will flee, but He also reminds us to flee immorality. Because the father of lies is so strong in his devices, it is a good practice to avoid places where immoral behavior is widespread and especially avoid situations where a man and woman are alone. A Jezebel-spirited woman, regardless of her age, can misconstrue these alone times and fabricate lies about an innocent man."

Jared felt sorrow for anyone harmed by such a powerful spirit, but he especially felt sad for the vulnerable child. "Sin is choice," Jared whispered. "Trauma is not.".

CHAPTER 44

Summary Court

Deborah smiled and Jared felt it. She asked if he would like to sum up God's laws or have her do it. Primary colors of blue, yellow, and red twinkled around Jared and intensified when he said he would like to try. He wanted to deliver his words as flawlessly as Judge Deborah might. He paused, thanked her for her kindness and service on his behalf, quieted his energy, and prayed for wisdom and understanding.

"Without laws to forbid something, there is no sin," Jared began. "For those who love Him, we feel no loss of freedom when we obey—we feel just the opposite. When God's standards of excellence are ingrained in our daily lives, we build a relationship with Him so strong that when adversity arises, we instinctively turn to Him rather than be overwhelmed with fear and panic."

"Whatever we know His laws to be," Jared added, "if we obey them with a pure heart, even when our motives are faulty, God knows the difference."

"Splendid summary, Jared," Deborah remarked.

Her words of praise were pleasant to hear and inspired Jared to quote something C.W. had read to him, "All you do ought to be done out of love. The end of our readiness to obey is the ability to love. The law is given not merely to be complied with but to be cherished."[1]

---

[1] A.J. Heschel's *God in Search of Man*

Judge Deborah knew that Jared had gained wisdom about God's laws and the meaning of being cherished. It delighted her to know that her service was appreciated. She asked. "Which realm are you visiting next?"

"Creation," Jared answered, and Deborah replied, "Oh, I believe the name of that realm has been changed to 'Can a Fetus Feel Pain?'"

CHAPTER 45

Can a Fetus Feel Pain?

Moving out of the law library, Jared drifted toward a small room with a tiny opening. He wasn't sure he could squeeze through but as he approached, the opening expanded and the room swallowed him up, not in a scary way but more like being embraced by a feather pillow mattress. Surprised by the ease with which he slid into the area, he grinned, glad for his accomplishment.

Jared snuggled in thinking that he was alone in the room until something brushed against his face. Its touch was delicate with a lasting sensation like the feeling of walking through a spiderweb. He didn't expect to see a spider, but as the room increased in size, it gained light and he looked around wondering who was in the room with him."

"Greetings, Jared," a kind male voice offered. "My name is Luke and assisting me in this realm is 'the woman of great loss,'" Luke said as an attractive dark-skinned woman with blue eyes approached. Her garment fluttered around her like cherry blossom petals lifted by an invisible puff of air, revealing the source of Jared's spiderweb-like introduction to the realm.

"Nice to meet you," Jared said. "I'm curious. Why was the name of this realm changed from 'Creation' to 'Can a fetus feel pain?'"

"FAQs," Luke responded.

"Frequently asked questions," Jared replied.

"Correct. Since 'Can a fetus feel pain?' is the number one most frequently asked question we get here, we felt it was a more appropriate name for the realm," Luke explained.

"So is there a number two most frequently asked?"

"Yes, we are often asked if it's okay to abort a child created from incest or rape."

"Whoa! That's a tough question. How do you answer that?"

"All life is precious to God," Luke said.

"But what about the horrors for the mother?"

"God understands," the woman of great loss offered. "Some women would rather avoid the shame, the guilt, or the constant reminder of what happened to them if they marry the father. These women abort because they choose not to take on the difficult work of being a mother to such a child or wife to a rapist."

"That's harsh!" Jared said rudely.

The woman of great loss added, "I know. We all prefer life to be easy."

Jared winced. He had experience with the brutal act of rape. His daughter Marcia had been raped when she was sixteen, but she did not reveal the attacker except that he was someone she knew. Jared remembered how upset he was that night when Marcia burst into the house, crying, shaking, and terrified. All she wanted to do was to take a shower, but Priscilla was able to stall Marcia with a few nonthreatening questions. Jared stomped around in the next room while Priscilla and Marcia had whispered exchanges. His pacing was replaced with running when Priscilla grabbed the car keys and told him to hurry. During a nerve-racking drive to the Greenville Hospital emergency room, Priscilla was quiet, but Jared grilled Marcia for details. He recalled how furious he became when his daughter refused to tell him the rapist's name.

Luke and the woman of great loss remained quiet as Jared continued his recollection out loud. "In the emergency room, the doctor gave Marcia a pill to halt any possible creation. He explained to me and Priscilla the importance of prompt medical attention and shared that if Marcia had waited days rather than hours to be examined, conception would have had time to take place. Two years later, before moving to Oregon, Marcia and her husband Greg visited me and Priscilla. They brought their one-month old baby girl Elizabeth with them. While she slept draped facedown across Greg's knees, the subjects of birth, death, and violence drifted into our conversation. Greg knew about the rape and Marcia's other secrets, so when Priscilla brought up the topic of the rape, he remained calm."

Jared recalled how gentle Greg was during this uncomfortable topic of discussion and how he continued to sway his knees with love and appreciation for the precious cargo they held.

"Priscilla asked Marcia how she felt if a pregnancy had resulted from the rape. I was stunned by my daughter's response: 'I would have the baby, Mom,' she told Priscilla."

"Why on Earth would you do such an idiotic thing?" Jared had shouted at his daughter who replied, "I tried to see this from God's point of view. He wouldn't approve of the rape, but He would approve of my willingness to do the very difficult work of looking after this child. He would have used this child for some purpose. I know it."

Luke did not remark about the pinched look on Jared's face as he continued recalling this conversation with his daughter, especially when she said, "I asked God to help me with this difficult issue Dad."

"And what did God have to say about it?" Jared's words were sarcastic because he had no tolerance for some pious answer he was expecting to hear.

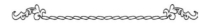

"Well, Dad, God and I talked about this a long time. He whispered to me that if the circumstances were different and I got pregnant and willing to take on the heavy burden of raising such a child, He would make it up to me."

"How stupid!" Jared hurled with anger at his daughter.

The woman of great loss interrupted the remembering. "What do think about Marcia's point of view now?"

"I just don't know," Jared snapped. "I can't understand how she could possibly be willing to allow a child of rape or incest to be born. It's crazy."

"When you look at it from a human's viewpoint, where we can't make sense of things, it can seem crazy," Luke said.

"Well, I'm eager to hear what you experts have to say about the matter," Jared snorted. He was convinced that he was right and Marcia was nuts to think the way she did. He didn't want to admit that what upset him was the fact that he would be a grandfather to such a child. The thought was repugnant to him. Since he would come to understand his daughter's position in a while, neither Luke nor the woman of great loss spoke. They allowed Jared to bob in neutral until something Sonny told him stepped up the positive charge in his energy.

"Sonny said that each realm leader was especially chosen for me."

"That's right," Luke said causing Jared to wonder if the issue of rape and incest were the only reasons the woman of great loss was part of discussion. Curious, Jared got closer to the woman. As he did, he read her thoughts: *twenty-eight abortions*. He grimaced and asked, "Is this why you're called 'the woman of great loss' because of so many abortions?"

"No," the woman said. "Even though the loss of those babies was terrible, the one loss that I didn't count on was my own life and future. I died prematurely on the operating table aborting the twenty-eighth fetus. I thank God for my childhood aunt who read His Word to me and who taught me about our Lord Jesus. So when the Final Offer was given, I knew His voice, asked for His mercy, and followed Him. It was here in the realms of understanding that I saw how my careless attitude cost me the life that God intended for me to have."

"Are you crying?" Jared asked.

"Yes, because here I know what it means to grieve. I never knew how to do that down there. My thinking was faulty. I believed that it was my choice to abort a child. It did not occur to me that I was God's choice to carry one."

She took in a quiet breath and continued, "The last child I aborted, number twenty-eight, would have brought me great joy. She would have inspired me to see things from God's viewpoint. I would have lived a long, rich, and fulfilling life with this child, my daughter, and a loving husband."

"How do you know all this?" Jared asked.

"Once I got here, Luke arranged for a session with the Advance-View Generator, and I got to see what could have been. Also, in the Realm of Empathy, Echo Chamber, I was given the echo of my own words about each child I aborted. My words were selfish, childish, ugly, and hateful. It was painful hearing myself say these things about a life entrusted to me. But for the last child, my daughter, I did not hear my own words echoed back."

"Whose voice did you hear?"

"Hers."

"And what did you hear your daughter say?"

"I forgive you, Mother," she said, soft crying, punctuating each word.

Jared's energy slowed to a low groaning sound. He ached for her. He could feel her pain and wanted to cry too.

"It's okay if you do," Luke said. "Crying is a great release and a sweet show of compassion and caring. We encourage it here."

The woman of great loss told Jared how much she appreciated his thoughtfulness. She sighed and resumed her story. "While in the Echo Chamber, I saw in Simulvision the potential of each child I aborted. I was grief-stricken to know what I had denied these twenty-eight blessed souls. When my daughter said that she forgave me and called me "Mother," the depth of my sorrow was so great that even here it was difficult to comfort me. The Master himself came to ease my pain. He held me in His arms, rocked me gently, and whispered that He would stay close as long as I needed Him to."

Jared could feel what she described: her pain and the comfort of the Master's arms. It was unexpected but effective because he was in her skin, knowing what she knows. "This must be empathy," Jared whispered to himself.

"You are correct," Luke said. His reply caused a tingling sensation in Jared as hundreds of holes were mended.

"Wow," Jared whispered. "Empathy is powerful."

"It is indeed," Luke replied.

Turning to the woman, Jared asked, "Do you mind telling me why you aborted so many babies?"

"Not at all," she said. "It was because of the way I lived and what I learned to trust." Momentarily she blocked Jared's awareness of her mission with an image of summer flowers growing alongside a red clay southern country road. She knew that while he was in college, three different young women claimed to be pregnant by him—in each case, he arranged and paid for "the procedure." He had set aside the memories of these abortions. Jared did not know that the woman of great loss through her story was about to help him recall these women and that she was especially chosen to help him understand this type of killing from God's perspective. She hummed in mellow, soft tones as she began her story.

"Mama was only fourteen when I was born and she never did know who my father was. To make a living, she pretended to be a seamstress, but she had a backroom where she entertained gentlemen. Often her customers would show up drunk and get mean, wanting someone to slap around or beat up. Most times, I was the one they chose for their twisted pleasures, but now and then, they chose my mom too. Mother would laugh and encourage their abuse of me, calling me a worthless bastard child and telling them that they could feel free to kick me around if they wanted to. Sometimes, Aunt Rose would show up just in time to stop the beatings.

"Who's Aunt Rose?" Jared asked.

"The aunt I mentioned earlier, the one who told me about Jesus—she's my mother's older sister."

"Aunt Rose took me to church, she taught me how to pray, and she read the Bible to me every day, until I was twelve. She died suddenly of a massive stroke. Only her doctor knew that she had sugar trouble and high blood pressure. She had not taken the medicine prescribed because rather than pay for these drugs, she used the money to buy us food, pay the rent, and household bills. I found the wadded-up prescriptions in one of her purses after the funeral.

"I blamed God for taking her from me. She was the only person in my life who loved me, cared about me, and protected me. I hated God. I hated His church and all the well-wishers who came to Aunt Rose's funeral. This is when I began to follow in Mama's footsteps. At thirteen, I got pregnant and the baby was taken from me immediately after giving birth. When I later found out that it was a little girl, I was numb with anger and this fueled my disregard for life. "Lee, a man from Aunt Rose's, church came regularly to our house. He wasn't there for favors. He came to see me. He told me that Jesus loved me and that if I wanted to be free of this life of selling my body, he would help me. In time we grew fond of one another, but during this friendship, I got pregnant by one of my clients. When I told Lee about the baby and the fact that I had no idea who fathered the child, he didn't flinch. He offered to marry me and raise the child as his own. He promised to take care of us, cherish us. I called him a liar. When I told him that I was getting rid of the child, he cried. He looked at me and told me that I didn't have to prove anything to him and for me to trust that he and God the Father would take care of us. I ignored him. I stormed out of the house, headed to the clinic, and kept my appointment. After the procedure, I bled so heavily that I went into shock and died. It was then that I had a wondrous experience."

"The final offer?" Jared asked.

"Yes, it came in a way that is difficult to describe."

"All at once?" Jared asked, his excitement growing.

"Yes. At the same time, in front of me were all of the expensive treasures, possessions laid out like a banquet, but from behind, I sensed a presence of love and peace that I felt with Aunt Rose. But this love was more lasting—permanent—it embraced me. I felt secure."

"Nothing can snatch you out of His hands," Jared whispered.

"Then I heard His voice," the woman continued. "He said, 'If you will, come to me and I will give you rest.' My heart desired to be with Him only. None of the material things mattered. It was as natural as breathing to decline the offerings before me, turn toward His voice, and be ushered by angels to the Waiting Room."

"I arrived so hole-filled that it seemed impossible that God could love me," the woman said. "But He did. I was oriented right away because Lee prayed for me. And now, I am here in this realm, eager to help others understand the value of life and to be with them when they go through the experience of the Echo Chamber and the Realm of Empathy."

"So can it? Can a fetus feel pain?" Jared asked.

"Yes, it can," Luke said. "Scientists experimented to demonstrate at what point in development an unborn child could feel pain. The parts of the fetal brain that control movement are not formed until around twenty weeks, so researchers stuck pins in fetuses much younger than twenty weeks and noted an elevated level of a hormone that is associated with pain. They knew that even though this creation could not move her arms or legs, she was experiencing pain.

"At conception, life is present, which is the ability to generate energy, grow, react to stimulation, and reproduce. Also at conception, the soul comes into existence for this life. On the twenty-third day, the first heartbeat is detectible. From there on, this life increasingly gains awareness. She can dream and respond to sounds, food, drink, medicine, stress, or trauma. She even has a level of knowing what her mother is thinking and feeling," Luke said.

"And because they are connected in this remarkable way," the woman added, "they are also connected to others who influence their mothers. You know, John the Baptist while in his mother's womb 'leaped' when Mary who was pregnant with Jesus came into the room."

Jared was jolted forward by the force of his own energy slowing down. He remembered at that moment what he had done. He could see the faces of the Bloomington, Indiana, "town-cutter" women and experienced a wave of nausea. He felt sick.

"Nausea is a side effect of realization," Luke told him.

Teetering and unstable, Jared wondered, *What had become of these women?*

"Only one was lost," the woman said.

"You mean she's in Hell?" Jared gasped, knowing exactly what she meant by "lost."

"It will not be easy to face the other two women or the sweet children they would have given life to, but our Lord Jesus will see to it that you are comforted in your sorrow, if you ask Him to. You can also ask for me to be present," the woman said. "It's what I do now."

The rich primary colors around Jared faded. His energy was barely audible. Realizing how little value he had placed on these women, he began to weep. Had he truly felt superior to them? He remembered having no respect for them, calling them low-life cutter women—a nickname given to noncollege girls whose fathers worked in the limestone quarries in Bloomington. Had he been so calloused, that he considered the babies disposable, worthless, inferior?

Luke wanted to comfort him, but he knew that Jared needed to finish experiencing sorrow.

"What becomes of aborted souls?" Jared asked, still weeping.

"Aborted souls, spontaneous or forced, go directly to the Master who guides them to perfection so that their souls can rise and shine. If their parents come here, they will meet their aborted children in the Realm of Empathy," Luke said.

Jared was weak with grief. These memories had long been buried. Quietly he asked Luke to carry on the discussion, hoping to restore his energy. Luke knew just how to get Jared back in tune.

"Only God creates a life," Luke said. "Although He uses a scientific process called biology to make it so for a man and a woman, each life is a creation in His image."

I always wondered about that," Jared said, his sorrow waning but still present. "How are we made in God's image? He doesn't have a physical body..." Jared paused remembering that God became flesh. "I stand corrected."

Luke smiled. He had witnessed that error in many souls trying to understand God. "God made us in His image, not so much in the physical sense, but as beings with the capacity for a conscience, the ability to think and to reason, to know, to show mercy, to forgive, and to love."

Luke added, "Our God is the beginning and the end: the Alpha and Omega. He created everything and everything carries His imprint. Down there, it is called deoxyribonucleic acid or DNA. Notice the first three letters? Used as a noun, 'deo' means God."

Jared once read that "deo" meant to bind. With his thought, the expanse brightened with the double-helix form of DNA. As the sequences rotated, Jared smiled. Verb or noun, only God could produce something this splendid.

Luke paused, allowing time to enjoy the remarkable display. Then he continued. "The discovery of DNA and later the mapping of the human genome caused a sensation and revolutionized medicine," Luke said. "Human beings found out that they were all related to one another, regardless of color or ethnicity. As men learned more about technology, some began to understand God better. They realized from these discoveries that they had proof of just how magnificent and creative God is. Some scientists went the other direction and decided this knowledge proved that God did not exist and declared that we all were created by aliens."

"Aliens. How absurd," Jared remarked. "Did they stop to wonder who created the aliens?"

"That's good, Jared," Luke chuckled and then added: "The Bible does have a few accounts that sound like spaceships and aliens to some people. The Old Testament book of Ezekiel is enough to make us wonder. Luke paused again, allowing a shift back to the topic of DNA. "God used DNA—His raw material—for all His creations, which means that as humans, we are all relatives. As for the rocks, the air, the water, and tonight's dinner, when we harm these things, we harm ourselves. We can actually alter our DNA."

"Are you saying that God is in the rocks, air, water, and tonight's dinner?"

"No, but he created all of these things, and so they too carry His imprint."

Jared thought about Luke's comment. He remembered a time when he and Priscilla believed that God was present in stone, metal, wood, and other inanimate objects. Now he understood that God is the life force that leads to the creation of such things.

"Okay, I have a question," Jared said. "Did God use a 'big bang' or evolution to create us?"

Jared heard a long sigh.

"I don't mean to sound disinterested," Luke replied. "Your question is a good one and among the FAQ for this realm. What concerns us is that God's beloveds can get distracted with the science-debate and end up fighting, arguing, and stirring up hostilities. The opposition loves it when we do this. The bottom line is that God likes science. He created it. And through His scientific processes, He created us, by whatever means He chose to use. If you are still curious, you can ask Him when you see Him face-to-face."

A tingling surged through Jared's energy; this was not the same as the sensation he felt when a hole was repaired. This one was like an alarm going off. He was looking forward to seeing God face-to-face but thankful for the opportunity to better understand things before that event took place.

"So is there life on other planets?" Jared asked, changing the subject.

"I suggest that you check with Galileo when you meet him," Luke said.

"I get to meet Galileo!" Jared declared. His childlike outburst amused his two discussion leaders.

"What realm do you plan to go to next?" Luke asked.

Jared hummed evenly and then said, "I'm not sure. Which one would you recommend, Luke?"

"I believe that you would enjoy the realm of understanding, end-of-life issues. A sweet lady leads the discussion—you will gain much wisdom from her."

"I appreciate the suggestion. Thank you, Luke, and thank you too," Jared said offering a welcome nod to the woman of great loss. "May I ask your name?"

"Bessie," she said and smiled. "Thank you for asking."

CHAPTER 46

Mercy Killing

J ared peered down a pine-scented corridor at a glowing amber bulb that indicated his destination. His energy sputtered when he discovered that as he advanced down the hall, it narrowed to a pinpoint. He knew that if he dawdled, claustrophobia would catch up with him.

When he reached the light instead of finding a door, he faced a pale-yellow plaster wall. Because of things discussed with Sonny, Ronnie, Martha, Luke, and Bessie, he revved his energy and was filled with confidence. So being, he floated forward and poured through the solid wall like an expert in physics.

"Nice," he said.

Inside Jared stumbled into a spaghetti-like mass of wires that tripped and bound him. Because he had just walked through a solid wall, he expected to feel freedom. He wanted to call out *"e ah qui,"* a signal he and his childhood friend Percy used to find one another when they were out in the woods. But before these words formed, a vibrant female energy emerged from the midst of the tangled bundle.

"Ah, relief," Jared thought as all wires, connections, and tubes dissolved into a lime green pool beneath him. While the entanglements disappeared down a nearby drain, Jared rocked and wobbled to achieve balance concerned that he might get sucked along and depart with the green goop.

"What would you like to know about mercy killing, Jared?" a sweet feminine voice asked completely ignoring Jared's instability. He didn't mind; he liked her directness. He found it refreshing. He wished he could be like that instead of sarcastic.

Jared regained his balance and said, "I thought we were going to discuss end-of-life issues."

"Indeed, we are. Mercy killing most certainly ends a life and the topic is a robustly debated subject on Earth and one that I want to lead with," the sweet lady said, and reading Jared's thoughts, she helped him frame his next question.

"Yes, Jared, mercy killing is the same as murder. It is a violation of the commandment 'Thou shalt not kill.' But many people do not think of it as murder," she added, "especially when having to watch a loved one suffer. These people do not think that they are taking a life as much as freeing a life."

"What's wrong with that?" Jared asked.

"Doing so is overriding God's timing for that being," she said. "Regardless of how right it may seem, it is a violation of God's sixth commandment."

Jared fidgeted. He didn't want to violate God's law, but he wanted an exception that made it okay to hasten death. Now her directness made him feel uncomfortable.

"What about capital punishment?" he blurted out.

"Violation," she answered.

"Crazy person?"

"Violation."

"Mutilated person?"

"Violation."

"Pedophile!" Jared shouted, feeling certain this person ought to be put to death.

"Violation," she said.

Regardless of how he spun it, this lady unraveled it. Feeling outmatched, he made one more attempt to deliver an exception.

"Well what about a person who's a vegetable?" Jared asked.

"You mean a person who is in a vegetative state?"

"Oh, yes," Jared said realizing he had used the wrong term. "I meant brain dead, totally unconscious, what about them?"

"It is still a violation," the lady answered in a softer tone. "There is no way to detect consciousness," she said. "Even when machines indicate that a person has died, their consciousness can still be present and the person can wake."

Her comment was unsettling. A fear of being buried alive haunted Jared as a young boy. He had seen thriller movies where this had happened and learned from Civil War books about being "saved by the bell" or "dead ringers." Even though these tales were considered urban myths, hearing about them made a lasting impression on Jared who as an adult struggled with claustrophobia.

"Today's medicine has lessened such a fear," the sweet lady said quieting Jared's anxious moment. "Doctors can look at images of brain scans and decipher intricate details about life. An image of a normal brain, for example, is colorful. Whereas the image of a dead brain is completely black. The ones in between, such as someone with a neuro-degenerative disease or who is in a vegetative state will show some color, not as much variety and not in the entire brain, but there will be color—and where there's color, there's energy, and where there's energy, there's life."

"But what possible good is that life?" Jared asked. "The person has no hope of being who they were."

"It depends on perspective," the lady said. "When viewed through the eyes of a bystander, this life can seem useless. From God's perspective, it's just the opposite. This life can be more meaningful in its disabled state than a life that is fully able to run, jump, shout, and lift. An individual with physical limitations can enrich the lives of those who care for them or those who want them to die."

Jared thought of people who were physically limited and Walter, his step-grandfather, came to mind. "Enriched" was not a word he would use to describe the impact Walter had on his life. Disgust and distain better described how he felt about this drunkard who lashed out with cruel accusations and leather belt whippings when Jared was a child. Jared could almost feel the pain of being whipped and the sting of bloody stripes. This reminded him of a time when Mom died. His recollection shined onto the plaster wall next to him; the sweet lady watched the experience take shape.

Walter sold the family home in Indianapolis and moved to South Carolina to an assisted living complex near Jared and Priscilla. Communication with Walter during this time was limited to holidays, and once in a while, 15-minute dutiful visits. Then Walter had a stroke and was moved to the Hope and Happiness Rehab Center.

After several weeks of rehabilitation Walter regained his ability to speak and walk, but he was not eligible to move back into the assisted living home, and his insurance for remaining in the rehab center was about to run out. As his only known relative, Jared resented being the one chosen to look after Walter.

Priscilla convinced Jared that Walter ought to live with them, a consideration that choked Jared with resentment and generated frequent fantasies of how to hasten Walter's earthly departure. In their home, Walter was denied "the drink," so this time, he bellowed out an endless string of demands. Priscilla was tolerant, but Jared wanted to smother Walter with the feather pillow that he insisted on having fluffed and tucked behind his head. Stretched out in Jared's favorite recliner, Walter hogged the television remote and barked or grunted orders for Kleenex, Q-tips, more blankets, and coffee refills.

On one outing that stole four hours of Jared's Saturday free time on the golf course, he and Priscilla put Walter in a wheelchair and took him to Waffle House where he banged and cussed as he navigated the wheel chair up to a booth and ordered two eggs: one over easy and the other one scrambled.

Jared was humiliated when the teenaged waitress asked Walter if he enjoyed his breakfast. Spitting tiny bits of egg white into her face, he hissed that she had scrambled the wrong egg.

Jared wanted Walter out of his life and thought that might happen when a second stroke provided a one-way ticket back to the Hope and Happiness. But irony had control and Jared was roped into helping feed Walter, buy his personal inventory of body lotion, special toilet paper, and difficult to find lemon candies. But worst of all, the center required him to do Walter's laundry, which Jared could never fold well enough to suit. Walter demanded a military way of folding clothes and Jared could not get the hang of it.

At the rehab center, surrounded by people whose personal freedom was defined by wheelchairs and the toilet-assist apparatus, Jared's fleeting desires for Walter to die remained, but seeing the simple tasks of having to ask for help to use the toilet was a sobering reminder for Jared of how fortunate he was to be able to care for himself. Walter had one more stroke and two weeks later lapsed into a coma. But before he did, Jared asked himself, "What possible use could God have for this slack-jawed, drooling man? I can sympathize with those who want to put someone out of their misery," Jared said out loud to the lady who lingered in silence while he recalled his experience with Walter.

"I know what it feels like to be emotionally and physically exhausted taking care of a dying person."

"Caregivers can feel hopeless and drained of energy, time, and money," the lady said. "They can fervently pray for peace, pleading for the end to come. Or they may want to hasten disposal of this inconvenient life."

Jared changed his tone and asked, "How do you know what to do? How do you know when it is time to let someone go—to pull the plug?"

"You don't. You have to lead with your heart. But doctors can help. On those who can have a brain scan, doctors can look at the images and report if the brain image is dark gray and black. If it is, the brain is dead and a breathing tube can be removed."

Priscilla had done exactly what the lady described. Earlier, Jared had been shown the moment of his decision to depart from his earthly body. With his breathing tube removed, whatever happened next was up to him. "And God," he whispered, humbled by the fact that God had given him control over the decision to stay or go.

The lady did not comment on Jared's realization of being in control of himself. Her responsibility was to share her wisdom of mercy killing. She floated nearby, waiting for Jared to conclude his moment of knowing.

"I don't mean to sound disrespectful," Jared said. "But why are you in charge of this realm?"

"Experience," the lady replied.

"So what happened to you?" Jared asked.

"My brain was deprived of oxygen," she said.

"How?"

"I was severely iron-deficient and didn't consider it to be a serious matter," she said.

"Iron-deficient? That's an easy fix. Take an iron pill. Eat liver," Jared said.

"Many doctors would agree with you, Jared, but iron deficiency can be more complicated than that. If it becomes too severe, a heart will fail. Mine did."

"Really? If your heart failed, how did that give you an experience with mercy killing?" Jared asked.

"My heart failed, but I did not die."

"How is that possible?" Jared asked.

"The heart can stop beating for a while and can be revived if someone does chest compressions or paddle shocks. My husband found me shortly after I collapsed. He did not know first aid, but he summoned an ambulance. The emergency crew did cardiopulmonary resuscitation—CPR. They got my heart started but my brain had been deprived of oxygen too long. Although neurological damage was extensive, I was still alive."

"You knew this because of brain pictures?" Jared asked.

"Yes. My brain pictures showed that I was in a vegetative state. This was simply terrible for my family. They argued fiercely about pulling my feeding tube especially when I persisted to live for nearly two decades in that condition. Eventually my husband made the decision to remove the tube. So I spent the next two weeks dehydrating and starving."

"Did it hurt?"

"At first it did, but then it felt like I was floating," the lady said.

"My last hours were most pleasant. My family was with me loving and caring for me and I was surrounded by kind women. One caressed my head with her hands and whispered words of comfort in my ear. She calmed me, dabbing my forehead with a cool cloth. Because of the tender words spoken around me by her, my parents, and friends, I died knowing where I would spend eternity."

"Are you angry at the ones who wanted you to die?"

The lady sighed, "End-of-life issues are complex, Jared. Even the issue of DNR—do not resuscitate—can be perplexing. In most circumstances, one isn't prepared to know what to do. Seeing a loved one collapse onto the floor instinctively prompts a person to call for help. That's what my husband did, and after that, the medical attendants took over. My husband believed there was hope that I would recover and be the woman that he fell in love with and married. That did not happen. For years, he suffered wanting a normal life. My persistence to stay alive kept him from that."

"Why didn't he get a divorce?" Jared asked.

"It's complicated, Jared, but in a while you will understand why he could not do that."

"In a while, in a while, everything in a while," Jared mumbled.

The lady felt compassion for Jared and she also knew that he was on the proper course, so she returned to the topic for which she was in charge of helping Jared understand.

"In the case of a loved one suffering with chronic pain, a caregiver might feel perfectly justified with assisted suicide. A hospice patient in a coma, lingering for days beyond expectations, might be given a patch to hasten dehydration. But the choice to do so depends on the heart making the decision. God knows the heart of that individual and knows who this person serves."

"So there is an exception," Jared declared.

"It is never okay to rush matters—but those who have chosen to do so will have the opportunity to understand when they get Here."

"In the Realm of Empathy?"

"No. In the Realm of Judgment," she said. "When we overrule God's timing for ending of a life by choosing life support for a loved one, then we cannot decide to remove this support because of inconvenience. The same applies to a person in a coma or on a feeding tube. If the decision to give that individual life support is made, then the time of dying is up to the patient and God."

Jared thought about his beloved Priscilla and how she had his breathing tube removed.

The lady helped him understand the difference. "When the physician explained about the brain images, yours were completely black. She still gave you the choice to stay or go. Unplugging the breathing tube did not end your life. It gave you the opportunity to make that choice on your own."

Jared appreciated this difference, but he made one more attempt to come up with an exception. "Well, what about pets?" Jared asked. "I thought it was merciful to put a pet out of its misery and suffering—why not the same for a person?"

"Animals are different. Although created by God, they are not in His image as are humans. God gave man dominion over animals and, as such, man can decide the appropriateness of retiring an animal from service."

Her answer made him think of a conversation he and his wife had with a thirty-year-old man with epilepsy. The lady waited as the memory came to light: The young man had the type of disorder where he was aware during the seizures and having one was terrifying—seeing, hearing, and knowing his heart could freeze and arrest in the course of the bone-shattering shaking of the seizure horrified him. For decades, he had been able to control the seizures with medicine but the availability of the drug became sporadic. The young man told Jared that if he could not get his medicine and had to endure seizures, he would just put a bullet through his brain. Jared and Priscilla agonized over what to do to change the young man's mind.

They prayed to God to help him.

"He didn't do it," the lady said.

Remembering that thoughts were shared, Jared asked what changed the boy's mind.

"Actually, he had a change of heart," she said. "God heard your prayers and sent one of His saints to direct the young man to resources that quelled his fear. He met a woman who was deteriorating with multiple sclerosis and wanted to kill herself. She begged the young man to help her with assisted suicide. His own words served to extinguish the fear he had about the unknown for himself. He told the woman that she had value regardless of the condition of her body and that through living she was laying her life down for a friend.

"He told her that most people think that laying one's life down for someone is to sacrifice it and die. But sometimes the sacrifice is not to die, in spite of great suffering. He pointed out to her that by living, she was laying down her life for Christ. Afterward, the young man prayed a prayer he had learned from a woman named Joni who was a quadriplegic. The prayer was, 'Dear God, if I cannot die, then show me how to live.'"

"Thank you for telling me that he didn't take his life," Jared said. "I suppose he blessed others by not killing himself."

The lady hid her knowledge of the outcome for this young man and the impact he would have on Jared. She knew that he would understand everything once he was able to see God's splendid threads and how He weaves His beloveds together with them. She turned to Jared and said, "When resisting man's mercy and trusting God's, this individual has exhibited the ultimate love and respect for our Heavenly Father. When they die, Christ reaches out for this soul and draws it to His heart where it is healed, perfected, and ushered directly to God's kingdom."

"You mean, they skip over all the realms of understanding?" Jared asked.

"Yes, they do," she said. "Before we part, may I share one of my favorite stories with you?"

"Sure," Jared said. Soft humming rose around him. He wondered if it was being generated by her or him. He decided it was coming from her since she had one more story to share. He liked the humming now; it made him feel connected to his surroundings.

"A woman named Virginia was in the hospital dying of cancer. Hourly, she called out to Jesus to give her strength to endure her dreadful pain. Her doctor, a gifted surgeon, was annoyed but intrigued about how this woman could exhibit calm acceptance of extreme suffering and agony. Declaring that he was an atheist, the young doctor stood by his patient, entertaining fleeting thoughts of putting her out of her misery. But he resisted as he administered the proper dose of morphine and watched her facial features change from twisted to peaceful. Following a pain-relieving dose, she opened her eyes, looked up at him, and asked if she could talk with him about something. Not knowing why, the young doctor agreed to hear what she had to say.

"Virginia assured him that her greatest accomplishment for God was about to take place. She told him that God had put the two of them together for a reason. Her purpose was fulfilled as she shared the gospel and touched the heart of this physician who dropped to his knees by her bedside and surrendered his life to Christ.

Jared was then given a glimpse of this gifted surgeon's path. Stressing the value of faith in the field of medicine, he reached the hearts of thousands of medical students assuring them that belief in God and prayer for their patients would make them better caregivers.

Jared smiled knowing that there was a difference between easing someone's suffering with medicine and putting them out of misery with it. He realized that as long as we're alive, we can be useful and change things.

"God's timing is perfect," he thought.

Simultaneous with his thought, the lady departed and joined a sparkling profusion of lights. The room went with her. This now seemed perfectly logical to Jared.

Because the lady left before he made his decision on the next realm, he returned to the bench and Doors of Wisdom to check his itinerary. An amber light on the map next to the bench blinked: "You are Here." Just above the map, he saw his schedule. Things had changed. Some names and realms were no longer on the list and some new ones had been added. One in particular seemed interesting. It was about the supernatural.

CHAPTER 47

Angels, Spirit, Saints, Ghosts, and Demons

Jared was excited to hear about things unknown. As a boy, he enjoyed ghost stories and playing with a Ouija board. He glanced back down at the map; the blinking amber light indicated, "Now you are Here." He smiled and as he rose from the bench to explore, a collection of tender voices rose with him. Their singing was high-pitched and exquisite like the hum of a fine crystal goblet when a damp finger is run around its rim.

"These must be angels," Jared thought.

"They're saints," a nearby being corrected him. "It's a common mistake."

"What is?" Jared asked.

"To call people angels, rather than saints."

"Hi Jared. I'm Chris and this is my good friend Channon."

Before Jared could respond, Channon spoke up.

"Welcome Jared, it's nice to meet you. Chris and I have been chosen to usher you through a discussion about the supernatural."

As she spoke, the singing changed to humming and a meadow filled with bright-colored wildflowers formed around them. Jared thought he saw a baseball diamond in the center of the meadow, but he wasn't sure.

"Thank you," Jared said. "This is a beautiful place you have here and those voices are so pure."

"Yes, they are," Channon replied. "Every soul who enters this realm says so."

"It's the innocence," Chris added.

"That's it," Jared remarked. "The voices are like brand new."

"That's because they are brand new. Their voice was not completely heard on Earth," Channon explained.

"Why not?" Jared asked.

"Their voice was silenced prematurely because of abrupt or cruel departure," she replied, and before Jared could ask for more detail, she added. "This chorale is comprised of the souls of defenseless children killed as a result of some act of violence by a 'faulty-wired,' misdirected, uncaring, or mean person. Abrupt departure occurs in the slaughter beds of the ungodly, from abortion, mass murder, abuse, torture, starvation, war, neglect, or by accident."

"You sound knowledgeable," Jared said.

"I have a great deal of personal experience," Channon replied. "Also, I specialize in sociology and have a deep love of children. I asked for this realm because I particularly wanted to work with these innocents," she concluded.

"And you, Chris?" Jared asked.

"Channon invited me to help. I'm good at baseball and teamwork."

"In the Doors of Wisdom," Channon interjected, "if you wish to know more about us and these saints, you can read our stories and multiple accounts of senseless loss of life and spirit due to the atrocities against children in Armenia, Iraq, Iran, Bosnia, China, Africa, Russia, Mexico, South America, Thailand, Cuba, Australia, and any other country you can think of including the United States."

Jared was not surprised that the United States was on the list. Without asking or understanding exactly how, he recognized voices of the children from Sandy Hook and Nickel Mines.

Channon anticipated Jared's next question and said to him, "When these children die, they are lifted up into Christ's arms instantaneously.

"These children have no memory of the fear associated with their departure," she said and added, "All they feel is love as they giggle and cuddle in the arms of Jesus."

"Are they given the Final Offer?" Jared asked.

"No need," Chris said.

"What if their parents are not believers?"

"That's not relevant," Chris replied.

"These are innocents," Channon began. "By no fault of their own, their earth journey was abnormal and simultaneous with their final breath, Christ reaches out for them. They know His voice and follow it. Whenever an innocent comes home, Christ holds and kisses them and takes them to Joy's Playground, which is the name of our lovely wildflower meadow."

Across the meadow, Jared saw little children twirling ribbons, climbing on to rocks, splashing in the water of a shallow creek, rolling, and jumping among blue, yellow, red, white, and purple wildflowers. Three of the children seemed familiar to Jared as he watched them bounce, flip, turn cartwheels, fall on the ground and laugh.

"Perfect," he said to himself and turned back to his discussion leaders.

"Earlier, you said 'common mistake.' What do you mean by that?"

"Calling people angels," Chris replied.

"Many people on Earth call each other angels, but the proper title for human beings is 'saint.' Humans are not capable of being an angel," Channon replied.

"Why not?"

"Angels don't have souls," Chris said.

"Why not?"

"They're spirit beings," Chris replied, and Channon added, "Angels are celestial—completely spirit. Humans are terrestrial and possess a body, heart, soul, and mind. Angels are instruments of God, His messengers. He commands them and speaks through them. Angels are instructed by God what to do. Human beings have free will and can choose what to do."

"What about Lucifer and the angels who followed him?" Jared asked. "I don't mean to sound smug, but this sounds like free will to me."

"God created humans to be heirs of His kingdom. It is their choice to inherit or not," Channon replied. "Heirs are powerful, but they vibrate at a lower frequency than angels. God created angels to minister to his heirs and to not leave their posts, but when they are disobedient and abandon their assignment, God will cast them out. As for Lucifer, he ignored God and lost his high arch angel position as a consequence."

"Heirs can tell Lucifer to scram," Chris interjected.

Angels that were fooled by Lucifer to follow him found themselves in a permanent prison—we call it the Abyss," Channon added.

In the Waiting Room, from the bench, Jared remembered seeing a great divide with an endless bottom. He wondered if this dark pit was the Abyss. Channon started to answer but before she could do so, Jared asked another question about angels.

"How 'bout wings?"

"Most angels don't have wings," Chris said.

"Examples of those that do are the cherubim and seraphim," Channon added and blended energies with Chris to call out in unison a list of angel characteristics.

"Angels can have temporary physical bodies when God so chooses. When He does, angels usually appear to be male around the age of thirty. They minister, wage war, usually have no wings, and some carry swords. Angels usher the righteous and the wicked, comfort people, and serve as guardians, and they can appear as lightning or brilliant light. They can abandon their position of authority by following evil, but that journey takes them directly into prison to await judgment and sentencing."

"Can animals be angels?" Jared asked.

"Oh sure," Chris said releasing his energy from Channon's.

"Are there angels here?"

"Of course," Channon replied.

"God's angels are everywhere," Chris added.

"If angels are spirit, is the Holy Spirit an angel?" Jared asked.

"What do you think?" Chris asked.

"*Hummmm*," Jared replied and thought. Other realm leaders had invited his opinion and he felt he had done a good job giving it, but this question was more difficult. He had not given much time to the characteristics of the Holy Spirit.

"Go ahead," Chris said. "Give it a try."

"Practice will build your confidence," Channon said preparing to pitch questions at Jared.

"Besides, God will correct your stance if it's out of plumb," Chris added and put on his catcher's mitt. He knew Channon was a good pitcher and she would make Jared stretch.

"Out of plumb," Jared whispered. This was a figure of speech Pop used to describe a person's point of view when it didn't line up with godly principles. Hearing the familiar phrase bolstered Jared's willingness to step up and try to deliver his understanding of the Holy Spirit.

"I believe," Jared began, "that the Holy Spirit is not an angel but a power that we connect with."

"Do you think we are born with the Holy Spirit?" Channon asked.

"No, I think we have to invite the Holy Spirit into our heart."

"And when do you think that happens, Jared?" she asked.

"At the moment of wonder?" Jared said, his voice rising as if he asked a question rather than made a statement.

"Wonder about what?"

"If God exists," Jared said.

"And how do think that moment comes about?"

Jared felt like he was in a fast-paced ballgame that didn't allow much time for thought. He recalled times Priscilla and C.W. invited him to Bible study—where he surely would have gained knowledge. Now, he was on his own, trying to explain things from bits of pieces of memories made with Pop or Grandma Robinette. He lacked skill because he had not practiced. With a sigh, he took a deep breath and said, "We are all born with a sacred room in our being, a place for the Holy Spirit to reside—but now we must ask for the Holy Spirit to live there."

"Regardless of a person's age?" Channon fired back.

"Well, that's a good question," Jared said buying some time to think. "A newborn or infant child doesn't need the Holy Spirit."

"Really? Why not?"

Jared sighed again. He realized that trying to see things from God's perspective was not straightforward. One question leads to another and the answers cannot be stated in a few simple sentences. But he wanted to try.

"Well, I think that God sends these children a helper in the form of an angel."

"Why?"

"Because they are too young to understand how to call upon the Holy Spirit."

"Really?"

"I believe that children are pure up to a certain age and then they can lose their connection with God, depending on who they are."

"For example?"

"If a child is self-centered they will demand, not ask for help."

"Then what?"

Jared stopped talking. Channon's questions were coming like fast balls over home plate. His energy felt pinched; he knew he was in a jam. He got quiet and prayed for wisdom. In an instant he was relaxed, warmed up, confident, and ready for Channon's next pitch.

"I believe that all human beings are born with spirit capacity," Jared began. "We call it the heart. And it is up to believers in Christ to make certain that anyone within reach knows of this capacity, especially children. The heart is like a receptor, where the Holy Spirit is the key. If this heart is filthy with hate, bitterness, revenge, lust, greed, or pride, the receptor is not able to receive. But when the heart is pure and spirit capacity kept steadfast through prayer, the Holy Spirit comes, connects, and resides as our helper so long as the heart does not become cluttered with worldly desires that quench the Spirit."

"Home run!" Chris shouted.

"Yes, indeed," Channon echoed and told Jared that soon he would be sharing his opinion with his Creator. Her comment reassured him that he had done a good job describing a relationship with the Holy Spirit and the idea of discussing it with God, now, was uplifting, not intimidating. *I know that He will expand my knowledge of His Holy Spirit and tell me things that are far beyond my ability to understand*, Jared thought.

Everyone enjoyed the sound of another hole being repaired. But knowing that Jared's time with them was limited, Channon asked, "Which supernatural topic would you like to discuss next?"

"What about demons or ghosts?" Jared asked.

"Both are spirit energy," Chris said, and Channon added, "Sensitive people can see this energy, usually with their peripheral vision—you know—what can be seen out of the corner of the eye. But earthly beings can also have a face-to-face encounter with either one of these energies—which can be dangerous. It is important to know the difference and to interact prayerfully not capriciously," Channon warned.

"The ghost of a human being is not the same as the Holy Ghost or an angel which are divine spirits," she continued. "Demons are the souls of Satan's offspring. They reside with the father of lies in hell and can be sent by their father to terrify, mesmerize, enchant, or entice people. When a person is capable of seeing these beings, they have the ability to align themselves with their frequencies. This is unhealthy but often irresistible since demons sometimes play winsome games with people."

"Well, if they can appear fun-loving, how can you tell that they are bad spirits?" Jared wondered.

"Just ask," Chris said.

"Ask what?"

"Spirit, do you come in the name of Christ?" Channon said. "An evil spirit will flee. A godly spirit will let you know its purpose. If a person does not ask for this clarification, they can become captivated by this supernatural experience, lose discernment, get stuck in a state of distraction, and end up with a permanent, harmful, and destructive resident."

Jared shuddered. "They become possessed?" He asked.

"Yes," Chris answered.

"And if the person does not get help from the Holy Spirit, they are doomed," Channon added and continued. "A ghost is a benign manifestation of the spirit energy of a godly man or woman. It is present to refresh and to help a person who is grieving and in need of reassurance that they are not forgotten. A sensitive person can manifest a likeness of the loved one, which appears like a holographic image—or ghost. Occasionally a fragrance can be detected—but the experience is being manifested by the earthly being."

"So it's not real?" Jared asked.

"Ghosts are real. Human energy is eternal and loved ones can feel this energy or see it as they might see a photograph or a movie."

"But it's just an image, right? Not the actual soul," Jared said a bit disappointed and then asked, "What about the meaning of 'crossing over' and 'earth bound?'"

"Hollywood drama," Chris said and Channon added, "Movies, books, and television programs are intended to attract followers who will become consumers of some product or money-making scheme being offered with the visual or auditory stimulation. So the idea being pitched is one of being able to talk with a person who has left this world and is in another—and this can be a powerful lure for someone sliding into depression caused by grief."

"But is there any way a person can talk with people who have died?" Jared asked.

"Not like they claim in these Hollywood or television exhibitions," Channon said.

"Souls that choose to inherit their heavenly home do not desire to leave Heaven and go back to Earth. Here they are divinely occupied and have deep respect for free will. They have no desire to interfere with worldly matters as the producers of such television dramas suggest. The idea that a person can 'see' or carry on long conversations with the spirit of a being who has chosen Heaven is nonsense."

Before Jared could comment, Channon added, "But there is a rare and sacred time when a loved one who resides in Heaven can be seen. It is a tiny sliver of reality just outside of the dream state when a person is waking but not fully awake. During this split-second moment, which seems like several minutes or hours to the dreamer, they see their loved one hovering above them or standing nearby. During this sacred time, a guardian angel is present.

"If words are heard, they come in the form of thought," Channon continued. "As the waking person blinks and becomes fully awake, they may say something out loud. As they recollect, they realize that the moment was real, and they are reassured of a life after an earthly one and that their loved one is with God. They are left with the sensation we call a heavenly hug.

They wake smiling, not frightened or longing for more encounters. They do not want to detain their loved one from heavenly service."

Jared felt better; the existence of a heavenly hug and sacred dream time made him hum with gladness. He could not imagine that God would permanently sever the connection between loved ones, and he decided that these encounters were rare and not ones that we could demand to take place but ones that would happen as a result of God's will.

A pleasant tingling spread through Jared's energy. He knew that multiple holes were being mended.

Chris and Channon waited for Jared to process the tingling sensation and to ask his next question about the supernatural: "What about people who claim to have lived past lives?"

"God doesn't recycle souls," Chris said.

"This may get a bit technical," Channon began. "Remember when I told you that seeing a ghost of a loved one is like seeing a holographic image?" Jared bobbed and nodded indicating that he remembered.

"And remember when I said that they are real?" Jared bobbed again.

"Should I call for Einstein?" Chris asked and Channon assured him that she could handle the matter. Chris moved out of her way so that Jared could get tuned in to Channon's frequency.

"Every person is born with a unique energy and fragrance. This energy vibrates at a speed specific to their soul. Every word, every action ever created by a person while on Earth remains in the universe permanently. We call this an imprint and every imprint has a frequency.

"Like dialing into a radio station," Chris interjected.

"That's a good example, Chris, thank you," Channon offered. "People who think they have lived past lives are sensitive and can merge their frequencies with these imprints. When they do, they are connected to that energy and can relive any moment in time as though they lived it themselves."

"That sounds dangerous," Jared said.

"It can be," Chris replied.

"It depends," Channon interjected. "If this happens unintentionally, the soul is protected and tethered to its temple. The experience will result in wisdom about the supernatural. But if the person craves more of these experiences and deliberately strives to leave the body, he or she can align with the imprint of some other soul. When they do this, they can become fascinated with the alignment, mistakenly believe the experience or words to be their own, which causes the frequency of their unique energy to change. This change is attractive to wandering or evil spirits, and a prolonged or repetitive out-of-body trip allows demons the opportunity to take up residence."

"Whoa, that's creepy," Jared said.

"You mentioned wandering spirits. What are those?" he asked.

"These are the souls of people who were never told about Christ. When they die, they wander about until they are claimed by evil or someone prays for them to turn to God."

"Do they haunt houses?"

"Only evil spirits haunt. The wandering ones are lost and need help."

Jared got excited. He remembered a conversation with Priscilla about haunted houses and evil spirits. "So an evil spirit might know about God, but reject Him, where a wandering spirit needs a prayful nudge to turn to the light."

"Well, that's another home run," Chris declared. "I'd say you're well on your way, unless you have more questions about the supernatural."

"Actually, I do," Jared said, remembering a neighbor who wanted to hypnotize him and Priscilla so that they could travel outside their body to discover who they were in past lives. Now that he understood the dangers of such a trip, he was relieved that he and Priscilla declined the neighbor's offer.

There was a time, however, that they allowed this neighbor to help. It was the worst time in their married lives. Loss had come like a rockslide, pushing their relationship to the breaking point; their drug-addicted son Philip had been missing for three years and then their daughter Marcia died out of their reach 3,000 miles away in Oregon. The grief was palpable in their home, and out of desperation to find Philip, Priscilla turned to the witch doctor for answers. She just wanted to know if Philip was dead or alive.

CHAPTER 48

Lost and Found

"The witch asked for an article of Philip's clothing," Jared told Chris and Channon. "Was this part of her performance?"

"Articles worn by or touched by someone will carry their energy," Channon said.

"And it is strong energy," Chris added.

"In the Acts, people used articles belonging to the Apostle Paul to heal others."

"So what did the witch doctor tell you?" Channon asked.

"We gave her a T-shirt belonging to Philip but I also gave her one of Marcia's hair ribbons—one she wore as a child."

Chris and Channon could feel Jared's energy slowing down. His favoritism for Marcia over Philip was being remembered, and this recollection could set him back.

"When a parent, a good friend, or a spouse dies, it is terribly sad," Channon said. "But when a child dies, it is torture. We can accept the natural order of dying, but this is not so when our child dies before we do—because this order is unnatural. Our grief is profound because we have been stripped of the future to see our child grow, marry, and have a family."

Channon's words made Jared feel like he was choking; tears sprang from his center and he blurted out, "But I wanted Philip to be dead. I didn't want to find him. He was not the sweet little boy we knew and loved. He was a junkie, a filthy blister-faced degenerate. I wanted Marcia back but not Philip."

Chris and Channon moved next to Jared. As he wept, they hummed and warmed his energy. "Do not fret, Jared. You are not alone," Channon said. "We do our best to raise our children and when they are snagged by evil and poisoned with drugs, they are not the same child. We are scared of them because they are strangers. Intellectually, we know them but emotionally we cannot connect."

Neither Channon nor Chris said anything more about children because they knew that soon Jared would come to understand the preferential feelings a parent can have for the easy to love child. To return him to the discussion, they blew a gentle, cool breeze over the meadow, creating pink-orange-colored mares' tail clouds, a favorite sight for Jared and Priscilla during their early evening trips from North to South Carolina.

"These are our favorite clouds," Jared said, his moment of sadness having passed.

"Yes, we know," Chris and Channon replied in unison.

"This time-space-energy experience takes some getting used to," Jared remarked. "I suppose that I'm somewhere between here and there, but I don't understand how that can be."

"Something Einstein told us about transition from Earth to Heaven was helpful for us when we were in your state of wonder," Channon said.

"We wanted to know about energy, frequency, and vibration and so we visited the realm where Einstein explained that vibration is the movement of energy and frequency is the speed of movement. He told us that matter can be broken down into smaller components of energy and that energy is permanent and can be in more than one place at a time."

"So matter has energy," Jared stated.

"Yes," Chris said.

"And the Soul has energy."

"Yes, it does, but it has a higher frequency," Channon said.

"And the Spirit has energy," Jared stated.

"Yes, it does, and it has the highest frequency of all," Channon replied.

"So when we no longer exist physically, I mean, when we die on Earth, we just change frequency," Jared declared.

"Correct," Chris and Channon said in unison.

"Then why do you think people are so afraid of dying?" Jared asked.

"Lack of practice," Chris said.

"Dying is usually a one-time experience," Channon said.

"And most think it will be painful," Chris offered.

"If one has never died, then he has only his personal imaginings or what he has learned from others as his only reference. Even when we know that our Creator is going to welcome us, we can still have fear of leaving the physical world," Channon remarked.

"I guess it would be a like a child making his first jump off the 20-foot diving board," Jared said. "He knows his loving father is in the water below him, waiting to catch him when he jumps, but he still has fear about doing something he has never done before."

"Another home run," Chris declared and Jared beamed in response.

"If people only knew the truth," Jared thought. Everything he had been told as a child made him afraid of God or afraid of dying. Being with Chris and Channon helped him to understand that before we can experience the splendor of Heaven, we have to shed our low-frequency heavy-body shells and allow the soul's high-frequency energy to rise. And if we choose Heaven as our eternal home, there is no such thing as loss.

Jared rose up and laughed as he flapped his arms, sending the mares' tail clouds out in different directions. Voices of the chorale heightened as the clouds dispersed and Jared returned to thoughts of the supernatural. Now, he wanted to know about guardian angels.

He wasn't sure if he believed that people had a guardian angel, but when he asked Priscilla about it, she had been emphatic that everyone has one and some people have more than one. Priscilla shared with Jared several examples of close calls where the only explanation had to include an angel.

Three stories in particular stood out: Kate Michaels, Baby Angela, and Marilyn.

Channon wasn't sure how much time she and Chris had with Jared. The three upcoming supernatural accounts needed to be played out for him; this meant extra innings, but Chris assured Channon that God would let them know when their time in the field was up.

CHAPTER 49

Our Guardians

"**M**arilyn and her supernatural experience didn't sound believable at the time she told the story," Jared began. "I felt like she was dreaming, but Priscilla assured me that what happened to this woman was not a dream. Marilyn said that she and her fiancé Daniel had gone for a canoe ride on a private lake. The area was secluded, surrounded by thick woods and hills filled with flat rock and timber-frame mansions. It was late autumn and most of the homes in the area were winterized since their owners only lived there in the summer months.

"Because of the time of year, it was cold enough for heavy jackets, which both Marilyn and Daniel were wearing. As they paddled across the water to the center of the lake, abruptly a 6-inch diameter column of water erupted from the floorboard of the canoe. There was nothing in the boat to plug the hole and it filled with water, toppling over too soon for words. Marilyn and her fiancé slipped into the lake and the heavy weight of their wet clothes dragged them to the bottom. She told us that the next thing she could remember was being lifted by something whirling, spiraling upward. As she looked up, she saw two good friends perched in a tree on the edge of the lake. She blacked out but woke to find herself safe on the shore. Priscilla remembered Marilyn saying that an eerie peaceful quietness surrounded her until she realized that her fiancé had drowned; gripped by disbelief, she looked back at the lake that gave no sign of having taken a life.

"When she told us this story," Jared said, "she couldn't figure out why she saw two friends perched in the tree and how she made it to shore. It tore her up that she was an excellent swimmer but was unable to save Daniel. Can you tell me what happened?" Jared asked. "How did she get to the shore? Did she swim and not remember it?"

"No, that would have been impossible in the water-soaked heavy clothes she was wearing," Channon said. "She nearly drowned as well, but before she lost consciousness, she called out to God to help her. He sent an army of angels who came up underneath her in the water and generated the hurricane force whirling strength required to lift her. Two angels perceived by Marilyn to be trusted friends sitting in a tree were there because God did not want to frighten her with the magnificence of the power required to lift her out of water and carry her to safety."

"Wow," Jared exclaimed. "I'd call that a miracle."

Channon smiled. It was a miracle, one of many supernatural displays witnessed by people in Jared's life but Channon did not list them for him—it wasn't necessary to the moment.

"Will she ever get to understand what happened?" Jared asked.

"She will," Chris replied.

"But first, she realizes that although she could not save her fiancée's life, she gave him what he needed to save his soul," Channon added. "Daniel accepted the Final Offer because Marilyn had just finished telling him about her relationship with Christ. She thought that he seemed disinterested in hearing the details of the gospel, but what she didn't know was that with her words she ignited the tiny spark of wonder in him."

"The tiny spark of wonder," Jared repeated recalling his discussion with C.W. and Ronnie about atheists.

"That's all God needs," Chris said.

"And will she get to see Daniel again?" Jared asked.

"Of course. She'll be here one day, but for now, Daniel will visit in her dreams," Channon said.

"Tonight, he will let her know how grateful he is that she knew to ask for help and fully understands that if he had asked God to help him out of the water, he would not have drowned— the same powerful force that lifted her would have lifted him. Together, they would have been devoted to God, to each other, and to their children, grandchildren, and greatgrands," Channon concluded.

"And hearing this won't make her feel sad?"

"Not at all. Her beloved is with God and she knows she will live a good life and see him again one day, not in a romantic encounter but in a spiritual brotherly loving exchange."

"I guess this is a good example of why some people are spared and others are not," Jared remarked thinking that if Daniel had prayed he would be alive.

"It doesn't always work like that," Chris said and Channon added.

"Sometimes when a person calls out to God for help, it may first appear that God is nonresponsive. You see this often in children's wards where a child is gravely ill and the parents are pleading for the child's life to be spared. Their prayers are answered, but they do not understand the outcome, especially when the child dies."

CHAPTER 50

Baby Angela

Above the meadow, a pink, orange, and powder blue blanket of fog formed and flickered with details about a family Jared knew when he was in high school. The parents were kind people, often serving as chaperones at sock hops and proms. They had three children, daughters ages twelve and two and a sixteen-year-old son, a popular kicker on the high school football team. Jared did not know the family well, but he admired the boy's ability because in spite of his small size, he could kick the ball nearly the full length of the field and drive it directly between the two goal posts.

"I knew there was a tragedy in this boy's family," Jared said. "News of his baby sister's death spread fast among classmates. I never knew all the details, but the child's name was Angela. She was about two years old and a late-in-life baby." Channon asked Jared if he wanted to know the story.

"I would," Jared replied.

"The football kicker's mom and dad became foster parents to a teenaged boy after hearing a sermon about how good Christians should be looking after widows and orphans.

"The boy, who was fifteen at the time, was in and out of juvenile detention centers for vandalizing businesses, stealing cars, and setting fire to churches. Multiple foster parents reported that he had too many behavioral issues and needed to be in a professional-run facility."

"His name was Carl, but the police called him the Delinquent," Chris interjected.

"Following the emotionally charged sermon," Channon said, "the parents were compelled to take in this boy, because no one wanted him. They felt blessed with three healthy children, a good home, and a prosperous business, a convenience store, within walking distance and where the dad worked six days a week. They decided God wanted them to share their blessings with this poor, unfortunate teen."

"The mom was nearly deaf and had poor eyesight," Chris said; then he and Channon teamed up with one voice to deliver the next part of the story.

"She wore thick glasses so she could see and powerful hearing aids in both ears, which made loud squealing noises when she tried to adjust them. There were two phones in the house, one was upstairs in a bedroom and the other on a side table next to the living room couch. The phone near the couch was special. It had an adapter that helped the mom hear better. But upon lifting the receiver, it emitted the same high-pitched sounds as her hearing aids. The sounds were shrill and hurt the ears of people who could hear normally."

"Carl was in great trouble with some hoodlums, but the family didn't know it. Also unknown to the family was the danger that Carl brought to their home. Carl's mother was a junky and a prostitute. She gave birth to him in a rundown trailer with no doors. She was too high on heroine to even realize that she had given birth—one of her customers had the sense to cut the cord and put Carl in a box. For weeks, no one held him or cuddled him—the only contact he got was when someone poured Pepsi down his throat or when he cried. Most times he was left alone in his cardboard box hungry, thirsty, and dehydrated, with only rats, spiders, and roaches as companions. A neighbor lady heard his crying early one morning and called authorities."

"Social services eventually found him but it was too late. Carl was empty and did not respond to people who attempted to show him love. During his years growing up, he dealt with his detachment by killing small animals, usually setting them on fire. As a teen, his coping mechanism was to destroy things. He liked to break windows of old commercial properties or churches, and if he had time to do so, he would toss a match or homemade bomb into the buildings. On several occasions, he chose a dilapidated structure owned by a man who had a reputation for being a thug. Carl had thrown concrete blocks through the windows of this man's building and set fire to debris outside. He did not know that the man had hired a security guard who was given a description of Carl and told to be on the lookout for him."

"In a short time, word on the street reached Carl, warning him that the security guard identified him and the business owner's sons were enraged and out for revenge. Carl knew that his life was in danger, so he stole a gun to protect himself. He kept it loaded and tucked in the back waistband of his jeans."

Channon and Chris continued to narrate as images of the scenes they described floated onto the pale clouds above the baseball diamond.

"Late one afternoon while the dad was still at work, the mom went down to the cellar to get potatoes for dinner. Their two-year-old child, Angela, was taking a nap on the couch. Carl needed to call a buddy to see if he could hide at his house until things cooled down. He didn't want to use the phone upstairs because he was in a hurry to make the call before the mom came up from the cellar. He picked up the receiver of the phone next to the couch where Angela was sleeping."

"Concerned that the loud squeal of the special phone would wake the little girl, he tried to cover her ears, which ironically woke her, where the squealing phone noise would not have— she had grown accustom to these noises. Angela now awake and sleepy from a nap rolled off the couch and waddled toward Carl with her arms up in the air, a gesture of wanting to be picked up."

"As he reached down for the child, the gun dislodged from his waistband. It hit the floor and discharged a bullet which entered the two-year-old's brain from the base of her skull.

There was no 911 system in place at this time and Carl wasn't sure if the child was alive. She had slumped to the floor and was not moving.

"About that time, the mom came upstairs. Seeing her baby on the floor, she thought the child had fallen. She had not heard the gun shot because she had removed her hearing aids before going to the cellar.

"Rushing to her little girl, the mom dropped to her knees and raised Angela up revealing a tiny pool of blood on floor. The mom assumed that Angela had been injured in a fall and was now unconscious. She screamed for Carl to call her husband. 'Tell him I am on my way with the baby!' she shouted."

"Scooping her lifeless child into her arms, she ran spastically toward the door, gasping for breath, screaming for God to open it. Holding Angela to her breast, the mom hooked one foot on the bottom of the front storm door which was not fully closed. It swung wide allowing the mom to press against the screen door—which was also unlatched. With awkward child-like advances, she hobbled off the front porch steps to the side-walk below.

"Their store was only two blocks away, but the mom felt like she was running through water trying to reach her husband. Her tears were so abundant that she was only able to recognize him by his shape. He stood next to the car, and when she reached him, his face exploded with shock as she stumbled into his arms. Instinctively, he grabbed the handle of car door and helped his precious cargo into the front seat. He spun around to get into the car and as he did, he glanced at his wife and his limp baby daughter. His legs buckled and ached with fear as he climbed into the car. When he asked what happened, his wife could tell him only that their daughter had fallen, because that was all she knew."

"With one anxious, violent twist of a key, the 1954 Chevy started and lurched forward in response to a floored gas pedal and the rapid release of a clutch. Trembling with fear, the dad's hands shook as he yanked the gearshift and prayed to God to keep them safe. Squealing tires announced their entry onto a one-way four-lane street, thankfully, void of traffic. Racing wildly toward the hospital, the dad felt that the car was being steered by someone other than himself. It careened through the streets, headlights flashing, horn blaring as it barreled toward the emergency room at Community Hospital miraculously missing other vehicles."

"The ER was familiar to the dad. He had been there more than once with his son for football injuries," Chris said.

"The commotion of the screeching tires and blaring horn activated the ER medical staff who ran to the car door, efficiently lifted the little girl out of the mother's arms, and directed her husband to an area where they could wait," Channon added.

Chris and Channon's delivery of the story was speeding up and as their words reverberated off the clouds, Jared lost his balance—he bounced like a ground ball smacking first into a wall of honeysuckle and then ricocheting back onto the baseball field. A blast of dust puffed out of his energy as he slid across the pitcher's mound. He wasn't sure he had the strength to finish this exchange.

Channon helped him stay in the game by assuring him that this event had great significance. She nudged him to think about reports on the news and details whispered in high school hallways. Feeling torn between wanting to know and not wanting to know details of this child's death, with reluctance, Jared asked Channon what happened next.

For impact, the images rolled onto the clouds in slow motion while Channon resumed narrating.

"In the hospital waiting room, overwrought by the unknown, the parents paced, crying, holding one another trembling and nauseated with fear. A quiet well-dressed man walked over and put his arms around the mother whose shoulders shook in rhythm with her sobs. She buried her face in his chest. 'Is it alright if I sit with you?' the man asked. Her 'yes, please' was faint, a weak voice smothered beneath painful tears. He guided her to a couch, where they sat in unison, and he held her while she cried. He gestured for the dad to join them. Stumbling, blinded by grief and worry, the dad dropped to his knees next to his wife and prayed out loud for God to take care of their child."

"After a while, a surgeon who attended to Angela, came to them and asked about how the little girl had fallen. Their details were sketchy because they did not witness the incident. They were unaware that their precious little girl had been shot. The surgeon had to give them the grim news," Channon said.

"When the surgeon's words penetrated their reality, the dad sprang to his feet. A look of horror replaced the initial look of shock on his face. The mom collapsed, falling off the couch onto the floor. The well-dressed man knelt by the mother until she regained consciousness. The dad paced back and forth piecing together what likely had happened."

"Where was Carl?" Jared asked.

"Trying to get away," Chris said, "but a police officer had been called to the hospital by an ER nurse who knew the dad, the family, and was suspicious of Carl. Within hours, the officer found Carl and put him in jail."

Jared knew that Angela died, but he did not know the details.

"God chose to bring her home," Channon told him.

"Wait a minute," Jared interrupted. "If God gives us free will, how did He choose to bring Angela home?"

"Good question, Jared," Chris said and Channon explained.

"When the dad prayed, he did not ask for his daughter to live. He asked God to take care of his child. Whatever the outcome, the dad would understand and be grateful."

"How can anyone be grateful for their child to die?" Jared asked, his voice stern and annoyed.

"Angela's brain was damaged so severely by the bullet that she would not have been able to function. Of course, her mom and dad did not fully understand this. They would have loved their child and tried to care for her, but the burden would have eventually destroyed the family financially, emotionally, and spiritually and this was not God's desire for them," Channon said.

"But He used their sorrow to change a community," she added.

"Hundreds of friends, neighbors, and members of their church shared in their grief—the local television news channel covered the story and the director of an adoption and foster care organization saw it and reached out to the family. Angela's life story brought awareness to the issue of mentally or emotionally ill foster children. Although offering to be a foster parent is a noble act, sometimes a child is best left with people specially trained to manage them," Channon said.

"These nice people thought that love could turn Carl around," Chris added. "They even said, 'If we love him enough, he will change.'"

"But they could not have known that Carl's wiring was faulty because he had not received the early infancy caring human touch to create a bond of trust. Unless these children get professional counseling, by the time they reach the age of three, sometimes four, they can no longer be helped—emotionally—they are destined to be sociopaths," Channon said.

"So what became of him, the Delinquent, Carl, I mean?"

"He died in prison," Chris said.

"You said, 'died.' May I ask..."

"Yes, he's here. His voice is one you are hearing in the chorale," Chris said.

"He's a teen. He's not innocent. How could this boy be the type of person that he was and end up here?" Jared protested.

"What spared him was God's grace and a social worker who understood the developmental problems caused by the abrupt departure of a mother's touch. The social worker knew that this act of neglect made Carl who he was, an empty shell void of a healthy voice or the ability to love or be loved. He prayed for him to recognize the voice of Christ when the Final Offer came."

"Wait a minute," Jared interrupted. "You said people on Earth aren't permitted to know about the final offer. So how could he ask for that?"

"This social worker was an angel sent to minister to this boy," Channon said.

"An angel, for him?" Jared bellowed—but his disapproval did not last long. He saw himself standing next to Carl as the social worker angel prayed with the boy. Jared felt the emptiness of this soul and understood. Now, he could hear this boy's sweet voice singing alongside baby Angela. Now, he was glad for the outcome.

"Were there others? I mean, did God send angels to the family?" Jared asked.

"Yes, He did. When the mom and dad raced to the ER, one angel paused the traffic lights on New York Street, which cleared the way to the hospital and kept them safe," Chris said.

"Traffic was stalled long enough for the family to make it to the ER and the delay also held back the regularly scheduled pediatric surgeon who was on his way to work."

"The well-dressed man and the stand-in pediatric surgeon were angels. The man ministered to the mom and dad. The surgeon took the place of the regularly scheduled doctor detained by the stalled traffic light," she concluded.

"On New York Street?" Jared asked.

"Yes," Chris answered and Channon added. "He did arrive in time to assist, but God's stand-in was scrubbed and ready to take the lead. This angel ministered to the emergency room medical staff weary from seeing so much violence and death. He also ministered to precious baby Angela as she died on the operating table. God lifted her up and delivered her directly into the arms of Christ, who brought her to me so that she could sing with us."

Jared blinked and sighed. "When you see this from God's point of view, the outcome is bearable, even preferred. I suppose if these parents could have made the choice, they would have chosen exactly what God did."

"God infuses us with the tenacity for life. We don't choose to die prematurely, even when our faith is intact and we trust who God is and we know that Heaven is our destiny—we still cling to life not because we fear dying but because we cherish the life God gave us and we want all the time we can get to show our love for Him through our love and care for others, especially our children," Channon said.

"What became of the parents?" Jared asked.

"These people of faith, in spite of their great sorrow, helped change policy for fostering children with severe emotional problems," Channon replied.

Jared thought about how God makes beauty out of messes: how He wastes nothing and how He provides comfort in times of sorrow and protection in times of great risk. He remembered how Priscilla coped with Philip's death by believing that he was spared the horrible life as an addict toothless, frail, twitching, blistered, and dull-eyed.

Another recollection rose on the clouds still hovering overhead; Jared instinctively looked up. Priscilla and the story she told him about Kate Michaels took shape on the soft surface above him. Channon and Chris knew the story but remained still so that Jared could have time alone with this memory. It was a good one.

CHAPTER 51

Kate Michaels

After he and Priscilla were married, she agonized through two miscarriages before conceiving twins. Priscilla was considered a high-risk pregnancy given her age of thirty-nine. Twins doubled the risk. Her doctor decided to birth the babies by Cesarean section—something went wrong and right before midnight of December 7, 1985, Priscilla died in recovery but she came back.

"About 4:00 a.m., Priscilla woke to a nurse who carried the babies to her bedside so that she could see them before taking them to the nursery. Priscilla was groggy and needed to sleep, but she noticed the name badge of the nurse. Kate Michaels was written in long hand because it was a temporary badge. After some sleep, Priscilla got out of her hospital bed and walked to the nursery to see the babies. Kate was standing next to the bassinettes that contained our little boy and girl. Both were premature. Philip who was born first weighed only four pounds. Marcia weighed one ounce more. 'We nearly lost you last night,' nurse Kate told my wife. 'I don't usually work maternity, but I was called in at the last moment.'"

"When she got back to her room, Priscilla wrote this name Kate Michaels on a piece of paper and during her week-long stay, she added the names of other staff that took care of her during her stay. After being discharged, and wanting to show her gratitude, Priscilla purchased ivy plants in miniature clay pots for each of the staff in the maternity ward. On the outside of each pot, she wrote the name of those who had cared for her and the twins.

"I helped carry the tiny plants to the hospital," Jared said. "We handed them over to one of the attendants who placed the pots on the counter of the nurses' station in the maternity ward.

"A few days later, the birth certificates arrived in the mail. Priscilla's mom was visiting and she noticed that the times of birth were wrong. I stayed with the babies while Priscilla went back to the hospital to get the certificates corrected. While she was there she decided to visit the nurses on the maternity floor. As she stepped up to the information counter, she noticed a single pot of ivy with the name Kate Michaels had not been claimed. Priscilla asked the person seated at the desk why this nurse had not picked up her ivy and was told that no one by that name works on that floor. Remembering that Kate Michaels said she generally did not work maternity, she asked the desk attendant if she would call Personnel. The call was made and the report was the similar: no one by that name works in this hospital."

"Kate Michaels was a bona fide guardian angel, wasn't she?" Jared asked.

"Indeed," Channon said, holding back the fact Kate was a man who appeared as a woman, because angels can do that.

"As you journey out of this realm into others, you will meet several souls with similar supernatural experiences," she added.

"They're common here," Chris said stirring up a question.

"The marquee includes 'spooky people'; who are they?" Jared asked.

CHAPTER 52

Spooky People

"Ah, spooky people," Chris said. "These would be our prophets."

Jared remembered the Old Testament prophets his grandmother talked about. Three in particular stood out: Isaiah, whose name Jared could never spell without looking it up; Jeremiah, who some called a God-intoxicated fanatic; and Ezekiel, Jared's favorite because his story read like pages ripped out of a Stephen King novel. These three, Grandma told him, were the major prophets and important to study. Jared preferred to hear Grandma's version rather than read how Jeremiah spent twenty-three years warning God's people who ignored him and eventually put him in a pit and spit on him.

"Who would want the job of a prophet?" Jared mumbled.

"Not many," Chris said.

"Prophets were around in your time," Channon said. "But they were sometimes called watchers, and like their Old Testament counterparts, they were ridiculed or ignored. Others thought they were extreme and so they tuned them out."

Jared had a memory of one man in particular that he thought must have been a watcher. This man had been prominent in the media and got disgusted because he was not allowed to talk about God on his television program. He quit his job and started his own network. Jared and his wife were early subscribers, liked the programming, and prayed for this man and his staff. They enjoyed seeing God at work in the changes to programming that promoted love, kindness, truth, and being prepared.

"Watchers pay attention," Chris said.

"They are avid readers with keen skills of observation," Channon added. "They try to warn people of danger—but it's difficult to think about preparing for a storm when the sun is shining and the winds are calm."

"Watchers know what's comin' because they know history," Chris said.

"They gather information like small pieces of a puzzle. The problem is when they see what the puzzle reveals, they get hysterical."

"They get wild and scary, "Chris added.

"Like the prophets, watchers can have the gift of prophecy. God speaks to them, which can be unnerving, especially when they tell others about their conversations," Channon said. "Most of them completely lose their composure. They do strange things. They rant and rave, get emotional, even cry trying to warn people to turn to God, to stop sinning, and to get prepared. It's easy to see how they get labeled crazy, spooky people."

"Just like Jeremiah," Jared remarked.

"And journalists inspired by the opposition only report a watcher's hysterical behavior. They are careful to glean out and ignore any acts of altruism," Channon added.

"I guess their aim is to discredit any messenger of God," Jared said.

"You got it," Chris replied.

"Tough life," Jared added, thinking of people he knew who were brave enough to stand up for the truth. Jared then realized that he had not heard the children singing for a while and asked why.

"They've gone fishing with Jesus," Chris said. "He plans to play a game of softball with them later. You're welcome to join us. I can show you the way."

Channon made an authoritative throat-clearing sound, reminding Chris that Jared had a few more realms to work through before he could play ball.

"Sorry, Jared. I didn't mean to get you off base," Chris said. "Where are you headed next?"

Jared squinted at his itinerary which was waving in front of him.

"Family aerodynamics," he said.

"Oh, you'll enjoy that one!" Chris said, but Jared was skeptical.

PART FOUR

Waking

Psalm 1: 4 "...The ungodly...are like the chaff..."

CHAPTER 53

Family Aerodynamics

J ared moved back to the bench outside the Doors of Wisdom. He thought about Chris's remark and tried to remember times he enjoyed being with family—but each happy recollection was followed by one of loss.

A *click-clop, click-clop* sound echoed around Jared as a man materialized; he was medium-height, slender, dark-haired, and wearing a lime green T-shirt, ivy league cap, knee-high argyle socks, and knickers, and he was carrying a nine-iron.

"Golf shoes," the man said matter-of-factly. Twisting one foot upward, he revealed spikes, the source of the *click-clop* sound. "'Specially made for my feet and my golf course," he added.

"You have your own golf course?" Jared asked.

"*Umm, hummm.* Sure do."

"I didn't think souls could own anything in Heaven."

"Oh, absolutely they can, but they share it freely with everyone."

Jared was listening but he could not resist staring at the man's funny-looking pants.

"I see you are curious about these pants."

"Well, now that you mention it," Jared muttered, feeling slightly embarrassed for staring, "I am."

"These pants belonged to a great friend of mine, a Scottish champion golfer who died in a 1999 plane crash. But he's around here somewhere. Probably hanging out with a few other heavenly golfing buddies."

"Does everyone here like golf?" Jared asked.

"You don't have to like golf to enjoy this course. Although the courses on Earth were beautiful, there is *noooo* comparison to this one."

"Is it because things here are more colorful?" Jared asked.

"Color's part of it—but it's the adventure that drives souls to this fairway."

Jared's energy revved. He liked this being and wanted to hear more from him.

"On this golf course," the man began, "a person finds the skills for flying tandem or soul-O."

"Tandem? Solo?" Jared wondered trying to imagine how these words applied to golf.

"In tandem with Jesus or on your own soul. Either choice is up to you, but He likes the game and comes anytime you invite Him. When you do, you are guaranteed a perfect score."

"Why play?"

"For fun!" the man said, his tone changing. "And also to refine the skills of patience, tolerance, respect, dependence, independence, consistency, respect for boundaries, following rules, having mercy, allowing failure, success, and joy. A player on this course will get the opportunity to understand the difference between interfering and interceding as well as responding calmly to spilled milk or skinned knees."

"This sounds less like golfing and more like..."

"Raising a family?" the man said, interrupting Jared.

"Yes, I guess it does," Jared answered.

"*Yooooou* guessed *cor-rect-ly!*" the man said, sounding like a game show host.

Jared looked back at the itinerary outside the Doors of Wisdom, wondering if he had gotten into the wrong realm. He had not yet discovered that this man was well-read, capable of being serious, and authoritative but enjoyed a good laugh and could get silly at times. Disregarding Jared's doubt, the man asked, "Would you like to meet your golfing teammates?"

"Sure. Are these people I know?"

Before he got his answer, a questionable-looking parcel of people appeared in front of him. Jared's energy spurted in disbelief. Staring at him, as if awaiting orders, were a three-year-old boy sucking both thumbs, a teenaged girl who was about eight months pregnant, a glamorous and well-manicured shapely woman who also appeared as a dumpy, short, obese girl with stringy bleached hair, dark-gray eye shadow, purple-painted fingernails and lipstick to match.

Jared grimaced and asked, "Am I expected to play with this bunch?"

"No, there are a few more joining your team," the man said cheerfully.

Momentarily Jared's energy was uplifted until he saw the remaining teammates. Straggling toward him was a Civil War Union soldier missing his left leg and all of the fingers on his right hand; at his side was a frail-looking ninety-ish-year-old man hunched over from arthritis.

"You must be joking!" Jared said. While on Earth, he was an excellent amateur golfer, invited to play in celebrity tournaments. This pitiful group did not look remotely like the teammates he had played with on Earth courses.

The man chuckled and said, "No, we are not joking. This round of golf with these teammates will help you understand the dynamics of family relationships."

Jared winced. He wondered why the realm included the word "aero."

"I suppose I'll find out in a while," he muttered as his players sauntered haphazardly toward the first hole, which was not only warped but it swayed. And no one had clubs.

"One thing you might like to know," the man said, "this is not like any course you played on Earth. This course is fluid and can be changed by thoughts or emotions of any one of your teammates. Grumbling and sour attitudes have the most impact on the stability of the course."

"That explains the movement I'm seeing," Jared grumbled sourly to himself.

"The lakes and sandpits are unusual too. You're able to go under water or under sand to hit your ball out of these traps," the man explained.

"Under water? Under sand? How are we able to breathe?" Jared remarked.

"Here you can breathe under sand and water," the man said. "One more thing, your clubs have to be manifested, that is created by your own energy. You will be given an endless supply of golf balls, our special brand, Kingdom Come∞. They really soar!"

Jared felt insecure having never-before-manifested material objects; he wondered if one of his teammates had this ability.

"Of course you are permitted to request the use of your teammate's special gifts," the man offered in response to Jared's doubt-thoughts.

"Special gifts? From what I can see, special handicaps are more like it," Jared moaned, thinking of the times he played in the Pro-Am tournaments. "This is unreal," he muttered to himself.

"Actually, it's surreal," the man said.

"Real, unreal, surreal," Jared said to himself and wondered about the players' special gifts. Promptly, he got his answer.

"Each one of your players has a unique ability, which you will discover is needed to complete the course. If these gifts are called upon and shared, your team will gain understanding about relationships and interdependence," the man said.

"I know, it's a lot like raising a family," Jared grumbled with sarcasm. But his tone changed as the man began to fade. Jared thought his sour attitude might have been the cause and called out, "Wait! Don't go. I didn't mean to offend you."

Jared called out again, "Please, please, don't go! Don't leave me alone. I have many more questions about this course and these players," Jared confessed as he shot a quick and doubt-filled glance in the direction of his strange teammates. But the real reason for his pleading had more to do with how much he liked being with this man.

With one more attempt to persuade the man to remain, Jared blurted out, "The clubs, how do I manifest clubs? By thinking? What are the rules? How many holes does the course have? And besides, I never got your name. I want to know who you are! Don't leave me! I need your help!" Jared's energy was shooting out in all directions. He was clearly agitated causing the humming noise to get louder—he didn't want this man to leave him.

As if turning up a rheostat, the man reappeared and explained his momentary disappearance. "I wasn't leaving. I needed to recharge."

Before the man could explain the process of being recharged, Jared said, "Thank you for coming back. I didn't understand why you left."

Jared missed the irony of his remark, but the man did not. He knew that it was time to reveal who he was. "Let me assure you, Jared, I won't leave you—ever again. I am here because I asked for this assignment so that I could be with you."

There was sadness in the man's voice and Jared thought he heard sobbing.

"Do I know you?" Jared asked wanting to console the Man.

"No," the man whispered.

Jared was completely unprepared for what he heard next.

CHAPTER 54

Surprise of a Lifetime

"I'm your dad."

"My dad? My birth father?" Jared squealed. His energy sparked and flared as sarcasm replaced compassion for the man. Thick volumes of kudzu, thistles, and crabgrass overran the golf course; images of lonely, anger-filled, and prideful moments when Jared wanted his father's love splashed onto the clouds. One poignant memory stood out: It was the day after Pop was killed. Forlorn, scared, aching, and lonely eight-year-old Jared climbed into the dining room window seat where he and Pop often shared story time. He understood that like his mother, Pop was gone forever. He held onto a glimmer of hope that his dad, who he was told might be missing in action, was indeed alive and would come for him. He cried "Daddy, daddy. Oh daddy, where are you?" Sobbing, needing comfort, the eight-year-old Jared called out through the windowpane again, "Daddy, please come get me." He pressed his nose against the glass, which fogged with his warm breath as tears gushed and soaked his white cotton undershirt.

His dad shared Jared's memory and he offered, "I am so sorry, son. I was young, foolish, selfish, and then matters got complicated."

"How complicated can things get to abandon your child?" Jared snapped, his bitterness pronounced in spite of the fact that he was feeling good about seeing his dad. He had a lot of questions beginning with why his father left. It had not yet occurred to Jared that he had done something similar with his son Matthew.

"I'll be helping you with your questions, Jared, and since souls understand better through experience than through lectures, this course is where you will get your answers."

Disappointed, Jared asked, "You mean I'm going to play this course without you? We won't be having any more conversations?"

"Sure, we will," his dad said. "You can ask anything you wish. But the refinement, the deep understanding of things, will come from the experience of playing this course on your own. You will walk in my shoes, the shoes of your children, and other members of our family. This is the best way for you to grasp what it is to fail as a parent and understand what it means to honor. Raising a family is like this course. It is full of surprises and there is no instruction manual."

Jared liked the authoritative and humble side of his dad and wondered about his father's experience with the course.

"Working here," his dad interjected, "helped me understand the honor and privilege of being a father, grandfather, son, and husband. With your mother, I was demanding, self-serving, and childish. I only wanted a family when it was easy going and convenient. When your mother told me that she was pregnant with you, I didn't want you. I didn't want the responsibility of another child. At the time, World War II was coming to an end, and after seeing so much death and destruction during the war, the thought of bringing another child into the world terrified me."

His dad's confession stung and Jared wanted badly to say: "You didn't want me? But he held back and said instead: "Tell me more about those days, dad."

"Everything you want to know about that time in my life is in the Doors of Wisdom," his father said and Jared knew that his dad did not want to talk about the war—but Jared's need to know was stronger than his father's need for privacy. At that moment, the overgrowth on the course disappeared and was replaced with a small pond that reflected images. He saw his dad register for the draft. Another paper his dad signed was dated January 20, 1942, when he volunteered for airborne training. A patch floated into view. It read 101st Airborne Division. Jared saw medals for bravery, injury, and photographs of soldiers gathered outside a tent. Some were suntanned and bare-chested with dog tags hanging around their neck. One soldier had a leg propped up on a tree stump, his arms dangling over his knee, and a cigarette hanging from his lips that were spread out in a wide smile. Others also were connected with smiles and arms around each other's shoulders.

Then he saw his father running across an airfield toward a petite, auburn haired woman. He grabbed her, swept her into his arms, and twirled her around. He buried kisses in her neck and the two giggled like children. Clearly they loved one another. He knew the man was his father. Jared wished he could see the woman's face.

"Was this woman my mother?" He asked himself and his dad spoke up.

"Not long after I got home from the war, your mother got pregnant. When I declared that I did not want another child, I insisted that your mother to get rid of you," Jared's dad said, pausing the images on the pond.

"Get rid of me? You mean give me away?" Jared asked.

"No, Jared. I wanted your mother to have an abortion."

"Oh," Jared whispered. Shocked, he turned from his dad and began to weep.

"Don't cry son," his dad said and wrapped himself around Jared. His father's embrace was strong and loving. It felt familiar even though it was the first time ever Jared was held by his dad. He felt completely safe in his father's arms. Together they rocked back and forth until Jared's energy quieted.

"After I made that impossible demand on your mom, I believed that God directed the full measure of His wrath on me. I lost everything. Your mother's pregnancy was complicated by high blood pressure and she was restricted to bed rest. Your

brother Mark and I had to take care of the house and your
mother and look after your sister Catherine who was just per-
fecting her ability in horseback riding. With all these demands,
there was no time for play. Your brother and I resented these
responsibilities and blamed our loss on you—even though you
were not yet born. While we wallowed in self-pity, neglecting
our duties, we both opted to let a neighbor take your sister for
her riding lessons. Attempting a jump, the horse stumbled.
Catherine fell and broke her neck which left her paralyzed. We
had to put her in a facility and the incident tore us apart. Your
mother's tears of grief made us feel worthless. Later Catherine
had a stroke and was no longer able to speak or eat. She had to
be placed on a feeding tube."

Jared felt uneasy. He wondered why Grandma Robinette
never told him much about his dad or his brother Mark. She
had told him about his sister Catherine and how her guardian
wanted to remove her feeding tube. He was not aware before
now that his dad was "the guardian." Until this moment, Jared
did not know that his father had been alive all along.

"Walter, the drunkard, and Mom, who had custody of you,
threatened your Grandma Robinette with loss of visitation if she
ever told you that your brother or I were alive. Their reason had
to do with money. Mom and Walter got a nice-sized check each
month as long as they retained custody. Your grandma Robinette
never directly lied to you about me—she was disgusted with the
way I treated her daughter, your mother, and especially how I
mistreated you. Besides the threats made by Mom, I begged your
grandma to never tell you that I was alive because I did not want
you to search for me. I just didn't want the responsibility. After
years of being silent, your grandma was ashamed of what she did.
She feared that you would hate her for withholding this."

His dad's words shocked him and he felt the pang of
betrayal discovering what his favorite grandmother knew and
never shared.

"Sometimes the ones we love the most disappoint us the
most. I am sorry that I put your grandma in this position, but

she loved you and wanted to spare you the influence I might have on your life, if we had a relationship other than a memory. Whenever I telephoned her to remind her of her promise to me, she would call me drugstore cowboy and your brother Mark, Satan's sidekick."

"Was he a bad person?" Jared asked his dad.

CHAPTER 55

Birth of a Brother

"No, your brother Mark was not a bad man, but like all human beings, he did bad things—some of them on purpose, some unintentional."

"Your brother and I had fierce, explosive arguments about your sister Catherine and one day in a fit of rage Mark left. I had no idea where he went, but that night your mother went into labor and I had no help to get her to the hospital. Frantic, I called a nurse who lived nearby and she rushed to your mother's side but it was too late. You were on your way and your mother had lost so much blood. She died after giving birth to you. It was more than I could handle. I hated you. I hated God. I hated everyone. On that night, staring at the blood-soaked bed, your first cry and your mother's last breath echoing in my brain, I ran as fast as I could to the farthest place I could go—Aurora, Colorado—more than a thousand miles from South Carolina. The nurse carried you to the hospital and remained there with you while my parents tried to find me."

"There you were, alone in your bassinette..." Jared's dad paused, with a hoarse voice he finished his thought. "I thank God for the nurse who cradled you and took care of you. When I played this course for the first time I met her. She was one of my teammates. I was able to express my gratitude to her for making certain that someone held you in a loving motherly way in the critical first hours and weeks of being born."

"Was she a guardian angel?" Jared asked thinking about his previous conversation with Chris and Channon.

"No, she was a saint, a caring neighbor who was fond of your mother and who had a sense about what I might do in a crisis. She never judged or preached. She would show up just in time whenever there was a tough situation and your mother needed help. I know that Pop exhausted all means of finding me, calling people and even hiring a private detective. You were placed in foster care for a time, but eventually my parents were given custody of you. Your Grandma Robinette would have been a good parent, but the courts wanted a mother-father influence."

Jared felt claustrophobic.

"I'm terribly sorry about the pain, suffering, and misery you endured after Pop died. I know that Mom was stingy and you believed that she hated you. I know that Walter, the one you call the Drunk, was mean to you and beat you. You could not have known that Mom was mentally ill. Nor could you have known that Walter had grown up in a strict, rigid home with a father who was a fundamentalist, religious tyrant. Walter, as a child, also endured many undeserved beatings from his father who daily bellowed distorted verses of scripture as he whipped Walter with belts, shoes, boards, branches, whatever he could get his hands on. 'Spare the rod and spoil the child!' Walter's father used to yell out as he thrashed on his son. He totally missed the point of Proverbs 13:24, 'He that spareth his rod hateth his son: but he that loveth him chasteneth him betimes.' 'Sparing the rod,' means indulging a child who needs discipline. 'Betimes' means when it's called for, not out of anger or cruelty. And to chasen does not mean beating someone into submission. It means to discipline for refinement, training, through standards, which sometimes calls for a father to just sit down and talk with a son—patient as God is patient with us. 'As a man chasteneth his son, so Yahweh thy God chasteneth thee.'"

Jared's dad was quoting scripture unfamiliar to him, but he liked it and he wanted to hear more.

"God gave us standards, His commandments," his dad said. "Christ showed us how to carry out these standards. He gave us a means of measurement and showed us what is good: to do justly, and to love mercy, and walk humbly with thy God."

Jared knew this verse of scripture. It was from Micah, the Old Testament, and one that Pop used to recite to him. He thought about "the rod" and got excited.

"The rod! It's a unit of measurement in a mile," Jared declared. "The rod could be a means measurement of living up to Christ's standards, couldn't it?"

"Excellent, Jared," his dad said with pride. "If a father sets up Christ-based standards which a child can endeavor to live up to, that father has given his son a good roadmap for being a dad himself. The values instilled in a child at a young age, when properly planted and nourished, are the principles that serve the child throughout life."

"And so, when he is grown, these principles serve him with his own children," Jared said surprising himself.

"Indeed," his dad replied.

Jared liked sharing with his dad and gradually he began to see similar patterns. Where his dad had abandoned him because he didn't want the responsibility, he too had deserted a son, Matthew for much the same reason.

"I was just selfish," his dad said sharing Jared's thought about desertion.

"So was I," Jared confessed.

"After the horrors of war, I wanted to have fun, play touch football with my army buddies, go golfing with celebrities, and later, hang-gliding."

"No kidding. Hang-gliding?"

"I loved the sky and the freedom I felt drifting to the ground. Those thrills fed and fostered an obsession with the sport."

"Did you ever get hurt? Did you win any awards?" Jared asked.

"I did. I lived through six kite failures, broke my collarbone twice and forearm once, had eight concussions, bruised a kidney, and won more than twenty-eight awards," his dad said but his words were not prideful. Jared was impressed and asked his dad to tell him more about the awards.

"When I was in my 80s, I attempted to become a Guinness World Record holder as the oldest person in the world to solo at two miles above Earth."

"Guinness World Record," Jared repeated with a mixture of laughter, wonder, and pride.

"Well, records are meant to be broken," his dad said. "And much to my disappointment, a man one year older than me claimed the title. It infuriated me because to retain the Guinness title for this feat, a person has to fly regularly and document it. Your brother and I suspected that this old guy was faking his flights."

"Excuse me, I don't mean to interrupt but..." Jared said and his dad assured him that interruptions were permitted, even encouraged in the process of discovery and refinement. "What is it you want to know?" his dad asked.

"It's about my brother...what was he like? I know you said you argued right before he left, but other than that, how did you get along? Was he married? Did he have children? Did he know about me?"

CHAPTER 56

The Family Tree

Jared's dad puckered his lips, drew breath through the narrow space to make a sucking sound. Knowing that Jared soon would be able to ask his brother these questions directly, he chose his words with care.

"Mark knew about you," his dad said and camouflaged the detail that Jared's brother wanted nothing to do with him because he blamed him for the disability of their sister and the death of their mother.

"Your brother and I were always at odds. We called each other vile names, yelled filthy profanities, and threw ashtrays, books, or blocks of wood at one another. Your sister used to cry and hide in the pantry when we got into one of our battles. Your mother despised our fights and had to be persistent to calm us and restore peace. She said the reason Mark and I did not get along was because we were so much alike. I didn't agree. Mark was an avid bodybuilder, a football player, and an Olympic-quality water skier—able to ski barefoot. He believed in global warming, green energy, and thought the moon landing was faked, but he touched a nerve when he became an advocate of gay rights. I despised homosexuals and it never occurred to me that your brother was struggling with that issue. One of our biggest arguments was over gay marriage."

Jared started to say something but was stopped when the light over the course dimmed and the sound of two male voices rose. At first their tone was even but within moments their conversation was replaced with words that challenged and provoked.

"So you believe that a loving, thoughtful, and kind relationship is reserved only for the heterosexual marriage," one man yelled. But before a response could be made, a third voice was added. It was feminine, gentle, and persuasive.

"If we thought that," the gentle woman said, "we would be cruel indeed."

Her voice was soothing to Jared; he felt a connection but he wasn't sure why.

"Marriage is God's creation for the purpose of procreation," she said. "A same sex partner relationship can be loving, thoughtful, and kind, but it cannot produce naturally by becoming one flesh, an offspring, which is what God intended the purpose of marriage to be."

Jared knew that there was more to the argument than what he was hearing. He remembered a similar argument with a homosexual man who wanted the church to redefine marriage so that same sex couples could do so in the church. The homosexual man asked that if marriage is defined as a loving, thoughtful, and kind relationship, then how you do define "friendship?" Jared attempted to present his side of the argument by saying that only a man and a woman are able to produce an offspring.

The gay challenger sneered at Jared and asked, "So! What about an infertile couple?" To which Jared delivered a mocking return. "A snowplow is still a snowplow regardless if it's moving snow in Buffalo or sitting in a vacant lot in Florida."

Jared remembered liking that comment at the time, but now he felt ashamed of it. Priscilla and C.W. helped him understand that sin cannot be ranked by degrees. She believed that the "thorn" in Paul's side was about homosexuality. That his disgust for this type of sin was the affliction God would not remove. C.W. added that these thorns do not come from God; they are placed there by our own doing, a consequence of sin acknowledged and a constant reminder of who we truly are.

Jared's dad smiled at his son's thoughts, which reflected his own intolerance and how he ranked sin in the order of his preferences. "Everyone sins daily," his dad said. "They might not see it that way but the sin of homosexuality is no different from the sin of gossip, lustful longings for another's spouse, feeling superior to others, offending another with hateful speech, eating enough food to feed an entire family, binge-watching television while an elderly parent sits lonely in a nursing home, or ignoring a brother who waits in prison for a letter, a card, or a visit. If you picture each one of these sins as a block of wood, they all look the same size to God.

"Heated arguments muddle our view," his dad continued. "Thoughtful discussion can clarify. Sincere dialogue that lacks judgment and partiality has the greatest potential for understanding a perspective other than our own. Dialogue does not mean agreement or a willingness to promote, but rather a desire to reflect Christ in our conversations with one another," his dad added. "And when we can depart from such an exchange without feeling superior, we have gained wisdom in showing mercy and God's type of love."

Jared felt good; he was glad to be having this time with his father but he wanted to know more about his big brother and asked, "Did you and Mark ever reconcile?"

"Oh yes, once I tracked him down in Colorado, we were able to talk about yearnings and how these choices can be driven by genetics..."

"What a minute," Jared interrupted. "Are you telling me that the desire for a same sex partner is inherited?"

"It can be. I learned from Mark that if the pituitary is damaged during early years of growth, a person can have problems of association and sexual preference. It's complicated, but Mark helped me understand that not all homosexual men and women are glad to be so. If given a choice, they would rather be in a relationship where they could love and have children of their own flesh and blood."

Jared remembered the first time he ever saw two men kiss. They were walking on the sidewalk in front of his house. He and Walter were sitting on the front porch when it happened. The way the men embraced made Jared feel queasy. Walter picked up a brick, hurled it at the two, and yelled, "Get out of here you queers!"

The recollection was not one Jared expected to have in front of his dad and more so not one he wanted to have in Heaven. He hummed louder hoping to camouflage his thoughts.

"That's all right, Jared," his dad said. "God has seen and heard it all. There is nothing that can be hidden from Him. Every word, every action, and every thought are known to Him. He also knows who will resist temptation of sin and call on Him for the strength to be compassionate with those who cannot."

"Why do I feel more disgusted with homosexuals than I do with a murderer or an adulterer?" Jared asked his dad.

"Because we are offended when we see a man who acts like a woman or a woman who acts like a man. We feel superior to this creation because we think we are behaving normally and know that they are not. We can all see ourselves as a murderer, thief, or an adulterer given the circumstances but we abhor the idea that we might be flawed, which is how we see these individuals rather than God's beloveds," his dad said.

"Priscilla and I wanted to be tolerant of others, but when government began to legislate morality and laws were written by people concerned more with offending man than offending God, it was a struggle," Jared said.

"That's not uncommon," his dad replied. "When rights erode and are replaced with special class privilege even tolerant people can feel contempt. You can of course visit the Doors of Wisdom and view this outcome, and you'll be glad to know that in time something was done to resolve the conflict between believers in God and believers in the self. The senator got this issue addressed."

"The senator? The one from South Carolina?"

"Yes, the very one. He introduced the 'Render to Caesar' bill, which permitted civil action, such as same sex unions and allowed companies that wished to do so, to accept a same sex spouse on insurance policies and health plans. This bill also preserved and protected individuals, churches, and businesses from reprisal for unwillingness to promote choices that were against their belief."

"But wouldn't that encourage discrimination?" Jared asked.

"Not at all, when people were freed of the fear of reprisal, and no longer forced to give up their rights because of someone else's wants, society did what it does best. People were kinder, more thoughtful, and generous," his dad said.

"And this bill, doesn't it encourage sin?" Jared asked.

"It allowed for choice, Jared," his dad said. "Something God gives us every step of the way. Do you remember when Christ was asked about the Roman coin?"

"I do. He said render to Caesar what is Caesar's and to God what is God's."

"That's right, Jared. Although the bill provided men and women who sought that lifestyle to have it, the bill also protected the choice of those who believed differently," his dad said.

"When you explain it that way," Jared replied, "I don't get so riled up. I understand."

"Glad you do," his dad remarked. "Controversial topics can stir up deep, hidden feelings. I was grateful for the conversations your brother and I had once we made an effort to dialogue rather than debate. We could see circumstances from the other person's perspective and we looked forward to talking with one another about difficult issues."

Jared felt a pang of hurt because he had missed out having such talks with his dad.

"Aren't we doing that right now?" his dad asked, surprising Jared. They both laughed and agreed that the thought-sharing feature of Heaven was a good thing.

Returning to the story about his life and his record winning accomplishments in hang-gliding, his dad said, "I remarried a woman younger than me. She was filled with the Delilah spirit, which produces a yearning to 'wear the pants in the family.' Her mission in life was to reshape our Father's identity and promote it as Mother-Father God."

"Is that the same as Mother Nature?" Jared asked.

"No such person, not here anyway. Also, not in the Scripture. There are great women in the Bible, mothers, sisters, judges, prophets, government leaders, or teachers, but none of them share the position of Creator with God the one and only Father. Scripture is very clear on our Lord's identity." Jared's dad said.

"So this woman you married," Jared began, "why didn't things work out?"

Jared heard a deep sigh before his dad answered. "Betsy and I married for lust rather than love, and once the romance department collapsed, the battle for control was all we had left. Little things grew into gigantic annoyances."

"Like what, Dad?" Jared asked.

"Betsy was an early riser, I was not. Each morning when I needed time to wake up, she would interrupt my quiet, coffee time with her lists of imperatives for the day. Mostly, she wanted to be shuttled around looking for other people's trash that she could use to clutter up our home. One Saturday when Mark and I had a flight scheduled, she pitched a conniption fit demanding that I drive 125 miles one-way to look at a cast iron bathtub she wanted to use as a planter in our front yard. As her lists grew longer, my desire for her was strangled by resentment. There was no room among her demands for playing golf or kite flying. When Mark and I managed to schedule a flight, if she didn't stomp around like a spoiled two-year-old wanting her way, she faked some acute illness or whined tearlessly about being left alone. I think she was jealous of Mark, but the more she tried to control my life, the more I wanted to get away from her. Eventually, I left permanently. I divorced her. Out of spite, during the divorce, Betsy tried to get my hang-gliding equipment, threatening to sell it for a nickel, but Mark anticipated her plan and removed the distributor cap from her Jeep which allowed us time to relocate my belongings.

"Once the divorce was final and I was again free to fly, Mark and I had some great times hang-gliding. We learned about the aero-tow method of being towed by a light aircraft. It was exhilarating to be lifted into the sky and released to descend to the ground in silent, effortless circles. The sensations of these flights became addictive. The more we flew, the more we needed to fly. Our obsession overtook us," his dad said.

"But you became close because of these flights together, right?" Jared wondered, feeling a twinge of envy for the time his brother had with his dad.

"Well yes, we did, at first, but as your brother became more skilled, he got reckless, defiant, and ignored my warnings about taking chances. Our heated arguments came more frequently and eventually turned lethal."

"Lethal, you mean you murdered someone?" Jared asked, his energy ramping up.

"No, we didn't murder anyone, but your brother was killed because of the sport and I believe it was my fault," Jared's dad whispered. He sighed and was quiet a long while before completing the story for Jared. The humility with which his dad related the details of Mark's insistence to test fly a kite prototype in spite of his dad's warnings and how he watched his son plunge to his death generated a swelling of compassion in Jared for his father. Jared realized that being a parent is a great responsibility; decisions made by a parent can protect or harm their child.

"But what does a parent do with a rebellious child? One that refuses to listen?" Jared asked himself as he thought of his son, Philip, who also had been defiant and ran away to live a life as a drug addict. Priscilla and he were torn over wanting their son back home. Secretly Jared was hoping that his son was dead. Philip was so changed by street living and habitual meth use that the last time they saw him, they did not recognize him. His hair was matted, his clothes dirty, ragged, and smelling like urine and vomit. Purple-colored halfmoon shapes framed the underneath deep-seated eyes of their son. His face was covered with blisters on one side and he twitched and jerked trying to pinch invisible pests he imagined were crawling under his skin. Remembering his own selfishness and contempt for his son, Jared understood his dad's feelings about loss and wanted to comfort him.

"You just have," his dad told him, warming Jared who felt love for this man but whose love he still questioned. Humble hearted and childlike, he asked, "Why didn't you ever try to see me, Dad?"

"I did see you, Son," his dad said, surprising Jared. "You were only three and not aware of who I was when I came for a visit. Seeing how much Pop loved you and especially how easily he made you laugh, I knew that I couldn't measure up. Pop was good to you and when he died, you were eight years old, too old for me to step into Pop's shoes and be a father to you. Besides, I lived alone at that time and didn't want the responsibility of raising a young child. After that, I made an arrangement with my mother to make sure you got the gifts I sent for birthdays and Christmas."

"The twenty-two!" Jared beamed. "That was from you, wasn't it?"

A soft chuckle seasoned his dad's response. "Yes, the rifle, the pocket knife, the cross bow, the putter, the track shoes, the compass, the baseball glove, the magnifying glass, the Magic 8-ball, the multicolored marbles, and the last gift, the Denver Bronco's socks when you graduated Howe high school. Do you remember the note that came with the socks?"

Jared did. A note tucked inside a pair of worn brown and yellow-gold striped socks read "From one hornet to another." He never knew what it meant.

"Your brother tried out for the Denver Bronco's, and part of his uniform was that pair of vertical striped brown and yellow-gold socks. Since you were on the football team at Howe and your school colors brown and gold and your mascot a hornet, I thought you would get a kick out of the socks."

Jared did not laugh at his dad's pun; he was remembering getting the socks in a box left with Mom and being puzzled by who might have sent them. She offered no clues. At the time, he believed his dad was dead. Now, it hurt to find out that his dad was alive and chose to remain a stranger.

"I told you, Jared, I was selfish. I convinced myself that you were in better hands than mine. Freed of the responsibilities of raising a child, I could pursue aero-tow hang-gliding, which was my passion. Taking care of a family was not."

Although his dad's words stung, curiosity about his father's love of hang-gliding dulled the pain and he asked, "Aero-tow— how does that work?"

As soon as he asked the question, shadowy images of a lightweight plane that looked like a dragonfly formed on a nearby sand pit. Tethered to the plane was a triangular shaped kite attached to a three-sided aluminum frame. Beneath the kite engulfed in a body sock, for stability, a man held onto a metal bar in front of his chest and his legs were close together stretched out behind him—held tight and still as if he was in a butterfly cocoon. The combination of straps and wings seemed too flimsy to trust soaring miles into the sky. Jared watched the plane lift off, the cocoon-bound man being towed behind. When the plane reached 11,000 feet, the pilot released its cargo. The hang-glider took charge of sailing the kite in silent, repetitious circles, each one decreasing the space between the man and his kite, and the earth. Jared was fascinated by the scene but more so by the fact that although he was next to the sand pit observing, he was also in tandem with the hang-glider—his father.

"It's breathtaking up there," Jared said.

"Indeed," his father replied but then his dad's next statement shocked him.

"Eventually, I died in a kite-flying accident."

"What happened?" Jared gasped.

"At a site about 100 miles from your home, I was trying once again to claim the Guinness World Record title."

"My home? You mean where Priscilla and I lived in Greenville?"

"Yes, often on my trips to Lookout Mountain, I would go to South Carolina and drive by your house to catch a glimpse of you, Priscilla, and the kids," his dad said.

"Why didn't you ever stop?"

"Pride, too old, too set in my ways, too obsessed with my kite flying," his dad said. "I was a member of a hang-gliding club in Chattanooga. I flew there often to keep my rating and it was there that I died."

"Did your kite fail?"

"No, I had a stroke on final approach. I didn't feel pain but I was aware that I had lost control of the kite. It veered and hit a tree and the impact broke my neck," he said.

"How awful."

"Not really. I died doing what I loved and this was for me, the preferred way to die. The thought of being a drooling, paralyzed man at 83 was not how I wanted to spend my last years of life."

"But you must have chosen God or you wouldn't have come here," Jared exclaimed.

"True. I accepted the Final Offer, because of the wonder instilled in me by your mother."

"I wish I could see her," Jared said.

"You will. I promise."

"Where? When?" Jared asked.

CHAPTER 57

The Psychology of Being

"In a while, you will see your mother," his dad said. "Right now, she is on duty working with some teenaged girls in the realm of empathy along with Abraham, Abraham, and Peck."

"Who are they?" Jared asked.

"Abraham is the father of Isaac, Abraham Maslow is the developer of the Hierarchy of Needs, and Scott Peck is a well-known psychoanalyst. You can read their dossiers in the Doors of Wisdom. Just be careful not to mix up Maslow's Hierarchy of Needs with Maslob's Narcissist's Hierarchy of Wants and Entitlements."

"Okay, I will," Jared said and they both laughed. He was enjoying his conversation with his dad. But the laughter stopped when his father's tone became serious.

"There's something you ought to know before I introduce you to your teammates," his dad said. "This realm is the most difficult because no two people remember an event exactly the same way. It is not easy to understand an experience from another's point of view, especially a relative. In the Realm of Empathy, you feel what someone else felt during the experience—in this realm you will see what someone else saw during an encounter with you. Sometimes these memories clash and jostle us. Disagreement and embarrassment are expected. But if you make it through, you will gain wisdom. Are you ready for that?" his dad asked.

"I guess so," Jared replied.

"Which end of the line would you like to begin with?" his dad asked directing Jared to the line-up of golfing teammates. "The easier one or the toughest?"

Jared hadn't expected to get a choice of where to begin and certainly was not looking forward to being embarrassed, but it was his nature to put off ugly stuff as long as possible and he answered his dad, "The easiest."

"We will begin then with the 3-year-old boy. This is your son, Philip, on a day when he wanted to ride in the golf cart with you."

Jared felt sick. He remembered this day. Philip begged to go with him, but Jared told his son that he was too little to ride along in the golf cart. "He doesn't understand 'too little.'" Priscilla told him. "He only wants time with you," she had said.

When his son pleaded for Jared to take him along on the golf outings, Jared ignored him, asking Priscilla to keep Philip busy while he golfed with his buddies. Jared watched several more moments that were nearly identical. Philip begged; Jared played. Then another moment took form for Jared to see.

Philip argued that he needed a night light in his bedroom. Jared told him he was "too big" for that. His son insisted that monsters lived in his closet and under his bed and they came out when it got dark. Jared scoffed and dismissed these night fears as nonsense. "Monsters are not real, Philip. You should know that at your age," Jared growled.

"The monsters were real to Philip," his dad said embarrassing Jared and in defense of himself, he blurted out, "This feels like judgment to me!"

"I can understand why you think that, Jared, but it's not judgment. This is a behind-the-scenes look at the answers to the tear-filled 'Whys?' you and Priscilla repeatedly asked God about Philip."

"The earliest years of a child are the most critical years and yet they seem to be the ones when we have the least amount of patience. We are frustrated and short-tempered when we cannot stop their crying or angry when they interrupt our conversations with other adults. When we're tired or in a rush, we can often respond to our children with a face of annoyance or mutter sarcasms like 'What now?'"

"We can trivialize their fears by comparing them with real concerns, such as taxes, mortgage, car repairs, unemployment, insurance payments, dwindling savings accounts, and debt."

"Children are more resilient than we think. If we make time in the day to hear about their experiences, listen with sincerity, reserve talks about adult concerns for family conversations where the children are included but not made to feel responsible for the problems—and if we allow them the opportunity to offer ideas for solutions, they will understand the challenges their parents are dealing with.

"When we can smile through our exhaustion and lean in for a comforting, reassuring embrace, and kiss, there are no guarantees about how they will live out their life, but if some loving person does these things when a child is very young, the child will have a reliable compass that will always get them home.

"An unresolved early hurt or fear can pierce the heart and send a child in the wrong direction. The longer the hurt remains unresolved, the more difficult it is to repair and the more off course the child will wander. When too much time gets between a father and his child the relationship lacks strength in its foundation, awkward attempts to be friends is like building a home on sand."

Jared felt weak and disappointed in himself. He wasn't sure he could lead this team through all eighteen holes of golf. His dad was pleased with his son's humility and showing mercy he offered: "If it helps ease the pain for you, Jared, I confess that my journey on this course was almost identical to the one you are about to experience."

"Every parent makes mistakes," he continued. "An occasional scowl and proper discipline will not harm a child. What will harm them is a pattern of disapproving looks, harsh critical words, or unwarranted punishment. Children are forgiving. They love their parents and will remain respectful in spite of blunders as long as a parent is fair and tells the truth. Children depend on their fathers to be leaders, people of authority, not their buddies. When a parent tries to be the child's 'best friend,' the child figures out how to manipulate into the position of authority, which has been abandoned."

"Now in charge, the child demands more and more, secretly hoping that these demands will push their dad back into the proper position of leadership. Often, a father fed up with the inability to control the strong-willed child ignores parental duties and drifts into self-absorption where the child has no access. Angry for being 'left out' fuels an extreme need to be noticed. Consequentially, some type of self-destruction takes place: lying, cheating, stealing, vandalism, bullying, drug abuse, immorality, isolation which leads to depression, or indiscriminate sex."

"Once this pattern of inappropriate authority is well-established, the child does not know what to trust and has to adapt. This is why Philip as a teenager was not enthusiastic to go places with you when you decided to make an effort toward a relationship. It was too late. He had lost respect for you. Your sarcasm had no effect on him. Instead of your time to establish an environment your son could trust with reasonable boundaries, fair guidelines, and rules you gave your son lots of things. He got addicted to it. Your relationship became about having things versus doing things."

"Stop it. Stop it. Stop it! I can't take anymore! This is awful," Jared cried. "This is too intense. I feel miserable."

"I understand," his dad said. "Just breathe," he added.

Jared sucked in a stuttering breath and glanced over at the scraggly bunch of golfing teammates. They were jumping, shaking, and rolling on the grass. "What a contrast," Jared groaned, thinking of the order and decorum of the golf games he was accustomed to. Resisting the desire to run away, Jared bowed his head and swung it side to side.

"I'm okay, now," he told his dad.

"Are you sure? This is going to hurt."

"I think I got that figured out," Jared replied.

"When your son knew that he would not get time with you, possessions became a substitute for security. He demanded the latest gadgets, cell phones, tablets, watches, designer clothes, and expensive shoes. When his demands became impossible for you to meet, Philip found ways to get these things on his own by stealing until he was caught and arrested. In jail he met five sons of the father of lies. All of them were extraordinarily damaged souls who taught your son how to live a life of depravity but one that assured ample money for anything he wanted."

Jared listened to his dad's sickening account of Philip's decline into habitual use of meth and selling his body or beating up and robbing helpless people for money to support his habit. Events described by his dad were difficult to accept as real happenings in the Wolcott family—they seemed more like the episodes of a dramatic television series.

"I was so frustrated with him, I wished him dead," Jared confessed and began to weep. "I wanted a child that was obedient and loving, not a jail-bird-drug-addicted bum. When I turned away thinking that if I couldn't see it, it might not be real, I abandoned my post, didn't I?'

"Parenting is not easy," his dad said. "We call upon what we know. But when our children are out in the world, they are vulnerable to people without scruples who give them drugs, booze, or show them porn—who mock authority by trespassing on private property and stealing or vandalizing in a show of power and defiance. Kids can believe this is appropriate behavior especially if it comes from an adult."

"Our best effort as a parent begins each day with prayer, asking God for the wisdom to assure that provisions are in place to keep our children safe. If we are blessed to have them another day, we are to show them how grateful we are to be their father or mother as we tuck them in at night.

"A child knows when the effort to be with them is sincere. A few undivided moments of attention given each day to a child's interests, curiosities, and concerns is what builds trust and trust builds character and character strengthens discernment. And discernment can help them make better decisions when faced with the taunts of unscrupulous people, dishonest bosses, a thrill-seeking fool, a con artist or prideful thinking," his dad concluded—and then he surprised Jared.

"Your son is here, you know."

"Philip is here? In Heaven? Oh, thank God," Jared whispered. "How did he make it here? He was so horrible. I heard that he was even involved in a murder robbery but I never knew for sure. Priscilla and I begged God to show us why He was punishing us with Philip's horrid behavior. But I suppose none of that matters if he's here," Jared said, his energy calming.

"It matters," Jared's dad assured him. "Like all of us, your son was given the opportunity to understand that God does not punish people but He allows us to live the consequences of our choices—even those we believe to be good ones."

"If you like, I can tell you the events that resulted in his coming here."

"Oh, please, yes. I would like that."

"Philip had been sleeping outdoors near the bus station in downtown Atlanta," his dad began. "A retired military passerby gave him a hundred-dollar bill tucked in a book entitled *God has His Own Watch* written by a man from Greenville, South Carolina. Your son used the money for a hot meal, a shower, shave, some clean clothes, and a bus ticket to Greenville in hopes of meeting this man. Sadly, Philip met up with members of the opposition before he could find the author. These scoundrels coaxed him into dark places where he was reintroduced to meth and heroin. One January night it was bitter cold and he was sleeping under a downtown bridge. He had nothing to keep him warm and was curled up in a ball shivering. He was hungry and thirsty and shaking from the need for drugs."

"Two men from the Greenville Rescue Mission found him. They reached out to him and took him to their shelter. One of the men cleaned your son's filthy face and hands, bandaged a cut on his head, fed him hot soup and coffee, wrapped him in a blanket, and prayed with him. This man was so caring that when he told your son the Good News about Christ. Your son listened."

"Philip did not feel he was getting a lecture. He knew the message was important. That night alone on his cot, your son thought about how much he had been given and how he squandered his life. He cried out to God to have mercy on him and God heard him. Sadly, so did the opposition, and when your son went back onto the streets, the temptations were too great to resist. He died giving into those temptations. His soul arrived here in shreds, but he was oriented as soon as he arrived in the Waiting Room because intercessory prayer for him was offered soon after he died."

"I wish I could thank those men and whoever prayed for my son. Can I see him as he is now? Can I hold him?" Jared asked, his energy aching to join with his child.

"Certainly, but not at this moment. We need to address the toughest player, your daughter."

CHAPTER 58

Marcia

"**M**y daughter? Marcia? I can't imagine that I failed her. She and I were so close. Don't tell me she's the pregnant one."

"Yes, she is. And you are correct. You were very close with your daughter, but this encounter will help you understand how parents can have a close, but superficial relationship with their children and how they can rob a child of an opportunity to gain wisdom."

"Each time your daughter came to you with a hurt or worry, you made it sound small, unimportant. She never learned how to work through problems. She counted on you to resolve them for her. She liked it when you told her that you would make everything all right. But this time was different. She came to you as a young teenager wanting to tell you about a boy who had convinced her to yield her virginity to him. She was feeling shame, fear—changed. She was very young, only fourteen, far too young to be in such an intimate relationship—she was too embarrassed to go to her mother but she was hurting and needed to feel your arms around her. She hoped that like all other times you would make the pain go away."

"I remember that night," Jared declared. "She wasn't pregnant. Was she? I thought I was there for her. I remember holding her. She crawled up in my lap like a little puppy."

"You remember correctly, but what you do not recall is missing the clues, the real purpose of her coming to you. Rather than being still and letting her talk, you told her how beautiful and good she was and that one day some young man was going to be proud to be her husband. She was thinking just the opposite of herself. She just couldn't face you with the truth after that. She buried it and turned to friends for answers."

"What did they tell her to do?" Jared asked, but he knew the answer before his dad could say anything; he knew that Marcia's friends had convinced her to get an abortion. "I'm seeing her as a pregnant teen, because that's what she would have been if I had just listened."

"That is correct. In fact, after aborting this child, she lost respect for herself and had frequent sexual encounters. Her rape was the consequence of her indiscriminate sex. She would have had another abortion when she was eighteen, but something changed her mind. She married and kept the child that is your granddaughter, Elizabeth."

Jared struggled to process how easily he missed clues. "She was always so good, such a joy. She had lots of wonderful boyfriends."

"That was her performance. She gave you what you expected of her, which was the 'good and beautiful daughter.' Inside, she was aching and longing to be complete. She hid a lot from you, even her cancer was kept secret from you until her prognosis was grim."

"I'm flabbergasted. I never knew this about my daughter," Jared declared and then wondered what other signs he missed. His dad helped him see his daughter as a woman in pain and suffering loss. Marcia had been his pride and joy. He did not know about the abortion. And although he knew about her rape, he did not know about the indiscriminate sex. When she was eighteen and declared that she was going to marry, he had mixed feelings. He thought she was too young, but he was glad because her husband Greg treated her with kindness.

Jared remembered getting the uplifting phone call from this excited new daddy when Elizabeth was born, premature but healthy. He and Priscilla had enjoyed only a few months with them before they announced that they were moving to Oregon. He remembered the shock of getting the sob-filled, gasping phone call from Marcia to tell him that Greg had died suddenly of a heart attack. And the worst of all, the call from Matthew when he and Priscilla were told that Marcia had cervical cancer. It was invasive and she died within two weeks of that call; she was only twenty-one.

"This is unbearable," Jared shouted. "I'm not sure I want to understand any more about family," he cried. "I feel small and selfish."

"I understand son," his dad said. "You're through the worst. Come, sit by me as we finish up."

Jared moved next to his dad and considered the preferential feelings he had for Marcia over Philip—Marcia who gave him a performance and Philip who was an innocent bystander. He had loved the easier one—that was his fault not theirs. An urgency pressed on him; he didn't know what it was but he sensed that his time in this realm was about to end. Glancing back at his rowdy bunch of teammates, he asked his dad about the attractive lady and why she also appeared as a slob.

CHAPTER 59

Rita and Matthew

"This woman is your first wife, Rita. The reason you see her simultaneously as a dumpy, short, obese girl with stringy hair and ugly nails is because this is what you thought of her after she became pregnant with your first son, Matthew."

The mention of Matthew's name triggered more memories of regret. He knew very little about this son. He had gotten Rita pregnant when they were sixteen and he was running with a wild bunch of high school dropouts who liked to gamble and talk dirty. Sometimes gambling paid off and he could drop a wad of cash in Walter's lap, but after a hard alley way beating that nearly cost him his life, he had to get a regular job. For two years he worked as a custodian at a community hospital, but the pay was poor, not like the hefty yield of a prosperous gambling night. Jared was miserable. During those two years, Walter wore Jared down calling him a slacker, a loser, a bum. Matthew cried every night and Rita seemed to take Walter's side when it came to lists of things he should do as a provider.

The idea of being strapped down with a screaming kid and ugly wife sent him running to the Army Recruitment Center to enlist—but he failed the physical because of a childhood heart defect. In an angry outburst, he yelled at Rita and threw a heavy shoe at her head—it frightened Matthew and sent Rita packing to live with her mother in Louisville. Jared kept his job as custodian for a while, but after a conversation with a chaplain at the hospital, he decided to quit work and go to college at Indiana University in Bloomington.

While he was in school, Rita asked for a divorce. She argued that if he cared anything about his son, he would make a trip to Kentucky to see him. But Jared was having too much fun as a college man. Meanwhile he reached out to his son with birthday cards and presents. Rita responded with snapshots of a growing boy. But when she moved, this time to Colorado, the updates and photos dwindled. In time, the distance between them expanded and the connection with Matthew tapered off. Jared knew that Matthew had moved from Colorado to Oklahoma, married, and moved to Oregon. He was perturbed when Marcia told him that she and Greg were moving to Oregon to live near her half-brother and his family.

Because Jared did not know the details of Marcia's relationship with Matthew and why she moved to be with him, Jared's dad activated clouds above the first hole. Rita stepped forward to narrate. She spoke in even, warm tones the details of a family estranged from Jared.

"Matthew was married to a Choctaw Native American Indian woman named Ona, who was knowledgeable about healing herbs," Rita began. "Marcia enjoyed long conversations with Ona about modoc weed, puccoon root, scurvy grass, and Jerusalem oak. The funny names made Marcia laugh. Right before Elizabeth was born, Matthew and Ona persuaded Marcia and her husband Greg to move to Oregon. It was a blessing because Ona had a special sense about the needs of Marcia, Greg, and Elizabeth."

Rita's words prompted Jared to remember the string of announcements: first the news that Greg and Marcia were moving and then the shocking news of the sudden death of Greg when Elizabeth was six months old, then Marcia's cancer, and then finally, the most terrible news of all, when Marcia died. As Jared recalled events, his recollection took holographic form above the golf course. When news of Marcia's illness reached him too late to make the trip to see her, Jared was furious with God. Until now with the help of Rita, he did not know that because of Ona, Elizabeth was in capable hands and Marcia's last moments before dying were peaceful.

He recalled that after Marcia died, years passed without meaningful conversation with Elizabeth, Matthew, or Ona. Talks about possible visits were exchanged but did not happen. Neither Jared nor Priscilla liked to fly so travel from South Carolina to Oregon meant several nights of staying at motels. Jared hated the idea of sleeping where some stranger had been but also, secretly, Jared thought Ona was a witch doctor and the idea of being in her company gave him the creeps. Eventually, they all relied on cards, emails, and brief phone calls on holidays and birthdays. Meanwhile, marriages, illness, loss, and grandbabies were entered into history without much celebration—at least not at Jared's house.

"I don't understand how I could have been so selfish," Jared confessed. He saw how Rita had threaded together all the necessities for a peaceful place of departure for Marcia. "I hope you will forgive me, Rita," Jared said but turned to his dad without waiting for Rita's response.

"I know that I have to deal with this but I feel a need to step up the pace," he told his dad.

His father knew exactly why his son was feeling this way. Time was running out but there was still a bit of work to be done.

CHAPTER 60

The Rest of the Family

Together Jared and his dad looked back at the soldier and the arthritic hunched over old man. Jared asked, "What about these two?"

"This soldier is one of your ancestors who fought in the Civil War."

"But he's black and I'm not," Jared blurted out in surprise.

"Once the human genome was mapped, we discovered that we're all related," his dad said.

"And the crippled old man?" Jared asked.

"He's the soldier's father."

"But he's white," Jared remarked.

"See what I mean?" his dad replied.

"This is your great, great, great granddaddy."

"The old man?"

"No, the soldier. The old man is your great, great, great, great granddaddy."

"So who is the other remaining player, the beautiful older girl?"

"Remember the time-space thing?" his dad asked. "This is Marcia at a different age. She is twenty-one. In this form, she is helping you understand something else. She wants to tell you how great her life turned out to be."

"But it didn't!" Jared blurted out. "Her husband dropped dead of heart attack when their baby was an infant. She got cervical cancer and died when she was only twenty-one. How could she call that a great life?"

Jared's eyes widened as the beautiful woman approached him. Without a doubt this was Marcia floating toward him. "Hello, Daddy," she whispered and kissed his cheek. "I see that you are learning a lot about our family. You didn't know much about us and especially about how I died," Marcia said.

Jared choked back tears, "I wanted to," he said.

"I would like to share that with you now, if I may," Marcia offered. She spoke so softly Jared could barely hear her and although her voice was filled with warmth, Jared felt a chill.

"Matthew's wife Ona was the one who took care of me," she began. "In spite of how you felt about her and her herbal remedies, she honored my wishes for traditional medicine. Ona helped me through my hysterectomy, chemotherapy, and eventually hospice house. She sat by my side, tenderly wiping my forehead with cool cloths until my last breath. Before I died, Ona and Matthew agreed to raise Elizabeth as their own.

"I'm sorry I didn't reach out to you and mom more often. I did not want you to worry about me—there was nothing either of you could have done to change my situation. I was at peace and knew where I was going to spend eternity," Marcia said.

"Your granddaughter Elizabeth learned from Matthew and Ona how to choose a mate. Ona helped her know the difference between marrying a godly man who will love her as Christ loves us and marrying a man for his potential financial gain. The man Elizabeth married exemplified love, respect, mutual encouragement, manners, and morals—he cherished Elizabeth. He knew how to handle money: to earn honestly, give generously, invest intelligently, save prudently, and to enjoy God's blessings. He understood leadership and how the father is the head of the family, the authority, but not a dictator or someone who exasperates his children. Elizabeth taught each of their seven children to begin the day thanking God and then to live that day only. She told them that no one finishes the day with a perfect score and before going to sleep to hand mistakes over to God. She said each day, 'Love God and then just be yourself.'"

"How do you know all this about Elizabeth since you died when she was an infant?" Jared asked.

"Here we know everything: the past, the present, and the future," Marcia reminded him.

Jared felt a loss of opportunity with his daughter, son, and granddaughter. "Oh God, forgive me. I see how much I missed. Have mercy on me now," Jared prayed.

"I believe that it is all right for me to tell you that your granddaughter Elizabeth and her husband, the senator from South Carolina become president and first lady. In time they restored decades of destruction caused by the opposition."

"President and first lady," Jared whispered with delight; then it registered with him: had Marcia aborted child number two, none of these happenings would take place. He gave thanks for the influence that kept his daughter from destroying this potential. Then it struck him. "Here, I can tune in. I can see my children at any age, any event, and I will be with them forever."

"Yes, for eternity," his dad said as his joy-filled energy expanded and merged with his son.

CHAPTER 61

Tee Off Time

"I think it might be time to tee off," his dad said as soft snow floated from overhead. It fell like lace blankets dropping from the clouds, but for some reason, the snow did not make Jared feel cold. Listening to his father made him eager to begin his game. As he looked through the snowflakes at his teammates, everyone looked different. He saw that his first wife was not the despicable being he made her out to be. With this memory, he expected to feel shame, but instead, he felt relief and love.

"Benefits of understanding," his dad told him and then asked, "Are you ready to play?"

With newly found energy, Jared said that he was.

Offering one final word of instruction, his dad said, "Remember that each of your teammates has a skill necessary to complete the course."

Jared took a deep breath and then announced, "I suppose since we all need golf clubs, I had better call a huddle and find out which teammate can help us manifest solid objects."

Jared's father smiled. His son hadn't yet figured out that he and everyone on the team was capable of that. Because he was concentrating on the huddle, Jared missed his dad's thought and found himself engrossed in how to manage the players.

Abraham, Abraham, and Peck joined Jared's dad and together they watched attempts to direct fellow teammates

toward the first hole. Team players were disorganized and separated. The three-year-old Philip trotted off toward the sand-
pit with three unidentified toddlers. Jared decided they were
neighbor children and he raced after the small players. While
chasing the wee ones, the other teammates were left alone to get
confused about the huddle they were to make. They too began to
scatter and soon Jared was chasing all of them. At that instance,
Jared looked upward and asked Jesus to join them in the game.

Like a magnet drawing iron filings to one point, all players
met Jared on the first hole.

"Organized chaos," Jared's dad said out loud to Abraham,
Abraham, and Peck. They all shook their heads but smiled
knowing that in a little while, the team would get on course, play
through, and return with all hurts understood and forgiven.

CHAPTER 62

The Letter

Jared's dad, Abraham, Abraham, and Peck watched the family team come into focus. Jared in the lead, his hair wild and perfectly white and as expected, all family members moving harmoniously as one being, fluid and steady, refreshing one another with laughter. His dad had not been able to join them on this game. He knew this was Jared's chance to understand, so he had to wait like a father concerned for the teenage son driving the family car solo for the first time.

His eyes watered with loving pride as his family returned united, all holding onto one another. He greeted Jared with a bit of humor. "Well, it took a while but I see that you are back in one piece." Everyone merged frequencies and shared a heartfelt laugh.

As the laughter quieted, Jared's dad leaned over and kissed his son. "I have a surprise for you," he said causing Jared to look up. "Remember the first soft feminine voice you heard during the conversation with me and your brother Mark?" his dad asked and swept his arm around as if making an introduction.

Jared did not need one. Approaching him like warm waves of a luxurious bath were his older brother Mark, his sister Catherine, and the being with the soft, feminine voice, his mother, Julia. Although on Earth he had never met them, now he knew them instantly. Jared's energy expanded, embracing them. Synchronicity of their frequencies created a shared delight, a result of their joy to be with one another for the first time.

Within moments Jared saw others coming toward him: his daughter Marcia and her husband Greg; he saw his son Philip, Pop Wolcott, Grandma Robinette, Percy, C.W., and Walter. Some of the people had been dear to him on Earth. Some had been mean but as they gathered around him, he couldn't tell the difference.

Meeting his family was a remarkable moment and Jared invited them to the bench outside the Doors of Wisdom. They told him to go on ahead and that they would be along in a while.

As he seated himself, Jared's attention was drawn to two beings heading his way. Because of his size and shape, clearly one was an adult male, the other one was smaller, a child perhaps? Both were radiant pure white light and they shimmered hypnotically as they got closer to Jared. His response to them was wondrously strange. From the center of his chest, Jared felt a massive, powerful shaft of light thrust out and reach for these beings. The connection was electrifying, yet peaceful and calming. The light reflected off the clouds, the bench, the doors, and the beings coming toward him. Jared lifted off the bench, prepared to be embraced by the Master when the being introduced himself as Adolf.

"Who?" Jared asked, surprised.

"You probably know me best by my last name, although I use it rarely here."

Before he spoke the name, Jared realized he was in the company of Hitler. Surprisingly, he did not have the reaction to this being that he did earlier. What Sonny had told him about being changed by God's love, Jared at this moment realized and understood.

Hitler positioned his energy next to Jared on the bench. He introduced the child with him as Sammie Baer.

"Sammie Bear?" Jared asked.

"Sammie B-a-e-r," Adolf corrected by spelling the last name. "His brother is one of the reasons, I'm here. During the war, when I was overseeing the persecution of this child's family, his brother Martin was praying to God for mercy and compassion, not just for his loved ones, but for me and my ministers of pain and cruelty. This kind of love was not known to me. I believed that all the hideous things I was doing to the Poles, Jews, and others was in service to God. When God showed me His point of view, I was crushed with sorrow for my horrid faulty thinking. It seemed impossible that someone like me could be here."

"And this is where Sammie Baer met you?" Jared asked.

"Yes, he was my greeter. He stayed with me through all of the realms, shared his love, and now is an integral part of who I am. I am grateful because through him I have been able to understand more clearly what it means to love, God's way. I saw that what I did, I did to God not for Him."

"You were a horrible person," Jared remarked. "You murdered innocent, precious people. Just the sound of your name used to make me shudder. How is it that I feel no hatred whatsoever for you now?"

"Only love can make that possible, Jared. I cannot offer any excuses for the vicious, evil things I did and you may find it completely inconceivable that while I did these things, I loved God too. I believed that I was doing a service for Him and I became intoxicated with the power of feeling superior. My version of service was twisted. I did not know how to love as Christ does. When I came toward you and the great light burst from your heart, did you know that is how Christ expresses love for us? You saw Him in me because He is in me now. Just as He is in you. This Agape Love Shaft emitting from your heart shows that you too have discovered God's love, the ability to love an enemy as Christ loves you."

Jared realized that the love exchange between Adolf and Sammie Baer was without emotion. It was graceful, peaceful, comforting, and compassionate. It was supernatural.

"You might not know the answer to this question," Jared said, "but if God loves this way and He doesn't waste anything, what about the people in Hell? Will He ever..."

Knowing that Jared was feeling compassion for souls agonizing in Hell, Adolf spoke before Jared finished.

"I cannot speak for God," Adolf said, "but I did overhear a conversation between Archangel Michael, Elijah, and Jesus. It sounded like they were making provisions for these souls sometime after Christ's return."

A warm wave washed over Jared, similar to the one he experienced seeing his mother for the first time. Knowing that the souls lost to hell might be redeemed filled him with joy. Then, reflecting on his own life, all of the realms he had journeyed though, and how he felt at this moment, it occurred to Jared that to align his frequency with Heaven, he had to understand God's love. Never did he expect to realize this from someone like Adolf.

"Once you experience this type of love, Jared," Adolf said, "you will know how much God loved His creations, all of them."

"By the way, I have a letter for you," Adolf said.

"A letter for me? Here?"

Adolf handed Jared a tan-colored parchment paper rolled up and held in place with a thin leather strap. Jared slid the strap off and rolled out the letter. It was from Einstein.

Dear Jared,

This will be one of many letters I will write to you. I know that you did not come to my realm. I missed talking with you. I knew that your progress would move quickly and soon you would be refined and ready to meet your Creator face-to-face. It's exhilarating, you'll see. For now, I want to ease your mind about the nighttime prayer that terrified you as a child—the Now I Lay Me Down to Sleep prayer. You should know that the author of this prayer was distracted from the original inspired words. The prayer was intended to

*be: "Now I lay me down to sleep. I pray the
Lord all fears to keep. If I should cry before
I wake, I pray the Lord a smile to make."
Your granddaughter Elizabeth was inspired
during a heavenly hug sacred dream time,
when Marcia gave her daughter the original version, which then was taught to your
grandchildren. All's well now, Jared. Be on
your way, my friend.*

Yours truly,
Einstein

Jared rolled up the letter, slipped the leather band in place, tucked it behind the golden thread that held his sword, and then lowered himself onto the bench outside the Doors of Wisdom. As he waited for what was to come next, he sat still among the delicate piano notes of Beethoven's *Moonlight Sonata*.

PART FIVE

Choosing

Psalm 1: 5 "Therefore the ungodly shall not stand in the judgment.."

CHAPTER 63

At the Gates

Undisturbed, Jared watched a fog-covered mirror form before him. Like a veil being lifted from the face of a bride, the opaque covering rose to reveal his own reflection. A smile spread across the face in the mirror when he saw Christ in himself.

Seamlessly, he released from one dimension and connected with another. At that moment, he understood God's time. During his arrival, he could have gone back and forth from his earthly body to his heavenly one. The instruments connected to him in his hospital room were neither capable of detecting consciousness nor recording the time during which he was able to be in two places at once: Heaven and Earth. What seemed like years were mere days, hours, or seconds. He realized that he had been in transition moving through realms of understanding to be refined and know how to love, forgive, and let go of his earthly connection.

A majestic presence wrapped around him. The loving energy that embraced him spoke to him, not in words but in thoughts. Jared remained still—he knew that he was not yet seeing his Creator face-to-face. It wasn't time. As a child he was terrified by the warnings of God's wrath, but here, now, he realized God's anger was His disappointment for the creations that chose evil and permanent torment over surrender and permanent joy with Him.

In this place of peace, where Jared chose to reside, he felt a type of love that could only be understood by experiencing it. And as he did, the Simulvision clouds next to the mirror filled with something splendid. Now he was being shown the many times he pleased God. He watched individual acts, words, and thoughts form into threads, rise, and weave together. Some threads were dull or thin and might otherwise go unnoticed, but as they joined others, a spectacular finished work was created.

Illuminated in the network of threads was an ability that amused him; it was his talent for spotting four-leaf clovers. During his time on Earth, he found no significance in this capability except to entertain. He saw himself on a grass-covered lawn next to the chapel at Lake Junaluska. He was kneeling down next to a young child who had gotten separated from her family. She was crying and he wanted to comfort her. He distracted her by plucking a four-leaf clover and handing it to her. In doing so, her crying was replaced with a look of surprise and then eagerness; she felt challenged by Jared's encouragement to find a four-leaf clover of her own. Tears turned to squeals of delight as she plunged onto the clover-filled lawn and discovered she had the same ability as Jared. Together they giggled and plucked until her small hands held more than a dozen clovers, most with four leaves but two rare finds had five.

Jared was shown that this otherwise insignificant moment shared with this child launched a brilliant career.

"Do you recognize her?" Jared heard the loving voice ask.

"Yes, I do. This is the little girl taken at birth from Bessie, the woman of great loss. How do I know that?"

The loving voice told him that in Heaven you know everything and that God's threads only make sense when you see them from here.

Jared watched a thin gold thread lift and float into the tapestry. This little girl became a radiologist, exceptionally gifted in deciphering complicated patterns created by imaging machines. She could spot a harmful tumor well before it reached the stage of irreversible destruction. Her ability to see potential harm spared countless numbers of people the suffering of disease.

Watching this encounter and its outcome, Jared understood that God sees things through a wider lens, always aiming at something not within our line of sight.

He watched as God's threads became illuminated with purpose. When Jared's mother died giving birth to him, God sent a saint, the nurse who attended to his delivery, took him to the hospital, held him, and responded to his first and immediate need, which was love. The kind next-door neighbor who halted his whipping in the shed was a guardian angel sent to curtail the backyard beatings Jared endured as a child. Old Curt, the Gaffney grocery store owner who introduced him to Priscilla, was an angel. The traveler's aide lady, and conductor also were angels who made certain he got on the same train with another guardian, the elderly man in the army uniform. Percy was a saint who gave Philip the hundred-dollar bill and the book that directed him to Greenville. The man whose car Jared had towed was a saint and the one who met Jared's homeless and drug-addicted son, washed him, wrapped him in a blanket, and prayed for his soul. The boy with epilepsy and the woman with multiple sclerosis who decided not to commit suicide were saints who became volunteers at a clinic that offered free ultrasounds to women considering abortion. Marcia's mind was changed and Elizabeth's life came into being because of this offering. Hundreds of other people appeared in the vast light-filled tapestry, some as passersby in his life, others as a strong influence.

Jared gave thanks to God for His splendid threads, for loving him through the willfulness of childhood, the waywardness of youth, the selfishness and vanity of his mature years, and the frailties of his final years of efforts to be a godly man. He saw that fear, worry, or anger are unnatural snags in our tapestry; and when we experience these, we need only to call out to Him and know that He is at the other end holding on to us and will not let go, unless we choose to sever the connection.

Enriched with gladness, Jared knew that judgment wasn't about ridicule, wrath, or punishment; it was about a relationship and mercy. He knew that the times when he felt the most important and self-reliant, he was the weakest in his relationship with God. He also knew that the only things we carry with us from our earthly life to our Heavenly one are relationships. As he held this thought, a gentle being joined him.

"Dearest one, greetings. I am Mary. I have been looking forward to this moment for a while."

With her words, Jared felt what he now knew to be a holy kiss and realized he had been receiving these all along. Without requiring an introduction, he knew the Mary who was with him was Mary the mother of the Lord, Jesus. Her voice was patient, kind, and reassuring as she explained, "Before you can enter God's Kingdom, you will go through the River of Perfection for Assimilation. Merriam will join us at the riverbank and we will help you into the waters."

Mary and Merriam held Jared but he had no sense of being bound. As he reached the River's edge he was invited to move into its pristine waters. Multicolored rays of light danced on the water's surface then penetrated to shine onto round-shaped rocks that lined the bottom. On each side of the river were lush trees with sturdy peeling bark that reminded Jared of the lace-bark elms of North Carolina. Their leaves displayed a profusion of vivid green, gold, and amber embedded with flecks of purple and copper. Branches bowed from the weight of ripe, sweet fruit dangling within reach.

"Eat now, Jared" Merriam said. "This fruit is blessed by God for the purpose of assimilation and healing which requires immense energy."

With her words, Jared's hunger increased, but it was not painful, rather it was a response to her instruction.

As he reached for a piece of fruit he noticed different varieties hanging from the branches. Each was perfect and unique in its shape, color, and size. Without effort, when he made his choice and when he touched the fruit, it tumbled and burst into his being.

Jared felt replete and gave thanks to God for this remarkable nourishment. He praised God, knowing that this food would be used for its highest good: perfection.

With tenderness and care, Mary and Merriam guided Jared into the river. As he moved forward and got deeper into the water, he felt a pleasant tingling sensation. Without concern, he pressed into the water until he was fully submerged and moving along the bottom of the riverbed. Immersed, he breathed effortless, strong breaths and tasted the water's saltiness. Fluid penetrated and flowed throughout his being, healing him, restoring him.

Golden and white light beings surrounded him, creating a buoyant sphere of love. He knew them. These were the Sisters of the Holy Family, the Sisters of Bon Secours, the Reverend Dr. Martin Luther King, Henri Nouwen, Henriette DeLille, Ruth Bell Graham, and Rabbi Akiba, who whispered to him that "even great stones are rubbed smooth by the force of the water."

Jared felt Akiba's words working on his scars.

"All of the holes in your soul were mended in the realms of understanding," Dr. King told him.

"But scars remained," Mary said and added, "In the River of Perfection, which flows from the throne of our Creator, you are experiencing assimilation from understanding and the healing power of the resurrected Christ. Soon these scars will be nonexistent and the residual of sin will be washed clean from your soul."

"Once assimilation is complete," Henri Nouwen added, "you will be perfect, restored to our Father's original creation. Breathe deeply, Jared. Let the waters work in you."

Jared was not afraid; he trusted completely, and as he breathed the salty waters in and out, he felt the process of perfection. His sarcasm was replaced with wit, God's original intent for Jared's personality. His earthly journey memories of sin were transformed into moments of joy, splendor, and magnificent gifts from God that prepared him for something of great importance: the new Earth and life eternal.

Brilliance encompassed him, reminding him of the glory he witnessed during orientation. With never-before-known strength, he emerged from the water and was lifted. Rising above the river, a multitude of angels surrounded him with wide swaths of radiant light swirling and expanding, uniting them. In unison with the angelic beings, he was carried to an exquisite set of gates that gleamed colors of gem stones jasper, sapphire, chalcedony, emerald, sardonyx, carnelian, chrysolite, beryl, topaz, chrysoprase, jacinth, and amethyst. Instinctively, he reached down and slipped the sword from the sheath that was fastened to a sash around his center. It was no longer a weapon but a key to the massive, gem-filled gates that rose before him. Unencumbered the sword unlocked the gates and they swung open.

Then the most awesome thing happened.

Jared saw Him, the Lord, Christ Jesus, walking toward him with arms stretched out in a gesture of welcome, as if he were the only soul in Heaven. His white robe and golden sash gleamed when Christ reached out for him and spoke, "Jared Hamilton Wolcott, I trust you enjoyed your journey through the realms of understanding. I have come to usher you, to our plenary session: a grand feast alongside your brothers Abraham, Isaac, and Jacob.

Christ embraced Jared, gave him a holy kiss, smiled, and told him, "After the grand feast, you will be shown our Father's Waiting Room, a place of readiness, limitless adventure, and exploration. It is where you will reunite with your beloveds to interact, laugh, garden, sing, and play until it's time for Me to go."

Jared understood that Christ was talking about His return and the New Earth. He thought how fortunate he was to be in Heaven at this time to be refined and ready to participate in such a blessed event.

Jesus wrapped His arms around Jared. "I have something for you," Jesus said and placed a pristine white stone in Jared's hand. "Hold onto this for a while, will you?" He asked.

Jared looked down at the stone; he knew it held his heavenly name. "Indeed, I will Father."

"Well then, before the family reunion, let's you and I take a trip into the universe to experience the splendor and the glory of creation."

"I'd like that," he told Jesus and caressed the stone.

"I'm glad you made the choice to remain in Heaven. Welcome Home my beloved child."

Psalm 1: 6 "For the LORD knoweth the way of the righteous..."

EPILOGUE

Matthew and Priscilla were weary from the two nights without sleep. They had remained at Jared's bedside, kissing him, talking with him, taking turns reading the underscored passages in his Bible, and sharing family memories with him. Most of the time, he was quiet, but with the mention of Hitler and discussion about the possibility of him being in Heaven, Jared produced the few signs that he was still alive. He bolted up from the bed, his eyes and mouth twitched in protest, causing Priscilla and Matthew to exchange wide-eyed looks of astonishment.

And to restore peace, Matthew played Beethoven's *Moonlight Sonata* for his father.

Priscilla knew the moment her beloved Jared decided to leave his body. The image of his face and peaceful blue eyes filled the room and looked down at her as she and Matthew walked out to meet Wesley, her best friend. She knew that life on Earth would have been intolerable for Jared in his impaired state. On the day he was taken to the hospital, she had prayed for God to take care of this man she cherished.

In the weeks before Jared was struck by lightning and died, they had talked about Heaven and her visit there when their twins Marcia and Philip were born. He had listened with a higher level of interest this time.

"Where do you think dad is?" Matthew asked Priscilla as they joined Wesley at the elevator to go home.

"Heaven, no doubt about it."

ABOUT THE AUTHOR

C heryl Garrison Garrett is a native of South Carolina; she is a mother and grandmother. Cheryl is a graduate of Indiana University, Bloomington. After twenty years of writing either Civil War, scientific, or medical content, *The Choice to Remain in Heaven* is Cheryl's first novel. She credits Stephen King with being her inspiration, not because of his beliefs, but because of his tenacity and discipline. *The Choice to Remain in Heaven* is the first in an intended series: *The Wretched Life of Priscilla Wolcott: Widow Wonderland; Be Perfect or Perish; Surviving Puberty, Boys, Siblings, and Hell; Marriage and Slave Labor.* Cheryl lives in Mauldin, South Carolina, and is married to Clyde Garrett

www.cherylgarrisongarrett.com

CPSIA information can be obtained
at www.ICGtesting.com
Printed in the USA
BVHW081158060121
596910BV00001B/55